Packing It In

David Rees was born in Surrey in 1936, but he has lived for most of his adult life in Devon, where for many years he taught English Literature at Exeter University. In 1984, he retired early in order to write full-time. Author of forty books, he is best known for his children's novel, *The Exeter Blitz*, which in 1978 was awarded the Carnegie Medal, and for *The Milkman's On His Way*, which, having survived much absurd controversy in Parliament, is now regarded as something of a gay classic - though in his own opinion it is not one of his more memorable novels. He also won The Other Award in 1980 for his historical novel set in Ireland, *The Green Bough of Liberty*. His most recent book is his autobiography, *Not For Your Hands*, published to considerable critical acclaim. An inveterate traveller (wanderlust is an inherited family trait), he wanted to write *Packing It In*, an account of recent voyages in Europe, Australia, New Zealand and the United States, because he has always felt dissatisfied with his previous travel book, *A Better Class of Blond*. He recently completed a collection of critical essays, *Words and Music*, an assessment of the achievements (and failures) of writers and composers, mostly contemporary, who are gay and whose themes and preoccupations are gay. That done, he has decided that his writing career, except for occasional bits and pieces, is quite definitely, and happily, finished.

Packing It In

David Rees

Millivres Books
Brighton

First Published in 1992 by Millivres Books (Publishers)
33 Bristol Gardens, Brighton BN2 5JR, East Sussex, England

Copyright © Peter Burton 1993
The moral rights of the copyright-holder have been asserted

ISBN 1 873741 07 3

Typeset by Hailsham Typesetting Services, Hailsham,
East Sussex, BN27 1AD

Printed and bound in Great Britain

Distributed in the United Kingdom and Western Europe by
Turnaround Distribution Co-Op Ltd, 27 Horsell Road, London N5 1XL

Distributed in the United States of America by InBook,
140 Commerce Street, East Haven, Connecticut 06512, USA

Some of these essays originally appeared in *Gay Times*:
'Couples and Metaphors' (October 1991); 'San Francisco: A
Valediction' (November 1991); 'A La Ronde'(December 1991); 'Barcelona
Days' (February 1992), Quotations from the will of Mary Parminter are
reproduced by kind permission of the National Trust.

for
Peter Burton
and
Richard Smith

. . . the clever hopes expire
Of a low dishonest decade :
Waves of anger and fear
Circulate over the bright
And darkened lands of the earth,
Obsessing our private lives;
The unmentionable odour of death
Offends the September night.

W .H. Auden
1st September 1939

From Lake Disappointment to the Loo

It is very red and very dead. Mesas like huge logs of ancient wood litter the sand; there are black scars – rocks or spinifex – and all rivers have failed; their windings are inscrutable messages scribbled in undecipherable alphabets. Lake Disappointment (the names! Bungle Bungle, Mount Hopeless) glitters with salt: dirty white, acid green, bilious yellow. There is nothing – not a house, a road, a railway line, a fence. The most inhospitable continent, the oldest, the most tired, the most worn out; sun-baked, sun-destroyed. It could be the surface of Mars, yet nowhere is more familiar. Because of books – this landscape figures in my reading more insistently than any other: Patrick White, Patricia Wrightson, Randolph Stow, Ivan Southall. 'Canyons, like great splits in the earth, as if about to split further.' 'The sun beats like a gong on red wind-drifted dunes.' 'Who can comprehend this country? Who can stand it?' Down there White's explorers – Voss, Palfreyman, the whole expedition – perished, victims of erroneous belief: that there *must* be an inland sea.

The flattest, driest place on earth. It is not difficult to imagine the astonishment of the pioneers; nothing had prepared them for this. The first meeting of European and Aboriginal – eighteenth-century man, product of Reason, convinced he was the apex of creation, appointed by God as supreme lord: confronted with aboriginals. Stone-agers. Utterly baffling. Who *can* comprehend this country?

Hours later a thread, absolutely straight, stretching it seems to infinity: the railway that crosses the Nullarbor. Red becomes grey, becomes brown, becomes red again; and there is the sea, the Great Australian Bight, the edge clean and clear as if an enormous shark had snapped off a piece of land and swallowed it. The sea is amber in the dying sun, and the darkness almost visibly gathers itself to extinguish day. We are heading east – the lamps of Adelaide flicker below; 'scattered brooches of light where the towns were clustered . . . but most of it, lying under the

1

edge of night, was in darkness.'

Sydney is one of the world's great cities: as vibrant and exciting as San Francisco a decade back. The weather, the season, reveal it at its best: early summer sun, the temperature low eighties, the air dry and clean, the breeze warm; and the blue of the harbour is intensely blue. My cousin Biff lives on the North Shore; we commute by ferry to Circular Quay – this approach to the city is stunning, spectacular – echoes of Venice, of Istanbul, and for a moment I really do think I'm sailing up the Golden Horn and that Pinchgut Island is Leander's Tower. But the chatter is English, and the houses, public buildings, the downtown skyscrapers are wholly and definitely those of Sydney. The opera house and the bridge, those clichés of so many postcards, symbols of Australia as well-known as Ayer's Rock, are there for the first time for me in the flesh; reality outstrips in magnificent fashion any photograph. The size of it all! The scale! The colours!

The opera house is one of the world's few great, modern architectural achievements; a fleet of yachts in stone about to slip its moorings and glide into the open water – where real yachts, even this early in the day, are triangles of white set in blue. How impoverished this spit of land must have been before it was built! Towering high above is the Harbour Bridge, Newcastle's Tyne Bridge copied, writ large, as elegant – as seemingly significant – as the Golden Gate. My eyes, all morning and the mornings to come, return to these two focal points; from any angle, and in any light, they fascinate.

When I can tear my eyes away I know I'm in a very different world: each bird, each tree, each plant is a new experience. Mynas squawking, a flash of red from parrots, which are in the open air – not in a zoo. Jacaranda trees, covered with dazzling blue flowers. Figs, Queensland bottle trees, varieties of eucalyptus unknown in Europe. Some plants I do know of course, bougainvillaea, agapanthus, and cheese plant, though the latter is not potted and in a living room, but adorns a flowerbed.

2

Even the Metro is weird, the first time in my life on a double-decker train, and the seats swivel round so you can look to the front no matter in which direction the train is going. And it's so noisy! It clatters, clangs and bangs like no other Metro, but what the hell: all Sydney is noisy, shouts as if in constant celebration. 'The city roared its song,' Wrightson said of the Great Going Home, 'pouring rivers of cars down every street and rivers of people into every station.' And so it does at noon, as we explore Victorian arcades and shopping malls, stare at verandas with their frills and fol-de-rols of uniquely Australian ironwork, admire the brownstone of house walls (I'd expected wood), exclaim at the odd position of sedate and neatly proportioned nineteenth-century buildings –a bank, a court-house – between huge, sober, skyscraping office towers.

It's a city for walking. Though its population is three million, and its suburbs straggle for ever (like Los Angeles, though more higgledy-piggledy, and with the worst freeway system in the world), everything the tourist may want to visit is a walk from Circular Quay: downtown is neat and compact, and full of surprises. No other city has placed its botanical gardens right in the centre, on what is prime office-building land, or has preserved a lived-in, residential Victorian quarter (The Rocks) where the port should be. I note the cosmopolitan nature of restaurant cuisines – here you can eat anything. We ascend Sydney Tower, higher than London's Post Office – the sprawl of suburbs, distant Botany Bay where Cook arrived, the whole extent of the harbour like a map, the Pacific Ocean on the horizon. Then, having packed so much into the day, we subside in a pub at The Loo (nickname for the district of Woolloomooloo); an Irish pub, straight out of Dublin it could be, with Irish men and women sipping Guinness and watching horses race on the television screen.

At night gay Sydney – the bars in Darlinghurst; the Albury, the Oxford, the Midnight Shift. Nothing specifically Australian in these – they are like the gay bars of anywhere, with the same disco music, the same kind of men; and though one may fantasise about the bronzed bodies and muscly legs of big, butch surfers, they are no different from the suntanned skins and hairy thighs one can see in all bars in summer. Sydney, we like to think, is as San Francisco was, the world's gay mecca, but only for Mardi Gras is this so – the great days are finished. The huge, all-night discos, the packed bath-houses aren't what they were. Anti-gay violence is on the increase; there are more and more unsolved murders. The shadow of Aids lies over everything . . . London is regarded by these people as more interesting; I check this by comparing the listings pages of Britain's *Gay Times*, Australia's *Outrage*, and New Zealand's *Pink Triangle*, and see that it's true. I'm surprised. But . . . it's easier to find available cock in Sydney. The saunas may not be packed, but they are still functioning; swishing queens and pretty youths mince down Oxford Street, and rugged, butch numbers loll against King's Cross walls. The adverts in the press are outspoken – 'Will drool over your throbbing weapon' – and the safe-sex literature is more explicit, with photos of cute guys being *very* explicit. Even the bookshops are overflowing with customers till late in the evening. My books are housed between porn and the novels of Iris Murdoch – enjoyable, laid-back chaos. But I should come for Mardi Gras, I'm told – *that* is the day: the streets crowded, the traffic diverted, train-loads of queens shrieking in from Melbourne and Canberra . . .

I head out to Manly with Biff in her four-wheel-drive Toyota, then north up the coast. The endless suburbs, neither beautiful nor ugly, but pointless and depressing, do at last come to an end; here are the well-kept gardens and wooden houses I'd imagined – their architecture not British, not American: something between. A hoarding outside a church (it seems peculiarly Australian) yells, 'Come to church now and beat the Christmas rush!' I'd forgotten it's only six weeks till Christmas; it is such an unlikely idea in the middle of summer. Each successive reminder is therefore easy to blank out, garbage the memory refuses to hold.

The most striking feature of this day in the country is I don't see a single field, not a sheep or a cow, hardly even a blade of grass, on the entire journey up to Palm Beach and Broken Bay. Primitive, ancient land: scrub and eucalyptus forest; writhing, twisted branches, an absence of the green that is England; instead the dusty, dry, tired grey-green of wattle and gum. But beautiful. Rudbeckia, orange and yellow at the roadside; oleander, bottle-brush, lilies, morning glory. Sandstone cliffs eroded by the sea into bizarre shapes: the sea rough, whipped up by wind, the light on waves hard, glaring, hurtful to the eye. I see no kangaroos,wombats, dingos, or witchetty grubs; I guess we'd have to go much further into the bush . . . A road-sign warns 'Koalas.' Biff screeches to a halt: "Kookaburra!" and there it is, on a fence-post, head cocked on one side, not at all fearful, most curious about *us*.

The texture of eucalyptus is as time-worn as the red rocks of the Australian interior; trunk and root are grainy like marble, look dead from an excess of sun-torture. Grey of all things that at home is green: yellow of sand at Palm Beach; not golden, not citrus, not buttery, not custard – just an extraordinarily dense concentration, as if only here was the real, original hue.

The absurdity, after miles and miles of bush, of a café – a solitary, isolated building – announcing that it serves 'Devon cream teas.'

Biff and I catch up on seventeen years. She, the youngest of our generation, and I, the eldest, were always close, and so it is now – we are completely at ease with each other; as if we are resuming a conversation that stopped yesterday, though she was a kid when I last saw her, and I'm now observing a middle-aged woman. She's done well. She came to Sydney in 1968 like some Victorian adventurer: nowhere to live, knowing nobody, unemployed, and a mere few pounds in her pocket. She had just graduated from Exeter with a degree in maths. Now she has a good job, money, a splendid flat with views of the Harbour Bridge, and a man to share it with – a relationship that's clearly successful. Unlike every other member of my family, she has no hang-ups about her eldest cousin being gay; she wants to know my story, how it has been and how it is. I wish those years had not been so separate.

The last time I saw her was in 1973 at my Uncle John's funeral. My Aunt Irene died in 1985, but I did not go to her funeral – I was working in California. A pity, for Irene was my favourite aunt; "And you were always the favourite nephew!"Biff teases. "How jealous we all were of *that*!" It's strange to find in Sydney things that belonged to my childhood, to a house in rural Hampshire nearly half a century ago. They seem out of key in this smart, bright flat at Kurraba Point, thousands of miles from their place of origin – the framed photograph of John that stood on their Alresford sideboard, the sampler Irene stitched of Winchester Cathedral, the portrait of my dead cousin, Biff's brother, Martin. Another world: I can't get used to them being here.

But it doesn't affect the enjoyment I feel in her company. I wonder, however, as we stare down at huge jellyfish floating like dinner-plates in the harbour, how different my perceptions of Sydney would be if I was alone. Travel, Theroux said in *The Old Patagonian Express*, ought to be solitary; other people's reactions get in the way of one's own. Yes, seeing it together is a kind of confusion; her perceptions do interfere with mine, and her knowledge of the city maps out how I observe it. But I also have the consolation of knowing that voyages into the bush would be impossible without her – I'd be spending the days not far from Circular Quay.

She drives us out west, to Katoomba, high up in the Blue Mountains. The Yosemite (on a much smaller scale) of Sydney's hinterland – a vast, sheer canyon, its sides, summits and floor covered with dense eucalyptus. These mountains, part of the Great Dividing Range, owe their name to the trees; the droplets of eucalyptus oil that fill the air give them their colour, a smoky, smudgy blue. We walk down a thousand steps hacked in the side of the cliff (the strain on my thigh muscles, AZT-affected, is appalling);

then, blessed relief, a path that is level through rain-forest: giant ferns, turpentines, native redwoods and sequoias that recall only a little their American cousins. Gelahs, pink and grey, whizz in the trees. On the ground is a spider, tiny and bright orange. "Don't touch it! "Biff warns.

"What is it?"

"I don't know . . . but leave it alone!"

Why does this land have more venomous creatures than any other? What fearful predators did its spiders and snakes have to deal with so rapidly and effectively they evolved the most lethal of poisons? Why, in New Zealand – which isn't that far away – are there no killer spiders, indeed no snakes or indigenous mammals at all?

We return to the car by ascending the cliff-face on what is said to be the steepest railway in the world. It is almost vertical, and the little train is in poor condition: I am absolutely terrified and dare not look down; I would scream. Fortunately the journey lasts a mere few minutes.

We stop for a drink in Windsor. Late afternoon, Friday. The pub is filled with macho, carousing men, shouting loudly: the six o'clock swill. Not at all like an English pub – it personifies the rough, mindless Aussie society of lager adverts and the anecdotes of disgruntled travellers. I feel intimidated, and say so to Biff: "You're the only woman in here, and I'm probably the only gay man!"

She agrees it isn't particularly attractive. "But if you hadn't mentioned it," she says, "I wouldn't have noticed. In twenty years I've got used to this . . . I think of it as normal."

Next day we go south. Suburbs, suburbs: car lots, fast food joints, American-style strip city. In the country – hours later, it seems – I become alive, more aware; this is a different landscape again. Thousands of years of controlled scrub-burning by Aboriginals have given this bush a park-like appearance; it is all grey-green field-grass, with here and there a eucalyptus that looks deliberately planted, as if to provide a focal point, though I'm sure it is not. Half a dozen cockatoos fly over a pond. "Pond?" Biff queries. "No such thing in Australia. It's either a billabong or a dam. That's a dam."

The restaurant where we have lunch is one of the oldest buildings in New South Wales, a spacious ranch-house miles from anywhere; its fireplaces, ceiling roses and mantelshelves date from 1827. I sense the life a well-to-do family must have had in those day – it's the kind of house one sees in films and TV serials about early Australia. In the garden is a huge pear tree more than a century old. The undulating, grass-covered land stretches to the horizon: flower smells, bees searching for honey, silence. Superb summer warmth. A drowsy dog opens an eye and stares at us, then flops back into sleep.

We approach the Harbour Bridge via Glebe, an inner suburb of tree-lined, Victorian terraces; the ironwork of verandas is intricate, beautifully carved. A publishing firm who once distributed our books in Australia has its headquarters here: they owe us more than five hundred pounds, and seem to have no intention of paying. They have, I guess, financial difficulties; but where is the thin division between hard times and dishonesty?

Momentous events are happening: Margaret Thatcher has resigned. Biff rushes into my room to tell me that people are dancing in the streets of London – champagne corks are popping. For a moment I wish I was there. The TV cameras find Bob Hawke; he's playing golf. Celebrating too, I imagine. He mumbles a few, non-committal words – this time he is far from tears.

I am on my way to New Zealand; these few days in Sydney are merely a pause. My appetite is whetted, not satisfied. I shall return; cost a fortune though it will, I want to experience the two great train journeys – Sydney to Perth and Adelaide to Alice. See Ayer's Rock, the Olgas, the Nullarbor; Canberra, Adelaide and Melbourne.

Meanwhile – I have stood under the Southern Cross. I'm amused that most people I ask are unable to identify it; I'd thought it would be as obvious to them as the Plough is to me. But there at last it is, a crucifix on its side. Impressive. And constellations that are visible in both hemispheres are upside down; Orion is on his back, legs in the air. As any decent man's should be. The moon seems to wax and wane in opposite directions to those I'm familiar with, and, yes, the bath-water does swirl round the plug-hole anti-clockwise.

I, too, am upside down.

November 1990

From Fuckarewarewa to Urupukapuka

First impressions of Auckland are of disappointment: sleepy city, cloudy sky, a hint of rain; landscape so green and English. Green English landscape isn't normally a matter for grumbling, but . . . one hopes the other side of the world will look different from one's own backyard. I'm wrong, of course: this Englishness is a superficial veneer. The vegetation shows that I really am on the far side of the world – mangrove swamps, greyish, their fruit small and looking like bitter oranges; tree-ferns ten, twenty, thirty feet high; kauri, cabbage-trees, and manuka; all quite unlike anything I know in Europe, and what I assume are bottle-brush shrubs that have grown into trees are pohutukawas. The forest is not gorse; it's matagouri – the Maoris once used its thorns, much bigger and more lethal than gorse prickles, to tattoo their skin. Bizzy lizzie grows here in immense profusion, and tradescantia is so common it's a weed. Another weed – and a great pest – is the ginger plant. Agapanthus (now in full bloom) decorates, as oleander in California, the central reservations of freeways. Harry's and Mark's garden is on the edge of a kauri forest; rosellas (a parakeet) fly about in the foliage. Bougainvillaea; cinnerarias and flax of gigantic size. At night I can hear the New Zealand owl – the mopoke – hooting in the kauris: "More pork!" it calls. "More pork!"

It's good to be, once again, with gay friends. I know I'm back among my own kind as I listen to some anecdote about a man who's been taken to hospital: the handlebars of a bicycle have got stuck up his arse; "I fell on them when I was having a shower," is his explanation. Not the chat I would have with my heterosexual cousin in Sydney. Strange to be here: I could never have imagined – not for one wild moment – when I first met Harry at a party in East London that eleven years later I would be in his house in Auckland.

I get to know Auckland piecemeal; there's no need to pack it in as I did in Sydney – I'm here for a month. And piecemeal is a very good way to approach

Auckland, for it's without an immediately obvious identity or definable atmosphere; its charms don't hit one as do Sydney's. It sprawls, imitating Los Angeles. Eventually I begin to like it as much as I like Sydney: but it takes time. Adjusting to a slower pace is the first requirement; a difference, I learn, not merely between Auckland and Sydney but between Australia and New Zealand in general.

It's devoted to water. Built on the narrowest neck of land in the country, it has two vast harbours – Manukau and Waitemata – and its people make full use of both. There are more boats per head of population than anywhere else in the world: yachts are almost as common as cars, and crossing from the North Shore by the Harbour Bridge the focus of attention isn't a cathedral or skyscrapers or monuments but the huge extent of the yacht basin, water crowded with masts. The bridge is typical of Auckland's self-effacement: it's much longer than Sydney's but is unremarkable to look at, a sort of stretched-out coat-hanger. Some years ago, when it become insufficient to deal with the traffic, a Japanese firm was asked to widen it on both sides: these extra lanes were called the Nippon Clip-on, and that has become the colloquial name for the whole structure. It has a moveable central barrier – a most ingenious device – so that during the morning rush hour the incoming traffic can use six lanes, the outgoing two: in the evening the process is reversed. I find I enjoy the views from this bridge as much as any from Sydney's or San Francisco's bridges; these early summer days the texture of the water is soft, milky, and constantly changing – very different from the hard, gem-like, unvarying blue of Sydney's water. I write a list of all the shades of blue I can think of: slate blue, fog blue (blue fog?), Delft blue, gentian, the blue of Renoir' *La Parisienne*, blue plum blue, Fra Angelico blue; delicate, virginal blue as in Mary's robes in medieval paintings. All of them – and none of them – fit Auckland's harbours, and the colour of the New Zealand sky, which has more shifting subtle blues than anywhere else I've ever been.

12

Downtown Auckland has some hideous skyscrapers, but the domestic architecture of the suburbs is most pleasant. As in California, wood is the chief building material, and nineteenth-century Aucklanders evolved a building style all their own, as did San Franciscans. No Victorian house is here exactly like any other, and though the vivid paints San Franciscans use are not in evidence, there is a similar originality in the decorative carving. A feature of these single-storey houses that one does not find in America is the gable – architecturally unfunctional, but a necessary focal point, often riotously designed. There are more trees than one would expect in a big city: in the most middle-class areas the houses are almost lost in woods. Parnell, an inner suburb, is the main Victorian showpiece; its nineteenth-century cottages have been tarted up to attract the tourists, and many are now boutiques – I prefer the more unobtrusive suburbs, still properly lived in. But Parnell is worth a visit for its splendid rose-garden. Auckland's house prices make one despair of what has happened in England : that 'over-housed and under-educated' country, as *The Economist* so rightly put it. Sixty thousand pounds in Auckland will buy an immaculate, detached, four-bedroom residence with a double garage, gardens, and stunning views of the Harbour.

I've never before seen Gothic churches built of wood, and in consequence find the old cathedral– the largest timber cathedral in the world – very strange. The reddish kauri makes the interior somewhat dark : but building in wood gives certain freedoms not possible in stone, the intricate dovetailing of beams and arches, for example – and it's warmer, less clinical than stone. And it creaks, like an old house at night. For some reason or other it was transported across the road in 1982, leaving behind and now looking purposeless, the bishop's palace which is also of wood and Gothic in style, with a cute octagonal tower and camp turret. Harry lived next door to the cathedral when it was on the opposite side of the road : he went to England for several years, then discovered on his return that it had been moved. It was, he says, as if a part of his life had been violently wrenched away.

Volcanoes are the most interesting natural feature of the landscape; there are about ninety of them in the Greater Auckland area, all of them, I'm assured, extinct. But, since Mount St. Helen's blew its stack on my birthday in 1980, I don't feel that any volcano is really extinct : I regard them with *deep* suspicion. Volcano talk in Auckland is as common as earthquake talk in San Francisco, and predictions of future activity are as vague as guesses about what shocks the San Andreas may provide. One 'expert' says a new volcano will soon appear, in the middle of Waitemata Harbour. The last time this occurred was six hundred years ago when Rangitoto shot up from beneath the sea: it erupted again in the eighteenth century and destroyed several Maori villages on an island nearby. I look at Rangitoto quite often (one can see it from almost anywhere in Auckland), and think how spectacular it would be if it did blast off again, now . . . Volcanoes, nevertheless, are good places for views; from the summits of Mount Eden and One-Tree Hill the whole of Auckland is visible. In the bottom of Mount Eden's crater a herd of cows is placidly munching grass; where on earth, I say to myself, in a city of a million people do they get milked?

The War Memorial Museum, grand and imposing, has a large collection of Maori artefacts, including a meeting-house and some impressive canoes; it also has a moa twelve feet high: the feathers, I presume, are not its own – moas were hunted to extinction nearly three centuries back. New Zealand must once have been dominated by these birds – skeletons of some ten thousand of them have been discovered in a single swamp in the South Island. It was extremely foolish of Maoris to hunt them to extinction, for they were the main food supply. (Which seems to disprove a fashionable sentimentality – that primitive races are more caring of the environment than we are. Aboriginals, I guess, may be more in tune with Nature than either we or Maoris, but even they caused major changes. I spend a long time staring at Auckland's moa: its great thumping feet, its huge neck, its tiny head and wings that lost the power to make it airborne eons before Maoris came to New Zealand. Victim of an environment in which birds were supreme and had, as a result, no ability to withstand the contact of mammals.

The forest beyond Harry's and Mark's garden – kauris, red pine, black beech, black tree-fern – is flourishing and extensive: not everything fell to the invasion of mammals. I'm reminded, looking at these trees, some of them a thousand years old, of how young is European New Zealand – no more than a gloss on the surface. I'm only yards away from Auckland and I hear no city noises, no traffic; just forest sounds: cicadas, bird cries, water dripping, and the rustling of unseen creatures. There isn't a human anywhere, but at night, perhaps, this could be a gay cruising-ground: it has that kind of feel. Now, in the day, it's marvellously atmospheric – a vivid pointer to what the whole country must have been like, once upon a time . . .

Out, by ferry, into the Harbour. From here Auckland's skyscrapers seem less intrusive; this city is built to be looked at from water – only then does it come together, is coherent, all of a piece. The marina is emptying: the sea is a mass of yachts, sails every bright colour bulging in the wind, like enormous birds. Some *are* enormous, stately as galleons. A group of six, keeping pace with each other, is as if Sydney's opera house really had slipped its moorings and floated off. Beyond the Harbour is Hauraki Gulf with its forty or so islands: the sea is the softest pastel blue, white-flecked in the yachts' wakes; when a cloud scuds over the sun, it is green, milky green, the green achieved with a crayon. The ferry lingers at Devonport – pretty wooden houses – then crosses to the southern shore near Mission Bay. On the horizon are the peaks of Coromandel: distant, mysterious shapes like the mountain-tops in old legends.

I disembark for another new experience – inside a glass tube, itself inside a gigantic underground aquarium; above me and at either hand are sharks and rays. *Huge* rays that lazily flap like black rags or black carpets being shaken; when still they resemble Stealth bombers. They have tiny,

15

smiling mouths. The sharks' mouths are not tiny, nor are they smiling; sharks are purposeful. They're hungry, busy, and extremely efficient.

The ferry moves to Rangitoto. Walking here is not easy; the ground is all clinker, dark rock, solidified lava. No soil, yet the entire surface is covered with pohutukawa forest – unlike the city's trees they are only just beginning to bloom. Some have been destroyed by possums, who have no predators in New Zealand; possums have multiplied so much it's estimated that the country has sixty-six million of them. (There are only three and a half million humans.) Visitors were banned from Rangitoto for two months in order to eradicate the possums; sixteen thousand corpses were collected: and the island is a mere three miles long and two wide. Under the pohutukawas is moss, in which kidney ferns abound. I had expected this plant to be big as a tree (ferns usually are in New Zealand), but it's four inches high – a beautiful, delicate, little thing. No one lives on Rangitoto : there are perhaps a dozen holiday cottages, at the moment empty. There is superb silence here, broken only by the soughing of the wind in the trees – consoling, satisfying. Again I'm struck by how easy it is in this big, urban sprawl to feel I'm miles from civilisation – as I do in the kauri forest, or the green interior of Mount Eden's cone, or my bedroom at Harry's and Mark's where the only noise at night is the soft cry : "More pork! More pork!"

The green hills dotted with sheep are deceptive: this landscape, hunched, bunched and scrunched – Earth's plates gouging at one another – is not English. This is obvious at Rotorua, unstable, volcanic, and riddled with fault-lines. But still the fields are green; the sheep look untroubled, and Lake Rotorua is a perfectly ordinary blue. In the town centre, however, steam rises from drains, and there is a smell of bad eggs. Years ago people came to take the waters; there is a wonderful, mock Tudor bath-house (now an art gallery) and almost every motel has a hot sulphur bath: twenty minutes in one of these is most pleasantly soporific – far more useful than any sleeping pill. Rotorua's domestic hot water is piped from the hot springs; until recently this service was free – the inhabitants are very annoyed with the government, who now make them pay for it.

The centre of attention here is Whakarewarewa: bubbling mud and spurting geysers, Whakarewarewa is pronounced Fuckarewarewa; 'wha,' a common prefix in Maori place-names, is 'fu' when spoken. So Whangaparaoa is Fungaparaoa. This is odd: the Maoris had no written language; these place-names are what Europeans thought they sounded like. 'Wha' for 'fu' is a genteelism – Victorian colonials aghast at the idea of writing down a syllable that might look like 'fuck', let alone saying it. There is a surprising amount of vegetation at Whakarewarewa: one would imagine the boiling water and clouds of steam would kill it – but the tea trees, though somewhat limp and scalded, endure. The mud pools slurp, plop, seethe and fart, forming thick concentric rings as baking ingredients do in a mixing bowl, The two geysers – Pohutu and the Prince of Wales's Feathers – perform magnificently, great spasms of blinding white hot water shooting upwards; the energy is colossal and a bit alarming. They really do shoot their loads: the sexual metaphor must occur to every tourist. The clouds of sulphurous steam are quite overpowering, and so is the smell – bad eggs, or pubes that have not been washed for months. I'm breathless: I have to move away.

No vegetation grows by the geysers – the ground here is covered with silica deposits from the water; grey, white and pink, and glistening like cake that's just been frosted. In the last century, on the far side of Lake Rotomahana, there were spectacular staircases of silica – the Pink and White Terraces – which were formed by a geyser much larger than any at Whakarewarewa. It was New Zealand's chief tourist attraction, the eighth wonder of the world: unique, a phenomenon of unsurpassed magnificence. But in 1886 a nearby volcano, Mount Tarawera, erupted with appalling violence – it ripped itself open. The Pink and White Terraces and the geyser were destroyed; the village of Te Wairoa was buried beneath an avalanche of lava, ash, and mud. One hundred and fifty-three people were killed. The village has been excavated; it is New Zealand's Pompeii – though without rude frescoes. The drive there is beautiful – the Green Lake and the Blue Lake, both aptly named, and hillsides thick with giant ferns: forests of green stars. At Te Wairoa one can see what was rescued after the eruption – blackened household goods, twisted bottles, even a baby's cot.

Fairy Springs is Rotorua's wild life reserve – mopokes, kiwis, tuis, native trees, pools full of gigantic trout, gentle waterfalls : the latter a contrast to the tremendous waterfall at Te Wairoa, which is reached through a dark, dank cavern. Kiwis, like moas, have great thumping feet and useless bits of wings. Immense beaks: I watch them forage – prodding under dead, decaying wood, searching out grubs. A pair of them asleep, curled up together, look strangely like hedgehogs.

The biggest cave at Waitomo resembles a vast Gothic cathedral – but as if the limestone had melted, then frozen again: bent, twisted columns, vaults askew, slipped bosses, drooping organ-pipes. Or as if liquid had showered down, then solidified in fantastic shapes—an elephant, a cat, a bird, Queen Victoria with orb and sceptre, a skull, a set of luxuriant African dreadlocks. Stalactites and stalagmites have fused centuries ago, have become a primitive radiator system, or were united so recently the join is as thin as a wafer or drinking straw, is fragile as barley sugar. In the lake at the bottom a punt transports us to the glow-worms: we are asked to keep absolutely silent – these creatures detest noise, and retaliate by extinguishing their lamps. There is not even the splash of an oar; the boatman finds his way through the darkness with his fingers, pushing and pulling on the walls of the cave. In the ceiling there are a zillion pin-pricks of light : we are drifting through the galaxies of the universe, clusters of unnamed constellations. But glow-worm light is not starlight; it doesn't twinkle – it's constant and muted, like faint pencil-torches. Weak, distant daylight filters through cracks in the ceiling or, occasionally, flues near water level: there is just enough to produce astonishing reflections in the water, which is utterly still. I'm reminded of Parnell's *Night Piece on Death*, the phrases about 'the livid gleams of night,' the churchyard wall which 'the silent water laves,' and I feel a similar contemplative calm:

> How deep yon azure dyes the sky
> Where orbs of gold unnumber'd lie . . .
> . . . The slumb'ring breeze forgets to breathe,
> The lake is smooth and clear beneath,
> Where once again the spangl'd show
> Descends to meet our eyes below.

Yes, a curiously eighteenth-century experience, The poets of nocturnal reverie and melancholic thought—Dyer, Green, Shenstone, Gray, Lady Winchilsea, certainly Pope with his enthusiasm for grottos – would have loved this place.

The bus returning me to Auckland stops for three quarters of an hour in Hamilton, New Zealand's fifth largest city. In the café where I drink tea the radio is on full blast, Harry Secombe yelling his balls off through every single verse of It Came Upon the Midnight Clear. There's nothing to say about Hamilton: it's incredibly dull.

I had assumed the winterless north would be quite different from the landscape south of Auckland – it looks, on the map, as if it should be drier, less green; this long, thin spit of island protruding far into the Pacific – but it is not: Auckland isn't a San Francisco, a great divide between temperate and tropical zones. Northland is green, and hunched and bunched and scrunched, with the usual sheep; but somewhat warmer – the season is more advanced. Jacarandas, acanthus, hibiscus, bougainvilla are in full bloom; there are great numbers of succulents and exotic plants I haven't noticed elsewhere.

I've come to see the Bay of Islands, said to be one of the most beautiful parts of New Zealand, and historically of great importance: the first Maoris settled here and also, by coincidence, the first Europeans; Waitangi is where the famous (or infamous) treaty was signed that established British sovereignty, and Russell was the Europeans' first capital. I'd misread the name as Bay of a Thousand Islands, and imagined that from here came the salad dressing – an idea that makes Harry and Mark guffaw. But if one includes all the rocks there are a thousand islands: I'm expecting a landscape like Scilly. Antipodean sunk Lyonesse.

It does indeed have resonances with Scilly—the same illusion of a still, landlocked sea – but it isn't so dramatic; no saw-teeth, and the islands are hillier and greener : it's a softer place. The sea lacks Scilly's blue intensity and copper tangleweed; it's cloudy green. I'd expected, too, a great deal of seaside tawdriness – it is, after all, one of the country's premier tourist regions – but I'm delighted to find it has nothing of the sort, not even in Paihia, the main servicing centre, which exists to provide hotels, motels, buses, shops and restaurants. Not that Paihia is particularly interesting: an old house or two, New Zealand's oldest Norfolk pine, and the site of its oldest church – nothing else.

Russell, on the far side of the Bay, is, however, a gorgeous little town, which, thank goodness, makes no concessions whatsoever to tourists : its waterfront, virtually unchanged in a hundred and fifty years, is a living anachronism. Russell has a laid-back, mañana atmosphere; some lovely Victorian houses with old-fashioned gardens; a huge Moreton Bay fig tree; and a charming, Gaudí-like police station built of wood, New Zealand's oldest. The oldest everything is here – hotel, church, restaurant; so on and so forth. In the graveyard is a memorial to a group of British sailors killed in 1845 by Maoris; the poem inscribed on it expresses the attitudes of the period – it amuses: and makes one cringe.

> The warlike of the Isles
> The men of field and wave
> Are not the rocks their funeral piles
> The sea and stone their grave?
> So stagger back the deep

> Free, free the white sails spread
> Where may not foam, and wild wave beat
> Where rest not England's dead.

I like the error of 'piles' for 'pyres.' A rock and a hard place . . .?

On the vast green lawn of the British Resident's house at Waitangi the treaty was signed. The house is the nation's most cherished monument, but there is only a handful of visitors this afternoon, none of them a New Zealander; it's a very modest affair, colonial Victorian, somewhat over-restored. In the grounds there is a Maori war canoe and a meeting-house, both excellent examples of native wood-carving skills. One has to remove one's shoes before entering a meeting-house; it is like going into a mosque. In the Residence there is a copy of the treaty, and I read it through. It's caused no end of problems down the years because of its supposed ambiguities, but it strikes me as being brief, clear and to the point. The most contentious clause isn't ambiguous – it's straightforward daylight robbery: the British sovereign has first choice in buying any land the Maoris wish to sell. This led to massive exploitation of the Maoris, who, like Aboriginals, had no concept of land ownership. To some extent reparations are now being made: the Labour government of the nineteen eighties, by means of the Waitangi Tribunal, decided to settle land disputes, and as a result great tracts have been returned to the Maoris. Guilty consciences. The Waitangi Tribunal has bipartisan support: the present National government is unlikely to abolish it.

I eat this hot, summer evening an excellent dinner in a Paihia restaurant – old house with a very English garden: roses, godetia, cornflower; the sweet scent of tobacco plant drifting into the room. The proprietor, middle-aged and chatty, is obviously gay – wrist-flapping, camp. I compliment him on providing chocolate mints with the coffee; he hopes, he says in answer, that I'll come back again. "I'm twelve thousand miles away from home," I tell him. He pulls a Frankie Howerd face, flaps wildly, and screams: "Oooooh!!" Then adds, as an afterthought, "Long

21

way to come, I suppose, for a chocolate mint." I stroll along the beach: cirrus clouds, pink with sunset; a gannet swooping low over the sea, which is like glass. Some cute young men are filling a boat with supplies – their radio is playing *When Will I See You Again?* New Zealand pop inhabits a seventies time-warp; I'm therefore constantly reminded of people and places, and lovers, and what I was doing on some particular evening fifteen years ago. How I'd like to share all this – this beautiful place – with a lover! A blond, suntanned youth starts up the outboard motor on his dinghy, and streaks off, direct as an arrow, for Russell: is he late, this modern Leander, for an assignation with *his* lover? Jesus! Why do we all, always, have to cart our personal garbage around? When . . . please . . . can I throw it aside?

Send my roots rain.

Perhaps I should, as my friend Martin did, buy myself a boat.

I console myself by spending all next day on water, in a catamaran bound for Cape Brett; it is partly for tourists, partly for commerce – mail delivery and cargo for the inhabitants of the outer reaches. The sea, inshore, is lime green, apple, olive, and crystal clear; further out blue-black, the texture of bottle-glass. Russell in the early morning mist seems only just this side of paradise. Sun, heat: and absolutely still. I see sponges, red coral; there are flying fish and shoals of blue mowie. Gannets and shearwaters. The beaches are those of imagined South Sea idylls – golden and empty, pohutukawas on the shore a crimson blaze. At Piercy's Island we meet the open Pacific: gentle swell, rising, falling. There is an enormous tunnel under the island – we drift through it slowly: magnificent striations of black and grey rock.

The return takes us to Urupukapuka, one of the inhabited islands; I land, climb a hill, and gaze at the far side. Silence, except for the wind. Then back to the dock where I venture into a submarine – it takes us beneath the water to look at fish. *Hundreds* of fish, but the only species I can identify is snapper; one, known locally as Jaws, is *huge*,

22

a grandfather of a fish – it looks remarkably like an elderly Australian I noticed on the catamaran. Curious the way fish move: wiggle-wiggle, wiggle-wiggle. Their mouths are like Bette Davis's, turned down and without humour. There are giant clams too, and rubbery, yellow sponges; seaweed which in the water currents shifts, sways, bends like hair.

Urupukapuka: a name from some fabulous myth of the South Seas.

Brochures advertising the Silver Fern, a first-class-only express train from Auckland to Wellington, specify its de luxe travel facilities – air-conditioning, seats covered in sheepskin for extra comfort, complimentary lunch, morning and afternoon tea all served at my seat, a bar trolley, complimentary newspapers and so on, but I do ask myself why a journey of four hundred and twenty miles should take ten hours; the London to Edinburgh Intercity, for example, takes about five. I soon learn. The brochure is not untruthful, but the train is a two-carriage, bone-shaking rattletrap, and the word 'express' must be some Antipodean idea of a joke. The railway is single-track, the whole four hundred and twenty miles of it; British Rail, one says fairly soon after leaving Auckland: all is forgiven. On this particular day the Silver Fern's brakes work much too well; they keep coming on when the driver doesn't want them to, so we grind to a halt – vey frequently. Other hold-ups are for a signal failure, and a rock that is stuck in some points. One of the carriages is non-smoking but the New Zealand Rail computer, which designates your seat, can't distinguish between smokers and non-smokers; so during the first two hours passengers who wish to smoke, and those who wish to avoid smoke, are scurrying about finding new places to sit.

At Raumiru we are told there will be a very long halt indeed; we're invited to get out of the train and take a stroll – look at the view. Another train, halfway up the Spiral, has broken down and has to be shifted. (The Spiral is a magnificent piece of railway engineering: the line climbs thousands of feet in zigzags and tunnels, emerging on a plateau beside the North Island's highest peaks, snow-covered Tongariro, Ngauruhoe, and Ruapehu, volcanoes all, two of them in excellent working order.) Raumiru, a scatter of houses miles from anywhere, is a pleasant enough place for a stroll: fresh mountain air, flower scents (lupins and broom), acres of pampas grass. And it's hot.

We arrive at Wellington two hours behind schedule; the journey has taken twelve hours, and not many passengers feel they've had a first-class travel experience. The North Island, I suppose, does not lend itself to smooth, quick railways: product of earthquake faults and volcanic upheavals, it's excessively un-flat, But at least the scenery is a first-class experience. Ferns that *are* silver; great buzzard-like hawks, their undercarriage blue and red; vast pine forests and spectacular limestone ravines; little one-horse towns – Bunnythorpe, Marton, Utiku – that inspire the question, as do similar places in Nebraska, Kansas and Iowa, what is their purpose? Who can possibly live in them, and why, and how? The end of the trip is extremely beautiful – the railway is on the edge of the Tasman Sea: rough waves glitter in the evening light; the mountains near Paraparaumu tumble into the water. I'm reminded of the Californian coast at Santa Barbara.

In Wellington I eat what I guess I should eat in a city so-named: Beef Wellington.

The capital, the Windy City, can only grow upwards – it is locked in by sea and mountains; one of its most attractive features is that its San Francisco-like suburbs, half-hidden in trees, seem built on cliffs, are clinging to ledges by their toe-nails – but, conversely, the huge downtown skyscrapers strike one as exceptionally intimidating, ugly, and dehumanising. Its modern buildings are in general without appeal; the new Parliament, for instance, which is colloquially known as the Beehive, looks exactly like its nickname – odd, and lacking real point. But the Victorian architecture is very pleasing. Old St Paul's, another timber-built Gothic church, as the guide-book says, is exquisite; a delicate, elegant

24

structure of rimu and kauri.

It's the only city in the world, apart from San Francisco, that has cable-cars, though the resemblance to their Californian cousins is remote: the principle on which they work is similar, but they're up-to-date, electronic affairs, much easier to drive, and they're not oblongs – they're built to take into account the steepness of the hill, so when they are at the terminus they look as if they're contemplating their navels. I ascend in one of these curious objects to Kelburn, where the botanical gardens are situated. The view is magnificent: the whole city, it seems, is spread out for my inspection; beyond is the sea, blue and sparkling, with wind-blown white crests, and fold upon fold of mountains, brown, green, purple. The inter-island ferry is steaming away from the harbour – I shall be on that tomorrow. But, for the moment, the South Island is invisible, hidden by Wellington's mountain peaks. I'm lucky to be here in such perfect weather – this city has a bad reputation for lashing winds and unpredictable squalls of rain. The sea between the islands, the Cook Strait, is the reason for this: it is a funnel.

The botanical gardens are the most interesting in New Zealand; steep slopes covered with shrubs and mature trees, fascinating vistas at every turn. Quiet, sweet-smelling herbs; the roses a blaze of colour; the begonia house hot and scented, with a fine display of blossom. There is a restaurant in a Victorian glass-house; I eat lunch – salmon salad with fruit, chocolate and almond cake. Refurbished old ladies sit drinking coffee; a myopic violinist plays the tunes of yesteryear – *If I Loved You; Isn't It Romantic* – and I'm reminded of a lunchtime also in December, at Emporium, San Francisco, the same (it seems) old ladies drinking coffee and toying with expensive, sticky cakes; 'Gaggles of old ladies,' – I wrote in *A Better Class of Blond*, 'a breed almost extinct, rich, in furs and hats and jewellery and garish make-up.' My lover, Tim, was across the street buying my Christmas present. Now –

I read, much of the night, and go south in the winter. My Aunt Noreen, I say to myself, would like this place, be of it, as I am. Not for the first time I think how similar to my aunt's is my own character, how our fortunes parallel one aother's. We both let all the men slip through our fingers . . . and read much of the night, and go south in the winter . . .

Colours are not the same as in Auckland; they're more intense – sharp, distinct, no blurring and blending of soft pastel hues. I go back down in the cable-car, then walk to the National Museum, which has, says the guide-book, an impressive collection of European paintings. If it has, it's on loan or been put in storage; in its place is an exhibition of contemporary Maori work, not much different from other kinds of modern, so-called 'art' rubbish. The galleries in Auckland and Christchurch (say the guide-books) also house collections of European painting, but again they've been replaced by contemporary trash. Auckland, Wellington and Christchurch have between them a population of a million and a half, but at the moment the only European paintings of interest people can see are one Turner and one Wallis. My advice to a young New Zealand art student would be to emigrate immediately.

If I enjoy crossing the Cook Strait, I've been told, then I'll enjoy sailing anywhere in the world. Not an encouraging remark, and I fear a very rough three and half hours. But I do enjoy it: except for a slight swell as we round the Heads, the sea is flat, and the weather still perfect. Dolphins companionably monitor our progress. In the distance is the South Island, its snow-capped peaks enticing, almost magical so full of promise do they seem . . .

Couples and Metaphors

Reading December's *Gay Times* in the sun-soaked garden of a house in Auckland, relaxing here with old friends, I'm reminded of British gay problems and miseries I haven't thought about for a month. For gay isn't an issue in New Zealand. There's nothing about us on the television or in rabid, tabloid newspapers or in Parliament, and the National Party didn't use us as a stick to beat the heads of the Labour government in the recent general election. The battles were fought in 1986 and we won; the victory was decisive; gay as an issue died and was buried. The new law lowered the age of consent to sixteen, and, among other liberal provisions, the foreign partners of gay men and women were granted the right to live and work here, thus making New Zealand the first country in the world to put such a concept on the statute book. There are loose ends – the law doesn't protect gays and PWAs from discrimination. But there doesn't seem to be much discrimination: I hear of no gay-bashings, murders, or people being evicted from their houses and losing their jobs because they have Aids.

Law reform has made the gay community non-political and very quiet. An editorial in *The Pink Triangle* sums it up: 'Many men now enjoy some measure of openness at work and with their neighbours. Some are turning away from gay groups to work as openly gay men in neighbourhood residents' associations and the like.' (And the like: I *loathe* that catch-all cliché.) 'A significant number of men,' it continues, 'are enjoying a full life.' Different, I say to myself, from that of our own dear queens . . . And, observing my friends in Auckland, and the gay men they introduce me to – middle-class, home-making, couple-orientated – I can see that it's so. But I wouldn't therefore assume gay life in New Zealand is all like this; what I see – as ever – is mere chance: circumstance. New Zealand's saunas, I'm told, are flourishing and are not raided by the police; I imagine, if I visited any of them (which I don't) I wouldn't meet my friends in there. Though I'm amused when Harry is driving me round Auckland – "You've pointed out more bath-houses than churches," I tell him.

'There is no apparent desire,' *The Pink Triangle* says, 'to join gay organisations or political groups any more. This lack of active support is hampering attempts . . . to help those fighting for better health services, particularly for sexually transmitted diseases and Aids.' This, I think, is also true, and certainly with the gay men I meet there is little talk of Aids; no news, as there would be in London or San Francisco, of the most recent statistics or medicines or dying friends and acquaintances. Again, I make no assumptions: New Zealand has its Aids patients, clinics and support services, as do – it would be pleasant to say 'anywhere else,' but that would *not* be true – do other white, reasonably affluent, so-called democracies. And maybe there are gay-bashings, murders and evicted PWAs. I simply don't know.

Harry and Mark belong to an organisation called *Couples*, which is affiliated to *International Couples Network*; but no branch of it, to my knowledge, exists in England: odd, for London, so Americans, Australians and New Zealanders say, has more gay specialist concerns, services, and support facilities than anywhere else. It provides a social existence for gay couples in a non-cruisy, non-bar/disco environment, sends out a newsletter to members, and arranges theatre trips, parties, sports activities and so on. It is, inevitably I suppose, middle-aged and middle-class. Harry and Mark take me to the *Couples* Christmas barbecue: I feel very out of place – I'm the only single man, and probably the only man with Aids. But not uncomfortable; these people are warm, open and welcoming. My gay friends in San Francisco, I remind myself, are nearly all couples – some in relationships that have lasted twenty, thirty years – and are middle-aged and middle-class. They don't, of course, know each other through an organisation: they are a group of friends who have similar interests (books, opera, bridge, academe) and temperaments. So I wonder what holds these New Zealanders together apart from a desire to advertise their coupledom, 'we' – the veneer of success, status and security: small talk about holidays, house prices, and Christmas presents. At this barbecue they all wear name-tags, their own name in large letters, their partner's in small letters. Grotesque . . .

But I'm not being kind; there are real friendships here. If such an organisation existed in Britain, and if I had a lover, I might just perhaps belong to it myself. Perhaps not: I have never been a joiner of anything. I do see that it is useful and obviously pleasant; and for Harry and Mark, who lived in England for years, it was, when they returned, necessary – they knew very few gay men in Auckland.

Coll-doll, the only single gay man I know in New Zealand, is sniffy about it, because, I suppose, it has nothing for him; he has a slight air of resentment around gay couples – I imagine because he isn't part of one. It's not easy to see him living with somebody. He's so houseproud: not a speck of dust is permitted on his carpets, and an unfortunate insect that strays into his living room the evening I eat with him gets instantly zonked with aerosol. He's very amusing, very camp – Liberace chandeliers on his piano, a reading-lamp that resembles a vase of tulips: and the shirt he's wearing he doesn't like, but he has to wear it, he says, because it's fashionable. He's the only person I've ever met who's been for his holidays in New Caledonia, of all places. After dinner he insists on doing his ironing – to show me, I guess, his ironing board cover, which has a picture on it of a *huge* naked man. I like Coll-doll: at this point in my existence I'm more au fait with his philosophy than that of *Couples*.

The Unity Bookshop in Wellington isn't specifically gay, but it has a very large stock of lesbian and gay literature; the people who run it are clearly aware of, and sympathetic to, our interests and needs. I find myself in conversation with the manager, who says if she'd known I was in town she'd have organised a party, a reading, an interview on the local radio station. I'm famous, she says – *dozens* of people would be thrilled to know I'm here. I'm read, she continues, by people in all walks of life (presumably she means gay and straight); Ive done so much for the young that's good and helpful. I'm intensely embarrassed – I cannot handle this sort of lionising praise. Thank God it's extremely rare. I clam up, giggle like a teenager; I'm very relieved she *didn't* know I was in New Zealand . . . It's a British kind of reserve, I suppose, a deeply engrained reticence – my friend Maurice would understand exactly what I mean. He and I have often said that beneath the apparent openness with which I write, under the frank exchange of feelings and ideas he and I share (and the bitchy camp of much of our conversation), we both have in our characters an inherently middle-class Britishness. It can manifest iteself in an inability to accept praise, gush – or help. Some months ago when I decided, because of Aids and increasing attacks of claustrophobia, that I could no longer do my shopping and house cleaning unassisted, he said to a mutual friend sthat I would never, in a million years, have asked for help unless it was absolutely necessary. I value that very much: because it's true.

I was hoping, in the Unity Bookshop, to buy the Penguin edition of Susan Sontag's *Aids and Its Metaphors*, but they've sold out. I look for it elsewhere with no success. I even try Whitcoulls, New Zealand's premier bookstore chain, an up-market W.H. Smith: the background muzak is *Rudolph, the red-nosed reindeer* . . . I'm referred to the paperback buyer. "*Aids and Its Metaphors?*" she queries. "Quite a mouthful, that. Is it a novel?" My initial reaction, amusement, is soon replaced by anger – what fucking ignorance. I eventually find it in another shop, and begin to read it immediately. It becomes an integral part of my tour round the South Island, inextricably blended with my images and observations of the Cook Strait, Christchurch, the Canterbury Plains, the Southern Alps, Queenstown, Fiordland, the rain forests and glaciers of Westland. I devour the whole thing in one go, with a huge feeling of intellectual excitement that is almost physical, sensuous – here, by far and away, is the most important piece of writing that has yet been done on the subject of Aids. Then I start at the beginning again, and read it slowly, a page or two at a time – it is so dense, so complex, that every paragraph needs to be carefully considered. I'm conscious of being two separate selves: the tourist enjoying days of marvellous landscape he's never seen before, in a country he's never visited before; and a PWA finding that all he's ever thought about Aids is here written down, discussed, and expressed in infinitely superior fashion to anything he could write himself. These two personae are both private and public. They eventually fuse when I meet a young German backpacker . . . which is also both private and public.

Aids and Its Metaphors is for me a catharsis: to detach Aids from meanings and imagery is liberating, a consolation, as Sontag herself points out. HIV as the 'enemy,' an 'invading host' that 'docking with the cell, penetrates the cell membrane' – the military metaphors, the language of *Star Wars* – she and I detest, for it 'over-mobilises, over-describes, and it powerfully contributes to the excommunicating and stigmatising of the ill;' it turns those who are ill into unavoidable casualties, or demonises them as the Saddam Husseins of medicine. Such stigmatising leads to an isolation (I've noticed it so often in others, and it is my own fate) that has happened throughout history when metaphor forms perspectives of illness; she quotes from Donne's *Devotions* to illustrate the point – 'the greatest misery of sickness is solitude; when the infectiousness of the disease deterrs them who assist . . . it is an Outlawry, an Excommunication upon the patient . . .' The metaphors applied to Aids add to the suffering of those who have it, stop people seeking early treatment or even from being tested for antibodies (how often we hear the suicidal "I don't want to know .. . I wouldn't be able to deal with a positive result"); the metaphors themselves kill us. Aids is a disease. Nothing more, nothing less.

Abuse of language is her theme. 'The general population,' she says, 'has been distorted to mean not the general population, but white heterosexuals who don't inject themselves with drugs'; 'infected but not ill,' an absurdity of clinical medicine, is an oxymoron that creates 'a new class of lifetime pariah, the future ill'; 'the gay plague is a Eurocentric presumption that lethal diseases originate somewhere or in somebody else, akin to the fantasy that people 'with little reason to expect exemption from misfortune – blacks, Hispanics, the poor – don't suffer as Europeans do. Were Aids confined to the Third World, Europeans would regard it as natural like famine, a part of the normal cycle of calamity – but Europeans have been astoundingly callous about the extent to which they have introduced lethal diseases to the Third World.' 'Full-blown' or 'full-fledged' as adjectives to describe Aids Sontag also rightly deplores: they are zoological metaphors implying the inevitability of an evolutionary process that lends support to an interpretation of clinical evidence which is far from proved.'

Only twice in her argument do I find myself disagreeing. Aids, she says, has intensified the questioning of sixties morality – 'The new sexual realism goes with the rediscovery of the joys of tonal music, a career in investment banking, and church weddings' – but I don't really think the reason why the Barbican may be full for Mozart and empty for Stockhausen has much to do with Aids. On the use of the word victims as applied to the ill, she says: 'Victims suggest innocence. And innocence, by the inexorable logic that governs all rational terms, suggests guilt.' For once her own inexorable logic has failed. We can be victims of circumstance – imputations of guilt are then without meaning. I am reasonably sure of the identity of the man who infected me, and though I may think of myself as a victim I don't view him in this respect, as guilty of anything. He didn't *knowingly* infect me. I am a victim of circumstance.

In France, Sontag tells us, Aids has become a political weapon; Jean-Marie Le Pen has accused his opponents of an Aids mentality, of being 'sidatique.' I rather like the word sidatique – it falls more trippingly off the tongue than Aids-ish – and I may use it myself in the perfectly proper context of replying to someone who asks how I am: sidatique, I may answer; not too well. But Le Pen's assertion that those who do not share his racist attitudes are suffering from some metaphorically acquired immune deficiency syndrome is an outrageous highjacking of language: tolerance, democracy, liberalism and decent values, it implies, are lethal, plague-like viruses. It's on a par with the American Moral Majority's response to attempts to outlaw discrimination against PWAs – 'Has America become a country where classroom discussion of the Ten Commandments is impermissible but teacher instructions in safe sodomy are to be mandatory?'

It is appalling, Sontag concludes, 'to attribute meaning, in the sense of moral judgement, to the spread of an infectious disease,' and 'It is highly desirable for a specific dreaded illness to come to seem ordinary.' As I travel about the South Island, I learn – not a new perception about my illness; I've always thought it – that my own ideas are shared by somebody else, and this is exhilarating; I'm not therefore, in one sense at least, an isolate. Disease – cancer, turberculosis, flu, Aids, the common cold – is nothing more nor less than itself. Ordinary. And I think of the praise I received in the Unity Bookshop: I could now, perhaps, handle it; it is, I suppose, rather nice to be told you've done a great deal for the young that's good and helpful. It should be ordinary too.

I came to New Zealand as a tourist and professional writer, as always, looking for copy; not as a professional gay – so there is not much else I have to add about my life here. I remark to Harry, in an Auckland bar, that whenever one sees drag queens in this country they're Maori – it's so, he says, and I remember Barry Nonweiler making a similar observation in *That Other Realm of Freedom*. They wear, many of them, two different kinds of dress in their daily lives – European and Maori; perhaps that makes it easier to don a third type of costume.

What is a PWA? At what point in the catalogue of HIV infection, I ask myself, does one become a person with

Aids? Different doctors give different answers. Sontag points out that dividing the course of the disease into stages – 'infected but not ill,' ARC, and 'full-blown Aids' – conflicts, because it implies periods of latency, with the notion that HIV inevitably progresses. ARC, she says, is becoming a term without meaning; it will disappear – it's even possible that the whole disease may be renamed. If Aids is impaired immune functioning (the most common marker of which is a count of T-4 helper cells considerably below normal) and a subsequent history of opportunistic infections, then I have Aids. I'm a PWA, though none of my opportunistic problems has so far been at all life-threatening. Thrush, leukoplakia, dermatitis and so on for me are merely a nuisance, and prolonged tiredness is best treated with sleep. Perhaps, in this absence of precise language, it becomes a matter of choice: I *choose* to say I have Aids, that I'm a PWA – even though my health has been better in 1990 than it was in 1989.

The day I arrived in New Zealand I was bitten by cat fleas. As I write this, nine weeks later in England, those bites still itch, have scabs, are not yet healed: my skin's immune system has almost ceased to work. I worry about toxoplasmosis – cats have long since been banished from my house. And the claustrophobia – a terrible attack one lunchtime in an Auckland restaurant – what is the reason for it? The virus affecting my brain? I think not. But something, virus, or AZT, has slowed my motor functions, my reactions: the claustrophobia is a log-jam in the mind; too many sensations and messages crowding in at once. As in this Auckland bar.

The German backpacker gets on my bus at Wanaka (I'm travelling from Queenstown over the Haast Pass to Franz Josef). Very cute; blond hair and extremely short shorts, a lovely length of thigh. He's with a girl: so I put him out of my head. Two days afterwards, on a train from Greymouth to Christchurch, a no-smoking train, I walk along to the caboose where other addicted smokers have assembled. One of them is the German. We exchange glances, eyes meeting for longer than is usual; where is the girl he was with, I ask myself, and – he smiles and winks: I know that you know, you know that I know. We are high up, above a limestone gorge – the view is superb. At which point we are unexpectedly swallowed by a tunnel, and I'm being groped. I think of Adela Quested in the Marabar Caves, but my reaction is not as hers; my hand is immediately up inside a leg of those short German shorts. Only one message, one sensation, crowding in here. Then the dark fades: daylight finds us standing separate – pictures of innocence. Until we are plunged into a second tunnel, and we begin again. There's a whole series of these brief tunnels – the episode is turning into a farce. After the final moments of blackness we're still a long way from an ending; he shrugs, laughs, and returns to his seat inside the train. I feel very frustrated. ("You'll have to call this story *The Tunnel of Love*," Mark says).

But at Christchurch's railway terminus I find I'm walking beside him. "Where are you staying?" he asks. We book in at the first hotel we see, and in our room throw off our clothes and leap into bed. His body is quite gorgeous. He has condoms; I have not – the charms I think I'll require these days against the perils of gay life are capsules of AZT. He hasn't had sex for eight weeks, and I haven't for eighteen months; given the difference in our ages (he's twenty-seven; I'm fifty-four) it's a moot point as to which of us is more in need.

Packing it in.

The girl is not his girlfriend: they are two of a party of Germans who've been in Fiordland since late October – they've done the Routeburn, the Milford Track, all the great trails. He'd noticed me, he says, staring at his thighs as he got on the bus at Wanaka. The girl, and the rest of the group, are travelling to Nelson; his reason for coming to Christchurch is sex: the South Island's capital, population three hundred thousand, has its gay venues.

"Why didn't you visit them?" I ask. "You could have found a man your own age – or younger."

He grins. "I couldn't wait," he says.

35

As the plane from Christchurch to Auckland lifts above the green and gold checkerboard of Canterbury I say to myself, those two selves I seemed to be are now one; there *is* life after Aids . . . no, I don't think I'm packing it in. Not yet.

December 1990

Sounds – Queen Charlotte, Milford, Doubtful and Silence

The boat noses through Tory Channel and into Queen Charlotte Sound: this landscape is like Scotland in summer – we could be sailing up Loch Duich. The fir forests on the mountains stretch down to the sea; once, every two or three miles, there is a boat-house or a cottage. The sun is superbly hot. Then Picton, reminiscent of Kyle of Lochalsh or Mallaig, but more bustling; and another train, as small and crowded as the Silver Fern – it doesn't run to time, of course, but today there are no absurd hold-ups. I'm sitting opposite a young Canadian; he behaves like the unspeakable Mr Thornberry who marred Theroux's journey to Limón with such comments as "Butterflies," "More herons," and "Look how green everything is." Whenever we pass a field, the Canadian says, "Sheep!" Now there are an *awful* lot of sheep in New Zealand . . . I eventually silence him by provoking an argument about his government's decision to close the Canadian Pacific Railway. "The last trains to Moose Jaw and Medicine Hat have departed," I announce, "left no addresses. By the waters of Huron I sat down and wept." He looks bewildered. If people prefer cars, he says, then railways have to be closed: business is business. "It's high time you Canadians and Americans," I tell him in my most professorial tones, "learn that you can't go on guzzling the world's oil and paying ridiculously cheap prices for it." I say it as if it's *his* fault.

The South Island: green, country lanes and sluggish rivers, lush river-banks shaded by willows and poplars; occasionally a road, but not a car or a house for miles. It is all asleep in the afternoon sun. In the distance, mountains more majestic, on a vaster scale, than any in the North Island: where they dip into the ocean we hug the shore-line – empty beaches, dark grey sand untouched by human print, littered with shrivelled sea-weed, tree-trunks, and branches as white as bleached bones.

Near the suburbs of Christchurch I decide to go to the loo; I am just shutting the door when it is thrown open, and a man grabs hold of me, starts ripping off my shirt, and pummelling me with his fists. "How dare you come in here before me!" he shouts. "It's *my* turn! Who do you think you are?" Where he's appeared from I haven't the slightest idea; he certainly wasn't waiting outside the loo. I'm dealing with a demented maniac: I could easily knock him down – he's old, fragile, and wearing a deaf aid – or I could summon the guard. But it's too ludicrous; I don't want to get involved – I want to be a tourist in Christchurch, not waste my time in a police station. So I let him pee to his heart's content.

I'm badly shaken by this – I've never been physically assaulted in my life. Is *everyone* like this in the South Island, I ask myself. It affects my impressions of Christchurch, spoils the whole evening: the city seems derelict, utterly provincial. By ten o'clock the streets are deserted. There are, I notice, a great number of seedy-looking massage parlours. Will I be attacked by some lunatic in a dark alleyway?

But, next morning, Christchurch proves to be very worthwhile. New Zealand's cities are remarkably unlike one another – Auckland has nothing in common with Wellington, and neither resembles Christchurch. Dunedin, I'm told, is quite different again. Christchurch doesn't have Wellington's switchbacks and skyscrapers, nor Auckland's love-affair with water; it is inland and flat. It claims to be more English than any city in England, as does Victoria on Vancouver Island; but both places, it seems to me, are not English at all. There are, I admit, superficial allusions: Christchurch is dominated by its cathedral, a pleasant and well-proportioned structure of grey stone designed by Gilbert Scott; the streets are named after English cathedral cities; and the River Avon, which winds through the centre, is a very passable imitation of the Cam at Cambridge – willows trailing in the water, and young men in white flannels and straw boaters punting. (The difference is that the young men are not students; they're employed by an enterprising firm to give Japanese tourists a taste of what is imagined to be the 'English' experience.)

Our cathedral cities grew haphazardly from Roman and medieval origins; Christchurch is grid-planned. it has preserved more of its nineteenth-century architecture than Auckland or Wellington, and that isn't remotely English – it's very New Zealand. Also the trees and flowers, apart from the willow-shaded Avon and those in the botanical gardens, tell us we're in the Southern Hemisphere; pohutukawas in full bloom are not exactly European. This exercise in nostalgia by the founding fathers doesn't really convince. It was never likely that it would – though one can sympathise with their homesickness, the need of upper-crust, Anglican immigrants of the Canterbury Society to establish their own values and traditions in a country on the other side of the world, from which most of them were never likely to return. Their feelings are well expressed in the ornate Gothic, pseudo-Oxbridge buildings of their university (now a flourishing Arts Centre), the botanical gardens, and in the faintly preposterous poem inscribed on the cathedral's font:

> Blest hour, in Akaroa Bay
> When England's flag first won the way,
> On these bright shores for British youth
> To grow in Christian grace and truth.
> O'er church and home, o'er fell and flood,
> The fount and origin of good.

The reductio ad tragediam of these sentiments was the killing-fields of Gallipoli: when New Zealand lost its innocence, and started to realise it could never be an exact replica of England. But I'll only believe it's really found its own image when shops in December no longer decorate their windows with holly berries and imitation snow, and their muzak is belting out something other than *I'm dreaming of a white Christmas* . . .

The earnest patriarchs of the Canterbury Society would have some difficulty in recognising Cathedral Square at lunchtime; in fact they would be appalled. Deserted it may be in the evening, but at noon it has some of the most entertaining street-life I've ever happened upon; the party, briefly, is *here* . . . It's crowded and polyglot – not only the local office workers taking their lunch-break, but tourists from all over the world: camera-clicking Japanese, middle-aged Britons, back-packing Germans, red-neck Americans, and from Sweden blond young Vikings with sixties-length hair and *huge* accumulations of thigh. There are jugglers, soap-box orators, a rock band, knick-knack stalls, hot food sellers – every Pacific cuisine is available: Korean, Japanese, Thai, Chinese, Malaysian, Singaporean, Tahitian. The largest section of the crowd is drawn to the Wizard – a New Zealander as famous as Dame Kiri Te Kanawa, Sir Edmund Hillary or Sir Robert Muldoon. Every lunchtime, wearing a long black cloak that reaches from neck to foot and a pointed enchanter's hat, he delivers his harangue; his only aid is a step-ladder which he runs up and down, but which he occasionally leaves to speak directly to individuals in the front row. He's intelligent and very amusing, a mixture of the sociology professor and the stand-up comedian. Today's subject, he tells us, is fun – but it's mostly an excuse to catechise what are obviously his favourite bêtes noires: Marxists, fascists, radical lesbian feminists, socialists, liberals, conservatives; academics; born-again Christians; workaholics; gossiping women and wimp-like men; mortgages, taxes, marriage, unruly children. But Jesus, he says, he respects: Jesus was fond of women, didn't do any work, didn't marry – in fact never said a word about marriage – and he disliked his mother. Only twice is he thrown off course: when the rock group gets too loud ("What on earth would Athens have been like if Pericles had had to compete with a rock concert!" he yells), and when a small girl climbs up the step-ladder and says she's going to fly from the top. "Where is this child's mother?" he demands. There's no response, and we all gasp as the girl throws herself into space – and lands unhurt.

It's hot and humid: the temperature is in the high eighties. I stroll in the botanical gardens in the shade of huge, mature copper beech trees, and when the afternoon has cooled I visit the Canterbury Museum. It has several moas of varying size (though none as impressive as Auckland's), and a fascinating Antarctica collection: defrosted dinosaurs; rocks, minerals, flora and fauna; Amundsen, Scott and Shackleton relics. It also has the skeleton of a blue whale, the world's biggest mammal, living or extinct – the vastness of this object is so amazing one says, how? Why? What ever can be its purpose?

From Christchurch to Queeenstown by bus is a long, long journey, ten hours of it, but good weather, good roads, and spectacular scenery make light of any discomforts. For the first two hours we are on the Canterbury Plains – sheep, fir plantations, more one-horse towns, and it is as flat as Holland. Then, as we near the foot-hills of the Southern Alps, the greenness is broken by patches of white and pink: foxgloves in bloom. Later, foxgloves are replaced by pink dog-roses, and thousands and thousands of lupins. The lupin was brought to New Zealand by early settlers as a garden plant, but today it's more commonly seen in the wild, particularly in the South Island; it obviously likes the extremes of heat and cold. It has spread over whole acres – at this time of the year producing a gorgeous riot of colour; red, yellow, white, pink, and every conceivable shade of blue. The air is filled with its hot, peppery scent.

We are lucky; the entire range of the Alps is visible: bleak, bare granite capped with snow that is dazzlingly white in the sun. Resonances with other mountains in Switzerland, Scotland, the Sierra Nevada in Spain. I stand in the summer heat, surrounded by lupins, and gaze towards Mount Cook – and become lost in a memory of myself a decade younger, in an orange grove at Lone Pine, California, gazing at snow on Mount Whitney: turning round, I was looking at a dried-up lake, a salt-pan. Here, turning round, I am again in a desert, or the nearest New Zealand has to a desert, the Mackenzie Country; beyond the lupins there is only dust and tussock.

The lakes are piercing aquamarine and beryl, their texture the milk or silk of pools in Cornish claypits: the water contains great quantities of very fine powder, the result of glaciers pulverising rocks. In the Church of the Good Shepherd beside Lake Takapo there is a memorial to a woman who died, quite young, in Exeter ... At The Hermitage we stop for lunch, but I spend most of my time staring up at Mount Cook, the Tasman Glacier, and the cracks in the snow that portend avalanches. The shape of Mount Cook is most pleasing: sharp, distinct, a smaller version of Everest. The wind is strong here, but hot. The sky is dark blue – almost black.

Queenstown, on the edge of Lake Wakatipu, mountains soaring on all sides, is like somewhere in Switzerland, though I guess a native Swiss (knowing the details as I did in 'English' Christchurch) would probably say it is not. It is devoted to macho sports like bungy jumping (tied to an elastic rope, you hurl yourself off parapets three hundred feet high); most of these activities require encapsulation in some sort of object that propels you at immense speed into the air, or on the surface of water, even *under* water: you can jet-boat, white-water-raft, paraplane and hydroplane (whatever they are), hang-glide, or whizz between peaks in a helicopter. I cannot imagine why anybody with a modicum of sanity would pay the huge sums required to do this ... My only macho adventure is to ascend a mountain in a téléférique – a very Swiss pastime, I suppose – and that is sufficiently terrifying: nothing but thousands of feet of fresh air below me. What if the cable starts to fray? (As it often does in films set in the Alps.) Or there's an earthquake? (Queenstown, in fact, isn't near a fault-line.) The view from the summit, which has a prosaically New Zealand name, Bob's Peak, is of course marvellous, and there's a restaurant where I can drink coffee and soothe my shattered nerves. Queenstown is a toy village miles beneath; the whole of Lake Wakatipu is visible, black in colour; and on the same level as I am a magnificent panorama of the Remarkable Mountains unfolds, summits once again covered in snow. But I don't feel safe until I've returned to my hotel.

The hotel is in Rees Street; there is also a Lake Rees and a Mount Rees. My curiosity is heightened when I discover this namesake was a sheep farmer who came from the same part of Pembrokeshire as my ancestors; my grandfather, I remember, told me there was a relative who emigrated to New Zealand and became a sheep farmer. William Gilbert Rees, it so turns out, was the first white man to set foot in what is now Queenstown. He arrived in 1860 with his family – from Dunedin, I guess – and journeyed up Lake Wakatipu in a whaleboat, falling in love with the scenery. In 1862 gold was found on his land, and he evidently saw the chance of becoming rich: he pulled down his sheep-shed and built a hotel, which is still here and functioning as such. Almost overnight thousands of miners flocked into the area. The Reeses didn't like this at all – they sold the hotel (I imagine at a very considerable profit) and moved away. There's a monument to William Gilbert in the park; on it an inscription, presumably from his diary or a letter – 'Nothing had been prepared by burning. Progress was not only slow, but often really painful – speargrass three feet high and matagouri impeded us.' A characteristic tale of early settlers' life, I suppose, or at least a settler with flair and imagination. *Undoubtedly* a Rees!

In a Queenstown lay-by is a red double-decker London bus, a 12, though that is not its real number, the conductor says; it's been painted on, and a piece of London's geography has been mis-spelled: Trafalagar Square. It was a 73 in fact, my local Stoke Newington bus. The route of this faintly daft souvenir is to a bridge that spans the Shotover Gorge (even Queenstown's place-names have a macho ring) where one can watch the bungy jumpers, then go to Arrowtown, which was built in the gold rush days and hasn't changed a great deal since. I sit on the top deck right at the front: we saunter along sleepy lanes, and I say to myself how bizarre it is to be sitting in this vehicle twelve thousand miles from where it should be; though nothing seems so bizarre this mad afternoon as the bungy jumpers. There's no shortage of macho men willing to part with eighty dollars (about twenty-five pounds) in order to be flung at petrifying speed towards the Shotover River, jerked back again, then left dangling upside down until a boat rescues them; fools and their money are indeed very soon separate ... If I were to indulge in such an activity I'm sure my last remaining T-cells would immediately die of fright ...

Arrowtown I'd thought would be a ghost town, as is Bodie in California, or only inhabited in part like Virginia City, Nevada; but many of its houses – carefully preserved nineteenth-century relics, small, wooden, and attractive – are either lived in or used as holiday homes. Its somnolent main street, lined with enormous old elms, and containing a splendid octagonal pillar-box, is the most beautiful in New Zealand. Strange to find myself excited by elms – once so common in England I took no notice, but now vanished from our landscape. Arrowtown had a thriving Chinese quarter; its shopkeepers and prospectors lived in minute shacks, now uninhabited, by the River Arrow – buildings almost hidden by ancient willows and profusely flourishing lupins. The sleepy afternoon is made all the more pleasant by the sun's warmth, the willow pollen drifting on the breeze, and the peppery lupin scent. Enchanted place – enchanted time.

The journey to Milford, the advertisers declare, is for scenery the *ultimate* experience, but, though the road to the head of Lake Wakatipu is interesting (the water storm-tossed, dark blue flecked with white, and the Remarkables very sinister – black teeth and rushing cloud) the landscape through Southland from Kingston to Te Anau is dull: sheep and fields. At Mossburn I am at my furthest point south; I'm nearer to Antarctica than I've ever been, or am likely to be. From now on it's north until I'm back in England.

After Te Anau the scenery, I have to agree, is superb, though perhaps not yet 'ultimate.' Te Anau Downs is a mass of golden flowers: broom, which, like lupins, was a nineteenth-century import; but in many places, such as here, its proliferation is wildly out of control – is as destructive to the land as rabbits or possums. The government pays farmers to burn it. On the far side of Lake Te Anau are the Murchison Mountains, out of bounds to the public since the discovery there of several tekah, a bird, it was thought, that became extinct centuries ago. Humans, however, are not the most likely predators: cats are the real enemy. It is not too astonishing that tekah were seen in the Murchisons – this is Fiordland, so wild and remote that whole areas of it have never been properly explored by either Europeans or Maoris; I would like to think that somewhere, hidden in its impenetrable interior, there are still colonies of giant moas tramping through the vegetation. It's not *totally* impossible: is it?

North from Te Anau Downs, forest – native forest of tree-ferns, silver beech, black beech and red beech, nothing European anywhere. 'Beech,' I imagine, was the name given by the first settlers because they saw a resemblance with our beech trees; but they're not related, nor do they to my eye look like the European specimen. They are small-leaved – no New Zealand native tree, I realise, is broad-leaved or deciduous: was it unnecessary, I ask myself, in a country without mammals for the broad leaf to evolve? For trees not to shed their leaves in autumn? The small leaf allows much more light into the forest than does our broad leaf: sylvan glades, delicate foliage, like the forest clearings we created in our imaginations when we read, as children, tales of woodcutters, witches and lucky youngest sons.

The bus carefully skirts the debris from a recent avalanche, then negotiates the Homer Tunnel – the most primitive of holes, a cylinder through rock with unsurfaced walls and road. The driver treats it with great respect. When we emerge into daylight we stop to look at a kea, a mountain parrot: a bird with no fear of humans, and a thief – it likes bright, metallic objects and is adept at removing windscreen wipers. It doesn't much enjoy flying – it prefers to hop and flap. New Zealand has, or had, a great many species of flightless or semi-flightless birds; the absence of mammalian predators meant that they didn't have to fly, and it occurs to me that there are also many European birds who enjoy other methods of locomotion – ducks, for example, would rather swim on a pond.

The landscape now really *is* ultimate: I've never seen

anything like it. We are in the Cleddau Gorge – vast, impenetrable overhangs of rock, and everywhere we look there are colossal waterfalls. It has begun to drizzle, and because there is no soil on the mountain peaks the water drops over the edges in torrential cascades. There are extraordinary holes and tunnels in the limestone, huge chasms, with – miles below, it seems – roaring torrents of water. The gorge opens into Milford Sound, glaciated mountain-sides towering vertically for thousands of feet, summits hidden in cocoons of swirling mist. There is nothing at Milford apart from a hotel and boats. I take the boat that travels the length of the fjord to the Tasman Sea, a journey that is more 'Romantic' than the Romantics could ever have dreamed of; it is like being inside a painting by Claude or Turner – rifts, flaws, abysses and cataracts, the trees and shrubs clutching impossible toe-holds on vast heights and depths seem like figments of the Romantic imagination, not reality. Wordsworth and Coleridge would have wanted to recreate this landscape in poetry; had they seen it I'm sure they would have tried. For me it has no resonance with anything seen, not even in Scotland or Norway; only what is given to the inner eye by literature and painting. Characters of the great Apocalypse . . .

These are the trees and shrubs of rain-forest, all the possible, subtle shades of green ('woods decaying, never to be decayed'); even that brilliant, wet, emerald green one thought one could only see in Ireland. Green because it *is* so wet – sometimes over one hundred and fifty inches of rain a year. The fjord water is as dark as Guinness. And silent. Milford Sound is the sound of silence . . .

On the return journey a gap in the mountains, but I can't see far – too much mist. Through there is Doubtful Sound: I'd like to explore that too; it looks magnificent in photographs, and the name intrigues. But it's a whole day's ride – I have to go on, tomorrow, to Franz Josef, eight and a half hours by bus from Queenstown.

Another hot morning – the rain didn't get as far as Rees Street. We follow the Shotover River, past the world's most southerly vineyards, and stop at a roadside stall that sells fresh-picked fruit. Standing by an orchard in the hot sun and eating cherries, I say to myself: but it's December. At Wanaka the German tourist gets on the bus. I've seen him before, in Arrowtown; each day there are familiar faces on the buses, in the streets – people doing the same circuit of the South Island as I am, though not necessarily in the same order. The Japanese don't use public transport – they chart their own buses. There are *hordes* of them in Queenstown, so many they seem to outnumber the natives. They relentlessly photograph everything. It's difficult at times to concentrate on the scenery because their cameras are clicking beside one's ear-drum and their flash-lights are distracting one's eyes. They photograph each other with it doesn't matter what as a background, a shop, a bus wheel, empty dinner plates. Why on earth do they do it? It's an incredible waste of celluloid: by the time they get home they won't remember half the places filmed, or why the pictures were taken at all.

We cross the Haast Pass and descend into Westland, New Zealand's remotest inhabited region – a long, thin strip between the Alps and the Tasman Sea. Only three roads lead into it; the one we're on, and two further north from Christchurch, Arthur's Pass and the Lewis Pass. Geography, one is told, has formed the character of West-landers: they're pioneers, battling against the elements, quite unlike most of the nation. Westlanders argue stoutly that they wouldn't live anywhere else, despite the rain they have to put up with; two hundred inches a year is normal. (They insist they also get plenty of sunshine, but it's difficult to believe.) The land is covered with huge tracts of forest: very luxuriant – ferns and beeches – and the under-growth is swampy as a sponge. There are almost as many shades of green as at Milford, and moss everywhere – emerald, rust, ochre, mud-coloured; there is lichen all over the trees and fence-posts. Rushing torrents tumble down the mountains, and immense boulders litter the river-beds. Houses are fifty miles apart.

It begins to rain as we reach the summit of the Haast – a

monsoon-like downpour, and it doesn't stop until we are out of Westland on the Canterbury side of the Alps a day later. The driver begins to worry about the swollen rivers – they often flood above the tops of bridges. North of Haast Town we are on the coast; to our left is the Tasman, grey and angry, its beaches grey sand, not a human in sight. Three hours of this, then we are at Franz Josef. It's minute, merely a staging-post for tourists who want to see the glacier; a little row of shops, cafés and lodging-houses. The bus terminates at a motel on the edge of town, and almost the entire company of passengers, though not the German, elects to stay the night here. It's a very smart establishment with a good restaurant, and incredibly cheap. A huge log fire is roaring in the grate. I may not get out of here tomorrow, the receptionist says; the rain may well have covered the bridges in both directions. I may even have to flee from my room in the middle of the night – rain like this often floods through the whole ground floor. From the garden, the scent of jasmine and lupins: beyond the garden, thick forest. As I fall asleep the only sound is heavy, drenching rain: I feel as if I'm marooned in the Amazon jungle – to be in Christchurch by tomorrow evening seems a ludicrous impossibility.

The bus to Greymouth, where I shall catch a train to Christchurch – the Tranz-alpine Express, which turns out to be anything but express – does not leave Franz Josef till mid-morning: enough time to see the glacier. But rain puts walking out of the question, so a young Australian couple, an American lad, and I hire the local taxi which conveniently takes us to the foot of the ice-field. This and the nearby Fox Glacier descend to a level not much above the sea, lower than any other glaciers in the world: because the mountains are so steep, and because the rainfall (snowfall higher up) is so immense that the tops of both glaciers are constantly being reinforced. The ice in parts is a mile thick. For two centuries the Franz Josef and the Fox receded, but since the early nineteen eighties they've begun to advance, several feet a year. Global warming, the taxi-driver says, has loosened the ice, increased its speed.

48

There it is: huge crevasses and massive ice-falls, great pinnacles of permafrost, and on either side, weirdly, because we are so near to sea level, tropical rain-forest. The colour at its foot is grey; the middle watery green, and higher up even in this damp – a dazzling white. A river gushes from ice-caves at the foot, battleship grey (powdered rock caused by the glacier's grinding); ice floes, spinning wildly, hurtle towards the sea. The only occasion I've witnessed a similar phenomenon was on a May morning – in Leningrad. An unexpected heat-wave had broken up the ice on Lake Ladoga; I looked across the Neva – the classic view of the Winter Palace, the picture on all the postcards; I was in shorts and tee-shirt it was so hot – and the river was full of ice floes rushing down to the Gulf of Finland.

The east side of the railway tunnel through Arthur's Pass is a different world. No rain-forest, no rain: to begin with it is like the gentler regions of Scotland – scree and mountain turf – then the man-made, European patchwork quilt of Canterbury; willow trees, lazy rivers. There's a *drought* here, and bush fires. The sun is shining. On the train's caboose we can smoke: the German, a Canadian girl, an Aboriginal couple and their three sons, an elderly New Zealander, and a Japanese TV crew who are totally inscrutable – they ignore all questions about what and why they are filming, questions that aren't without reason for the camera is pointing *downwards*; they are photographing the rails. Drifts of heady, Canterbury scents: hay, fresh air, lupins, and the old thatch and honey smell of broom.

My last full day in the South Island. Its conclusion I've already described – a different taste of honey; couple as a verb: a most enjoyable climax. Several of them.

December 1990.

Takapuna Transfer

I notice the sign on a bus, and I think of another, more famous Transfer – Manhattan – and half expect this Auckland driver to serenade his passengers with *Chanson d'amour* . . . No destination-board on a London bus would announce that it is the Tottenham Transfer. Un-British English; and though we are not so divided from New Zealanders as we are from Americans by our common language, I listen every day to something I haven't previously heard. "Do you want a short snort of grog?" I suppose I look bewildered, for the invitation is explained – "a large whisky." A bottomless cup of coffee means you get a free re-fill; and a fish dish on a Christchurch restaurant menu is 'battered with beer.' Do I want my raspberries, Coll-doll asks, "drizzled" in cointreau? A hoarding outside a church proclaims, 'The reason for the season: Jesus!' A frequent road-sign, 'Peds crossing', leads to a number of jokes about child molesters – as, in busy American down-town streets, 'Violators will be towed away' makes one think of rapists more than illegally parked cars. Another road-sign announces 'Ducks crossing' – and I remember in Orkney 'Otters crossing.'

It isn't only the language that tells me I'm far from England: the patronising cliché that New Zealand is just like Britain, but fifty years back in time, is not remotely true; and even less true is the joke about the History professor, whose speciality was the Victorian age and who liked being in New Zealand, he said, because he could *live* in the Victorian age. New Zealand is decidedly twentieth-century, though it regards the here and now somewhat differently from the way we look at it.

Yes, there is an absence of oomph in its cities; no one in their right minds would say of Auckland and Wellington, as one would of Sydney, London, Paris, Amsterdam – even Glasgow, Salamanca, Seville or Budapest – that the party is here. New Zealand is *not* the hub of the universe. Which is why, I suppose, one sees generation after generation of its young people stuffing all their belongings into rucksacks, and taking off for a year or two to sample what they hope is a more exciting world. We don't return the compliment, but we should; for New Zealand has some of the most beautiful scenery in the entire planet, and probably more variety of landscape than any other country of comparable size. It's so far away, we think; but the difficulty of getting here is psychological, not actual. Thousands of British tourists fly to holiday destinations on both coasts of the USA; it really isn't a tremendous hassle to pay a bit more and fly a bit longer to Auckland. The problem of cost is solved when one's arrived – everything here is cheaper than in Britain. There's also the attraction of summer during our winter; it's a real lift to the spirits to stop at a roadside stall in December and buy fresh-picked strawberries, raspberries and apricots.

New Zealand's summer, in fact, brings plenty of holiday-makers, but the British contingent are here to spend time with relatives; the real tourists are Australian, Canadian, American, German, and – in bigger numbers than from anywhere else – Japanese and Swedish. There are so many visitors from Japan that brochures, menus in restaurants, even direction signs, are in some places printed in two languages, Japanese and English. Why hordes of Swedes should come here I find very puzzling. Scandinavia and New Zealand have much in common: mountains, a small and scattered population, fjords, remoteness – and also political neutrality and strong conservationist movements. But why people should travel half-way round the globe to be somewhere that is very like the place they have left is a mystery to me.

There are no French tourists. Not surprising: New Zealand, since the French secret service blew up the Greenpeace ship, the *Rainbow Warrior*, in Auckland's harbour one quiet Sunday morning, is not exactly Francophile; and France's refusal to stop testing nuclear weapons on her Pacific atoll – which isn't a million miles away – is a perpetual source of annoyance. New Zealand is the most anti-nuclear of countries. The present government will not reverse its Labour predecessor's policy of closing

New Zealand's ports to American nuclear ships: anti-nuclear is bipartisan. It is also the greenest of countries, deeply committed to environmental protection. Maybe the accident of geography – being on the edge of things – which was once considered a handicap is now a virtue: if the world should be devastated in a nuclear holocaust, then New Zealand is probably the safest place to be; so the desire to preserve it as it is has become very strong.

The other side of this particular coin is a 'happy valley' mentality. New Zealand is the Switzerland of the Southern Hemisphere, without that country's financial skills – the kind of place that does nothing in six hundred years except to invent the cuckoo clock. Everywhere the peaceful, green farm-land snoozes in the sun; the roads – which are excellent, though curiously devoid of adequate sign-posts – are, outside the cities, almost empty of traffic, a pleasure to drive on. We've reached where we should be, it all seems to say: why struggle to do anything else? It's lotus-like, the atmosphere. The news on the TV is not much concerned with imminent war in the Gulf: farm prices, what will happen to exports of lamb if the GATT talks break down, are the headlines; and the media is more obsessed with the details of an extremely unusual murder trial than the postures of Saddam Hussein. It's an interesting case, in which I too become absorbed – a man found guilty of double murder, but the bodies have not been discovered. It is, I have to admit, a brilliant piece of detective work, and its nasty side – the victims, a young Swedish backpacker and his girlfriend, were raped, tortured, and brutally done to death – is a tale one doesn't want to know about but can't resist, the material of nightmare.

New Zealand television, I say to myself one evening, is like an insidious poison filtering into everyone's houses – endless advertisements, *Blind Date* and *Sale of the Century* five times a week. Yuck! Maybe its awfulness is why this country seems to be a great nation of readers; the worse, I suppose, the media, the more will people turn to books. (The newspapers, however, aren't so bad: *The New Zealand Herald* has good world coverage, and a nice line in the ridiculous – one story concerned an old woman, wheelchair-bound, who robbed several shops at gun-point; the police said they were unable to find her, even though the wheelchair had a maximum speed of four kilometres an hour.) The bookshops are numerous and flourishing, and there are many more published writers per head of population than in Britain. In every small town, Harry says, there's a writer successfully scribbling away at something; authors have status here, are noticed, are reviewed and interviewed frequently, are read – it explains, I suppose, why the manager of Wellington's Unity Bookshop gave me the kind of fulsome reception I'd never get in an English bookshop, gay or straight.

Crafts are alive and well here too, pottery in particular: the originality of design and the quality of the work are much more interesting than in Britain. But music and theatre are neglected. The big cities have fewer concerts and plays than some provincial British towns with populations of no more than a hundred thousand; there is no opera company of any repute (the National Opera went bust), and in Auckland no symphony concert between the end of November and the beginning of February: imagine London – even Exeter – in summer without music!

The public transport system is also neglected, but nobody seems to care: it's a nation devoted to cars. Driving, as I said, is a pleasure – the country roads little used, and very good freeways where they are needed, in Auckland and Wellington. But to travel the length of both islands, as I did, on public transport, requires patience: nothing – plane, train, bus or ferry – departs or arrives on time. The railways, in particular, are inadequate. Auckland has only two commuter lines and no Metro; the inter-city trains are slow and infrequent. It seems odd for a people so conservationist: one would have thought there'd be a powerful anti-car lobby, dire predictions concerning the greenhouse effects of so much carbon monoxide, and questions about what may happen when there's no more oil – but none of this seems to figure in anybody's thinking.

New Zealand is more preoccupied with the effects of

cigarette smoke. I meet no one who smokes, and, as a result, am constantly hassled about my reliance on the weed. The law says that public places – cafés, trains and so on – must provide proper accommodation for people who do not smoke, but many establishments and institutions have banned smoking altogether. At times I become quite irritated in this most non-smoking of nations (is it another Swiss tendency, I ask myself); I feel I'm a pariah. But I have to say that Harry and Mark are extremely tolerant when I pollute their house – even though their one ash-tray has, carved on its pottery, the words 'Thank you for not smoking.'

Ten per cent of New Zealanders are Maori, and one is often told that Maoris are full participants in all walks of life – the implication being that there is no racial discrimination *here*. The outgoing Governor-General is Maori, and the country's most famous citizen, Dame Kiri Te Kanawa – also the clerk at the bank, the woman who owns the hotel, the tour operator, and so on. But it occurs to me that the least attractive jobs – driving the buses, mending the roads, disposing of the garbage – are for the most part done by Maoris, as in England the work we don't want to do we give to blacks. I'm not aware of racial discrimination as I am in Australia, and certainly New Zealand's record is fine in comparison; but – I wonder. The health of Maoris is less good than that of Europeans (an inability, perhaps, to withstand our diseases), and their infant mortality rate is much higher. Arguments about land ownership continue, despite the deliberations of the Waitangi Tribunal, and some young Maoris are militant and very extreme in their political stance: they would like all the land returned to them, and the Europeans expelled. One symbol that suggests an inferior status is the home of the Maori Queen – Queen Te Ata-i-rangi-kaahu – which is nothing like a palace; it's a modest, suburban affair in a small town near Hamilton, with few of the trappings of the Governor-General's residence in Wellington.

Maoris have always preferred to live in the North Island; before the Europeans came they used the South Island as somewhere to hunt moas and quarry greenstone rather than to colonise in large numbers. Whakarewarewa has strong Maori traditions – an important art and craft centre and a famous meeting-house; almost the entire population nearby is Maori. Wood is their chief medium of artistic expression – the decoration of meeting-houses is elaborate and highly sophisticated – but I find it most bewildering: it has no echoes or resonances in my experience; I don't know how to react to it, I don't know if I like it or not. The limitation is mine, not theirs; culture which isn't European – music, literature, painting, architecture, whatever – confuses me, leaves me puzzled. Japanese art, or Chinese – African, Indian, American Indian, Polynesian – I have no ability to appreciate or enjoy. In saying this, I'm admitting to a blindness of vast proportions, a lack of skill and sensibility that reveals me as a total Eurocentric. I can't help it: it's how I am.

I admire the skill as I look at the carving on Maori meeting-houses and on their war canoes, but I realise I'm noting penis size on their male figures instead of being struck by apprehensions of beauty, originality, conception, achievement: and I'm embarrassed to think that a huge cock may be the only detail I'll recall.

In Rotorua, Harry and Mark take me to a Maori dinner and concert, a hangi; and I suffer the same bewilderment. Maoris in Rotorua often cook their food by wrapping it in cloth and plunging it into the nearest boiling spring or pool of mud, but this hangi is at the Sheraton Hotel – the food, which is European (roast ham and vegetables) except for kumara, New Zealand's sweet potato, is cooked in the Sheraton's kitchens. There's something wrong about a hangi being organised in such a place; I feel we are being invited to observe creatures in a zoo and that the concert will not be the real thing – more like the 'stage' Russian entertainment in a smart Leningrad restaurant, or the 'stage' Irish served up at Jury's Hotel in Dublin. Rich, elderly tourists – red-neck Middle America on a package tour is what this audience chiefly consists of. I feel, if I really want to enjoy a hangi, I should be out of doors, in a

Maori village, under the stars. No concessions to Europeans. Would a Maori audience be found goggling at Yankee square dancers? I don't think so.

But the Maoris evidently enjoy their own performance – some of them, afterwards, tell me they *love* doing it – and indeed they are an innately musical people. Chord sequences and rhythm are not genuine (more like Country and Western); real Maori music is plainchant, without harmony, but the quality of the singing isn't European, particularly the male voices. The finale, in which we all have to link hands for a rendering of *Now Is The Hour*, is an embarrassment: I feel as awkward as I did joining arms and singing ho-ho-ishly at a German weinfest, or in Honolulu being photographed, lei round my neck, with a scantily clad Hawaiian girl. ("If she'd been a boy," Tom said, "you'd have loved it." I'm sure I wouldn't – it was a similar adulteration, transforming a piece of meaningful tradition into tourist grot. I remembered Dorothy Parker's words on returning from Hawaii to San Francisco – "How nice to be in a place where a lei is *not* a flower greeting.")

The impact of European civilisation on Maoris, I can't help thinking, is sad, though I guess a great many Maoris, pointing to the benefits, would not agree. But Uncle-Tomism is emasculation. St Faith's, a Maori church in Rotorua, is for me another uneasy experience – European building with Maori décor superimposed, or a meeting-house Christianised? I'm not sure. All I do know is that the two, aesthetically, are an unpalatable mix. (Though I'm aware the Maoris, like many Polynesian races, took to Christianity – and still practise it – with immense enthusiasm.)

I sometimes wish we'd never discovered the Pacific peoples, that Cook – a genius I greatly admire and respect – had never voyaged anywhere; or that the impact we made, and are still making, had left Polynesian culture and customs untouched, that everything European had been strictly confined to Europe. But of one thing I'm certain: had I annexed New Zealand for the British crown some two centuries before Cook discovered it, I'd have imposed very severe penalties for slaughtering moas.

Returning from the Bay of Islands, I get off the bus at Takapuna; I need the Takapuna Transfer – it will take me to Harry's and Mark's house on the North Shore. The usual syndrome when you want directions in a strange place – the people you ask for help are either ignorant tourists like yourself, or they haven't the foggiest idea of the street names in their own town. Takapuna, this Saturday lunch-time, is busy with shoppers. It has the largest supermarket I've ever seen: there's an amazing variety of meat and fish; whole counters of take-away hot dinners; all sorts of coffees, teas, mueslis and baking necessities you can shovel, to your own requirements, into bags; and so many free food samples – cheeses, chocolate, even deer-meat sausages – I won't have to buy lunch. Middle-aged men who all seem rather alike: there's a New Zealand kind of face; long, with pointy nose and chin, weather-beaten, short hair and toothbrush moustache. Sir Edmund Hillary clones. Classless. I like this nation's egalitarianism, the no-standing-on-ceremony, the absence of forelock-touching – tips, for example, are unheard of – and its cheerful, slightly muddled way of doing things. Muddle: I can't find the Takapuna Transfer anywhere. Not in Takapuna.

I arrive at Harry's and Mark's in a taxi.

December 1990

San Francisco: A Valediction

In memory of Dick Brownlow

I am, of course, being a PWA, a prohibited alien. Since 1987, when Congress voted in favour of the homophobic and reactionary amendment to the immigration laws proposed by Jesse Helms, the Senator for North Carolina, I have been barred from entry to the United States. It counts for nothing that in my passport I have a J-I visa ('exchange visitor allowed to work'), an H-I visa ('distinguished alien whose work skills cannot be matched by an American citizen'), and a tourist visa which has printed on it that it lasts indefinitely, and that the number of entries I can make into the USA is 'multiple.' But . . . when did the Immigration Service of the United States – the great melting-pot, the land of opportunity, the land of the free – last welcome immigrants or even visiting tourists? Never. 'Give me your poor,' all that Statue of Liberty stuff, is a load of crap. Hostility and ostracism throughout the ages are the hallmarks of American attitudes to immigrants.

I wouldn't be coming here if it weren't a convenient route home from New Zealand. And there's someone I particularly want to see: for a year he has been dying, and if I don't see him now I never will again. I also want to say my own private goodbye to San Francisco, a city I love and where I was loved, and worked, and was happy. I shan't come again – there are other parts of the world to explore; my health makes the future too big a question mark; and Jesse Helms disgusts me so much I feel I demean myself by setting foot in the country at all. I *do* demean myself: to make certain I can get in I have to divest myself of my identity as a gay man. Immigration may search my luggage (it's happened to me before) so I can't take the risk of AZT being found in my sponge-bag, or the dapsone and pyrimethamine tablets I take as a prophylactic against pcp. I've had to ask my ex-lover Tom to hunt through his friends' bathroom cabinets for spare AZT capsules; he's done so, and the supply I need is waiting for me at the house in Berkeley where I shall be for Christmas. I daren't have anything else in my cases that suggests I'm gay – it might arouse suspicion. So all kinds of material I've picked up in Australia and New Zealand (copies of gay newspapers, magazines such as *Outrage* and *The Pink Triangle*, Aids literature, a photograph of an extremely cute naked man, publishers' catalogues and so on) I've mailed home from Auckland. The postage for this was twenty-three New Zealand dollars (about seven pounds): it hurt to pay it. *Aids And Its Metaphors* I've left in my luggage – objections to *that* would create such a brouhaha that even *The New York Times* could be interested . . .

So . . . I fly from Auckland on the hottest and longest day of the summer, which I spend in shorts beside a swimming-pool with a marvellous bunch of Queens; "As you're travelling United," they say, "take care you don't sit near the door." (A United door recently fell out on a trans-Pacific flight, taking a steward with it. 'Steward sucked through plane door,' screamed one dubious headline. United – it goes without saying – puts me beside the door.) I cross into yesterday like Phineas Fogg, and so experience December the twenty-second twice; I reach San Francisco several hours before I've left Auckland, on the briefest and most frozen day of the winter – the cold is unprecedented, record-breaking: snow on the Oakland Hills, frost, ice, the citrus crop ruined, the jade dead, the bougainvillaea withered, and Arctic blasts hit me at every cross-road with a truly Siberian ferocity.

It all sounds as if it should be tremendously significant in some way or other, but it isn't. Nothing very awful occurs – Hawaii is the most likely place for that, for the plane stops at Honolulu for three hours, and I have to go through the rigours of American immigration and customs there, not at San Francisco. US immigration officials have a reputation, justly deserved, for being ruder and more un-helpful than those of any other country. The Honolulu man who deals with me is no exception – a great contrast with the Australian and New Zealand people who stamped my passport and wished me an enjoyable holiday; they were polite, to the point, and welcoming. It is, in fact, easier to get into Russia than the United States, and more pleasant – Moscow immigration is merely concerned that your face matches the mug-shot on your passport. Even pre-1989 Czechoslovakia posed no problems, and Budapest is as simple as if Hungary were already in the Common Market.

"Where are you staying?" the official demands. "Who are these people? How long have you known them? Where did you meet them? What do they do for a living? Did you meet them in the course of business or pleasure?" I met Marian, a Professor in the English Department of San José State University, on the first morning of the fall semester in 1982, but I feel like saying I was screwing at the time in a Rio de Janeiro brothel, or was being sucked off by a gorgeous man in a back room at the Sydney Sleaze Ball. The official notices my H-I visa and becomes slightly less belligerent. "It solves the problem," he says. I mention that the US government abolished the visa requirement for British tourists – and I'm entering America as a tourist – last year. "That's true," he says. "Perfectly true. But with a visa in your passport you can stay for six months. Without a visa . . . well, only two weeks. And I'd have to ask you a lot more questions than I have done. A *lot* more." What those questions might be I don't think it prudent to inquire; eventually he stamps my passport, and I'm allowed in. My luggage is not searched. I breathe a sigh of relief and feel . . . angry, and unclean. As a black may who, at some cost to himself, has successfully pretended to be white.

And discover what I should have known, but I haven't seen it reported on the TV or in the newspapers, gay or straight; Congress repealed the Helms amendment two months ago. But (there's always a but in these matters) it won't become law until the Health Department removes HIV infection from the list of diseases that forbids immigrants and tourists to enter the United States. This in fact happens while I'm in San Francisco two weeks later, but (another but) a further snag remains. The repeal of the amendment has to 'pass muster' (whatever that may mean) with the State and Justice Departments, and only if

61

they approve will the new policy come into effect. This is not likely to occur – Heaven knows why – for another six months. So I'm still an illegal immigrant.

But I'm here, and I may as well enjoy myself. My spirits lift as soon as I arrive at Katya's – there is a splendid log fire burning in the grate; a huge tree all lit up, at its foot scores of presents wrapped in their Christmas paper; the house is full of old friends, excited and welcoming; the vodka is opened. Suddenly – the Antipodean summer has successfully blotted it out of my conscious mind – it's Christmas! And a marvellous Christmas it promises to be, with dozens of people I know, about twenty of us for Christmas dinner, stockings above the mantelpiece (one has my name on it, and it's already bulging); "It will be Dickensian," Marian says. "With a goose. No . . . *geese*." It will be more like Christmas at Barbary Lane, I say to myself; for Marian, though she was not the model for her, is the living personification of Mrs Madrigal.

But the bubble is soon pricked. "Bad news," she says. The friend – Dick – I'd particularly wanted to see that important last time, died a fortnight ago. I was in New Zealand, and nobody knew my address. Why . . . why couldn't he wait?

It *is* as good a Christmas as I'd hoped, and so is the rest of my short stay here . . . a non-stop round of dinner parties, alcohol, games of bridge, and conversation. Christmas Day itself is hectic: everybody at one time or another in the kitchen doing something, in charge of a certain dish or course; my job is the geese (I volunteer as I can't quite believe Americans know how to roast a goose); Marian presiding over the whole shebang, brandishing ladles. Conversation between so many people preoccupied with cooking is conducted in fragments: half-finished sentences to Marian about A.S. Byatt's *Possession* and Monet's garden; to Stephanie about New Zealand flora and fauna; politics with Kevin; San Francisco bars with Sean; with Molly the size of the rat that got into the house we lived in at Los Gatos, and she *did* nick my Mystic Mints; all interrupted when dog, cats, children and the stove demand

62

priority. But I do hear, in detail, everyone's personal earthquake story, and see, in their eyes, the re-living of the horror that evening in October 1989 when the Cypress Freeway and parts of the Bay Bridge collapsed. I notice too, during the subsequent days, how nervous every Californian I know has become; how they'll start mentioning earthquakes when we're stuck in a traffic jam beneath a San Francisco fly-over; how aware they are it could happen again at any time and be a lot worse. There's nothing they can do to prevent it . . .

The cold weather has forced two raccoons, a whole family of possums – opossums Americans call them, as if they were Irish immigrants – and a skunk to take up residence under the house, in the furnace room. We hold a committee meeting to decide what to do with the skunk: the unanimous verdict is absolutely nothing, in the hope that when the weather improves it will simply go away.

I, once again, during this holiday so surrounded with people, am aware of my isolation. "How are you, David? You look fine! You look great!" And the talk moves to some other topic. Yes, I do look good – Aids-related dermatitis makes a face seem perpetually suntanned, and I've also just had six weeks of summer. But leukoplakia has turned my tongue and the bottom of my mouth into a landscape that resembles a set of working volcanoes; my ears need treatment (the dermatitis causes an excess of wax that irritates and can temporarily make me deaf); my remaining T-cells, not numerous when I left England, are probably shot to pieces as a result of wandering three quarters of the way round the world. I *could* say all that, I suppose, but it's inappropriate to the occasion, and, anyway, do my friends really want to listen? They know, of course, how it is with me – sidatique – for I've told them from time to time, but they won't want to discuss it, to get involved . . . how do we respond is the question they ask themselves. And they're lost for an answer.

Only with Monty are there minutes of really deep feeling. He and Dick were lovers for thirty-four years: now he's a widow. "If you say how well I'm looking," is his

63

greeting to me, "I shall scream!"

"If you say how well *I'm* looking," I answer, "I shall scream too."

"I don't want any sympathy."

"Nor do I. None offered. None taken." And we are in each other's arms, clinging, both of us in tears. Neither he, nor I, at this moment, is alone. That's comfort, and, of course, sympathy.

I'm glad a little part of Dick is preserved in my books. He's in the story, *Sacramento Blues*, and in much of *A Better Class of Blond*. I say this to Monty: he nods . . . but it's too soon for words.

Words I'm hoping for with my ex-lover, Tom; if there's anyone in California I can talk to on the subject of Aids, it should be he. But I'm shocked that it doesn't happen, all the more unprepared for it because he has left AZT for me at Marian's, and a Christmas present, and what she calls a 'care bag' of things I enjoyed when he and I lived in Castro – Safeway's Raisin Bran, Mystic Mints, and two pairs of Safeway socks: dear, darling Tom, as thoughtful and kind as he always was. But when we meet he is embarrassed, reserved, positively hostile. What I have to say to him he rejects totally; "I can't take your cynicism," he tells me. But there's nothing cynical about my words; pessimistic, yes – altogether different from what he thinks he hears.

Later, trying to explain, he says he can't listen to another word on the subject of Aids: he's Aids-ed out. Two close friends of his (friends of mine, also) are not expected to live through 1991; with one of them it will only be a matter of weeks. HIV negative himself, he feels not fortunate, but guilty.

He is full of reproaches about the ending of our relationship in 1984, ground we've tramped over many, many times in the past; it has no relevance now. I don't want to waste time deflecting his hostility: all it does for me is to confirm the rightness of my decision to leave him. Though the regrets I had were many. These moments should be of tender, loving care. What *is* his problem? He lives with a lover of five years' standing (a relationship, he

64

assures me, that is excellent); he has a house he likes very much, supportive friends, and a good job; he does not carry the virus. So why does he prefer recriminations to counting his blessings; shouldn't he, both loved and lucky, be one of the few people left who has reserves of love to give?

When we part, I'm saying goodbye for ever. I shan't come here again, and he's not likely to come to England, though he says he may do so. I don't want to see him.

New Year's Eve finds us not at San Francisco but Inverness, fifty miles to the north on Point Reyes. Marian has rented a house for three nights, and the entire party – plus dinners, vodka, bridge games, and conversation – moves up there. From the windows we have a magnificent view of Tomales Bay, an inlet caused by the San Andreas; Point Reyes is on a different plate of the earth from the rest of America – zillions of eons hence it will detach itself and float off into the Pacific. The countryside is wild and beautiful, and the weather, during the day at least, has warmed up a bit – we can stroll on the beaches without becoming frozen. Miles of sand and no other humans in sight; a gentle sea; cloudless, sunny. Sandpipers, those little birds that look as if their metabolism is of clockwork, scurry after the receding tide. On the horizon columns of water spout: whales migrating. I have to ask the others to walk less quickly – my AZT-weakened leg muscles.

New Year's Eve brings the lowest and highest tides of the year; there is a full moon and it is a blue moon. A blue moon, I learn, is the second full moon in a month, a rare event, and this is the only occasion in our lives when we'll see it on New Year's Eve. At midnight we are out of doors in the frost, drinking champagne and toasting the moon, which, because of the clear, sharp air and the absence of cloud, is enormous and spectacular. The tide is out; there is no water left in Tomales Bay: just vast mud-flats glistening like pewter in the moonlight. "It all seems tremendously cosmic," someone says. "What does it signify?" A superb 1991 is the general opinion, and I hope, as I make my New

Year resolution (the same as it has been for some years now: to live until the New Year in twelve months' time), that it will be so.

But I don't feel very sanguine about it.

The sun has shone all day, every day, these two weeks. Mist has lingered the whole time round the edges of things; there has not been a breath of wind. I don't think I have ever seen San Francisco looking so stunningly beautiful, so bewitching; and I've seen it in all weathers and at all seasons. It has never looked ugly. Driving across the Bay Bridge from Oakland, the spires and pinnacles of downtown looming through the fog, still makes the adrenalin surge; out to the west the Golden Gate this winter is gossamer drawn with a thin, fine pen; from Berkeley the city is a faint etching achieved with the most delicate precision. The houses are still a riot of decoration and colour. Castro is livelier than it was three years ago: not up to 1980 standards, but I'm glad the circus continues – the passing parade goes on passing. In Castro there will always be a celebration of gay life. Aids cannot totally destroy us.

This is the last time I shall see it. I have no regrets about that: I lived here, enjoyed myself here, loved and was loved here. I am a different me now. Some friends I shall not meet again; others – the European travellers – Marian, Bob and Jim, Dan, I will meet. Monty has promised to come. Dick: you would not want me to think this an occasion for disappointment. It isn't.

Goodbye!

January 1991

Six months later the Bush administration, bowing to pressure from the Moral Majority and the conservative right – 'forty thousand letters of protest,' it says – reversed Congress's decision. The Helms amendment stands; people like me will continue to be prohibited aliens. As far as I'm concerned the land of the free, the great melting-pot, can go fuck itself.

66

Our Man in Montenegro

There have been twenty politically motivated killings in Yugoslavia this week. Only one – a policeman murdered in Split – was headline news; and that is because Split is a major tourist centre. The Yugoslavs, however, do not want the tourists to be frightened: prosperity would suffer. The other murders, in remote mountain villages – Serbian enclaves inside Croatia – were off the tourist beat, and therefore not so newsworthy. Echoes of Spain in 1936: Slovenia, Catholic, respectable but dull (the Austrian influence), wants to secede and nobody would mind if it did; Croatia, Catholic, with a fascist history, also wants to secede and everybody objects (it has large racial minorities who are anti-secessionist); Bosnia/Hercegovina, Moslem, quondam Bogomil, is neutral, vague; Serbia, Orthodox. Communist and militant, Serbia has the most to lose if the country breaks up (it has dominated Yugoslav life since World War Two and seventy per cent of the army is Serb – its dislike of Croatia dates from 1941-1945 when thousands of Nazi Croats and Communist Serbs slaughtered each other); Macedonia, half Moslem, half Orthodox, has its own difficulties (a large and increasing Albanian population – the Albanians are accused of breeding like rabbits); and Montenegro, the most mixed of the lot (Orthodox, Catholic, Moslem *and* Communist), though quiet, is pro-Serb and against secession. Its Moslem minority keeps a low profile.

Is all that clear? Nothing is clear in the linguistic and religious Babel of Yugoslavia, a country in which twenty different languages are spoken, and which does not even possess an agreed common alphabet – in Serbia, Macedonia and Montenegro everything is in Cyrillic. 'The Civil War has begun!' screams a headline in a Montenegrin newspaper, but it isn't true. Yet. It's May 1991, not Spain in July, 1936. The army is not desirous to intervene, and the central government in Belgrade is most reluctant to ask it to do so; that's the verdict of my Montenegrin acquaintances, but I get the impression that some of them want to talk themselves into war: it would be exciting, relieve tedium. They're a volatile lot – Mediterranean, noisy, courteous, helpful, honest, very likeable, and a bit mad. Some extremely cute men too: tall, dark, macho and moustached. In pubs – as in Turkey, the women work and the men drink – they sing most musically, lugubrious folk-songs in four-part harmony (faithless girls and lovers' vows broken, I guess); the rhythms and melodies sound Arabic. As in Turkey, men walk hand in hand in the street, kiss when they meet each other. It's a chauvinist society; it's important to produce male children. A Montenegrin man who only has daughters is looked down on, laughed at. And – I was told amid gales of laughter – the Hercegovinans have much smaller cocks. I'd like to suck Montenegrin cock: but I don't know how to set about doing that.

In my hotel there are so many waiters, polite and hovering, in identical black suits and ties, that I could be forgiven for thinking that this is the chief profession Montenegrin males follow: but there's only one maître d' (fat, waddling and brow-mopping), so when a waiter yearns for promotion, what, I ask myself, does he do? Emigrates, I suppose. Meanwhile they attend to the needs of the tourists, mostly working-class British who for decades have flocked to the Yugoslav costas for the riviera experience – sun, sand and good living – that they could never afford in France. These Brits, at once identifiable by the drab dowdiness of their clothes, are salt-of-the-earth, well-intentioned and eager to enjoy anything, people who would be marvellous in an air-raid or on the *Titanic*; but whose utterly inane comments on a bus journey (no, I'm not being classist, but I am being snobbish) make me snort with derision. "Cor, look at *that*!" they say of the most unremarkable sight – a car with a British registration plate, a field of potatoes. "We'll know where to come next time," a woman says to her husband of a municipal park in Titograd (a second visit to *Titograd*??); a man walking down a hill "must know a short cut," and, of a view from the top of a mountain pass, "You have to see it, Eth. If you'd been told, you wouldn't have believed it."

The views from the tops of the mountain passes are certainly magnificent, but not beyond credulity. Almost anywhere along the Petrovac-Titograd road there is a splendid panorama, in one direction of the sea and the coast from Budva to Bar, in the other of mysterious, grey-green Lake Skadar (Scutari) and the snow-capped mountains beyond it in Albania. South from Budva the road is a corniche – massive summits on one side; the Adriatic, blue and gentle, hundreds of feet below on the other, and, every so often, an ancient, idyllic little town near the shore: walled fortresses with clusters of terracotta roofs, grey stone houses, and a Venetian-style church – square tower with pyramid spire – or a Serbian Orthodox monastery. Easy to imagine the Romans still here, or the Illyrians; it's so unspoiled. There are a few blemishes, modern hotels for the most part, but not the hideous rash of them one sees on Spain's coasts, and the port town of Bar, totally destroyed in the Easter Sunday earthquake of 1979, is now a hideous concrete fantasy: *awful*. I prefer the fifties socialist realism of Titograd (originally Podgorica, destroyed in battles with the Germans and the Italians in World War Two); at least it's had time to mellow, and it's well-planned, full of flowers and huge, mature trees. Bar and Titograd are exceptions, however; Montenegrin towns and villages are, almost all of them, beautiful, the domestic architecture, both old and modern, some of the most attractive I've ever seen, and Yugoslavia hasn't suffered the usual blight of Communist societies, the collective farm. It's a country of yeomen peasants: small plots, small fields; a few chickens, cows, goats; patches of corn, vegetables, little orchards. Along the coast the land is extremely fertile. Every garden has fig trees, orange trees, every patio a well-tended vine, and between Virpazar and Titograd – the only flat land in Montenegro – the wet lushness amazes: wild flowers, a riot of colour; sweet scents of choisia; the drone of bees; the richness of early summer. Yugoslavia – here – seems without poverty.

The best views of all are from the Cetinje-Kotor road. Cetinje, the ancient capital when Montenegro was a tiny, independent kingdom, is three thousand feet above sea level; you climb away from it another thousand feet to the summit of the pass, a col under snow-covered Lovčen on the top of which is the world's loneliest, most dramatic tomb – the mausoleum of Petar the Second, the last and greatest of the prince bishops who ruled Montenegro from 1697 until 1860. He is also said to be one of the world's greatest poets, but I have never seen his work in English. And my Serbo-Croat is zero. The other side of the pass is astonishing: it is a wall, as upright as the north face of the Eiger, and it drops four thousand feet to the sea. Down there at the bottom is the port of Kotor. A road threads down this wall in a zig-zag of hairpins: it's no surprise, one says to oneself, that Montenegro was the only part of the Balkans the Turks never conquered. They tried many times, but Lovčen was impenetrable. Just marching up this road (it's called The Serpentine, and is said to be the most horrifying in Europe) almost killed them; the Montenegrins simply waited at the summit and cut their heads off. Going down this road, one's safety in the hands of a Yugoslav bus-driver, is an experience of sheer terror – but not to be missed. The row of ikons above the steering-wheel doesn't inspire confidence, nor the absence of crash barriers on the hairpins. If I had not, at certain moments, shut my eyes I would have wet my knickers.

Cetinje is a delightful place, a nineteenth-century museum-town; here are Serbian Orthodox monasteries, the palace of the prince bishops (known as the Biljarda because Petar the Second installed in it a full-size billiard table imported from England and dragged up The Serpentine on mule-back), and the palace of Petar's successor, Nicholas the First, who ruled Montenegro from 1860 to 1918. Nicholas was not a bishop. He proclaimed himself king after defeating the Turks in 1878 in a brief series of battles that gave Montenegro, after six hundred years, a much-coveted outlet to the sea at Bar: the European monarchies were impressed, and allowed his daughters to marry into their families. Nicholas became known as the Father-in-law of Europe. Unfortunately the monarchies with which his daughters allied themselves did not last very long – Italy, Serbia, Russia, for instance – but one married a Battenberg and was therefore a great-aunt of the Duke of Edinburgh. The rooms of his palace are filled with portraits of most of the crowned heads of the day, including the Tsar Nicholas, Alexandra, and a youthful and improbably handsome Franz-Josef of Austria. It has the only photograph I've seen of four British monarchs taken together: octogenarian Victoria, Edward the Seventh already a grandfather, George the Fifth in his prime, and a child Edward the Eighth. Among this surfeit of royals is an incongruous outsider – an enormous painting of Verdi.

Nicholas and his queen, Milena, are sumptuously entombed here in a heavily restored, twelfth-century Serbian Orthodox church; it is a place much venerated by Montenegrins, even though Montenegro is a Communist republic and Nicholas was a nasty, ruthless, treacherous fellow. Other fascinations in Cetinje are the villas that housed its foreign embassies: palace-ettes – the French covered in mosaics, the Serbian a delicate shade of pastel blue, the Russian easily the grandest and painted coppery brown, the Austro-Hungarian rather hideous and miles away from the others. The British Embassy, a most elegant mansion of camp pink stucco, has a brass plate still on its door that says, in English, with disarming simplicity: 'His Majesty's Legation.' As with our postage stamps, *we* don't need to announce the name of our country – *any* idiot knows which country His Majesty rules!

Kotor, at the foot of Lovčen, is on the boundary between Catholic and Orthodox Yugoslavia; it is also the most southerly point on the Adriatic of Venetian influence. A stone lion of St Mark commemorates this distant edge of the doges' empire. It's a very attractive medieval city, a warren of narrow streets and sudden, surprising piazzas. No wheeled traffic is allowed within its walls, a major blessing: as in Dubrovnik. Both cities are (or were) ports – they are strongly reminiscent of Venice, but without canals. Kotor has churches galore; St Luke's, Serbian Orthodox and about the size of a small dining room, has a marvellous medieval iconostasis. When the bells and clocks of these churches clang out at mid-day, the cacophony is indescribable. Both religions have cathedrals here – the Serbian Orthodox is pleasant but dull; the Catholic, however, is exquisite twelfth-century Roman-esque, its baldachino a masterpiece. It was badly damaged in the 1979 earthquake, and is, unfortunately, still closed to the public, so its macabre treasures are not on view – an agonised, cadaverous wood-carving of Christ (given to the widow of Uroš the First, a thirteenth-century Serbian king, by Baldwin the Second, the last Latin Byzantine Emperor), and the head of Tryphon, the patron saint of the cathedral and of gardeners. St Tryphon is a very obscure person indeed: nothing is known about him except that he was a gooseherd and had his head chopped off at Nicaea in the year 250. The inhabitants of Kotor bought his head in 890 for three hundred pieces of gold from a ship carrying a cargo of relics that happened to dock in the port – there was, presumably, a brisk trade in such things at the time, and any city that could acquire a whole saint's head no doubt vastly improved its status.

Kotor, shut in by huge mountains, is at the innermost point of a fjord: it reminds me of Queenstown. If one travels therefore Herceg Novi, which is almost on the sea and is full of mimosa and other sweet-smelling flowers, the fjord appears to end at Kamenari; but beyond that village it suddenly opens out to reveal a huge inner lake, old towns (including Kotor) on its edges, and little islands as flat as rafts, each with a Catholic church or an Orthodox monas-tery. In times of war, chains stretched from Kamenari to Lepetane, the narrowest point, which kept out the ships of hostile Turks: the Venetians had a special interest in preserving Lepetane, for they built there Europe's biggest and most well-known brothel. The name, Lepetane, is a corruption of the French la putain. Today, chains and prostitutes have been replaced by a car ferry; less interest-ing, I suppose, but probably more useful to the modern traveller.

The road to Ulcinj and Albania takes one into Islamic Yugoslavia; from Sutomore onwards there are almost no churches: in each village a mosque, a delicate minaret. The boundary is marked by two ruined Turkish castles, Haj and Nehaj (which mean Fear and Fear Not); it's the old frontier between the Ottoman and the Austro-Hungarian Empires. There is a more impressive ruin at Stari Bar, once a walled town but in 1878 reduced to rubble by the Montenegrins when they drove out the Turks. A lovely name, Stari Bar; the resonances – Starry Vere! It hasn't been excavated or rebuilt, and is all the more atmospheric for being left in weed-filled desolation. It reminds me of Seljuk, near Ephesus in Turkey. Wild flowers grow profusely in the dilapidated houses and streets; it's wind-swept and silent: gazing up at the sky, then down into the arid ravine hundreds of feet below, I think of an old proverb; 'If it were not for the wind, spiders would weave webs over the heavens.' The Moslem graveyard nearby has tombs shaped like phalluses, their tops carved stone fezzes painted bright red.

Ulcinj is true border country, an amazing jumble of different races and cultures: in part old walled citadel (Turkish, with a Turkish fountain), mosques, flat-roofed Turkish houses, streets as noisy with bargaining as a Rumelian bazaar – and an elegant Serbian Orthodox church which I'm looking at when the dreadful ear-bashing squawks of the Moslem call to prayer blast from a nearby minaret. The people are a mix of Montenegrin and Albanian, some of them very dark-skinned, the Albanian women out shopping in traditional costume – coloured baggy trousers if they are Moslem, white skirts and white under-trousers if they are Orthodox, all head-scarved. The men, in non-descript jackets, stand around doing nothing. Portraits of Tito decorate the cafés. There is a tiny black colony, the descendants of slaves brought from Africa centuries ago by the Turks; one of them owns a photographer's booth on the quay. He speaks Serbo-Croat, but I hear Albanian more often in Ulcinj. The frontier, the Bojana River, is eight miles to the south: it is not a crossing-point. Modern Albania's self-inflicted isolation Yugoslavs regard as a tragic joke. It is the only country in the world that has made atheism its state religion (Shkodër – Scutari, Skadar – its third largest city has one of the finest monasteries in the Balkans, but it is now a Museum of Atheism); religious literature is forbidden, and so is importing political and pornographic material. Presumably to annoy the Albanians, the Yugoslavs have built on the frontier a very large, de luxe holiday camp for nudists.

You can cross into Albania at Božaj, which is on the road from Titograd to Shkodër, but I decide I won't even try; the hassles will be too many, and the rewards, other than saying "I've been to Albania!", are likely to be few. Instead I look down from a high mountain road on the frontier near Ostros (where people come to market on donkeys); a Montenegrin border-guard – cute, young, friendly, but armed to the teeth – warns me not to take a step further. The view is marvellous; the whole of Lake Skadar is visible, snow-capped peaks beyond, and it's obvious Albania is a different country – the huge fields of collective farms. The Yugoslavs enjoy bringing bus-loads of tourists to this spot: it irritates the Albanian soldiers, particularly if you stare at them and point. One third of Lake Skadar is in Albania, the rest in Yugoslavia. Its wild life is its attraction, and the day I spend on it (the Yugoslav part) in a boat is certainly one to remember – thousands of frogs croaking in the reeds; all kinds of marsh birds crying plaintively; pelicans – just like their Californian cousins, but white, not brown, and bigger – swooping for fish; water-snakes laboriously chugging along the surface; willow trees half-submerged; marigolds and kingcups in bloom, and a million Monet-like lilies, their white and yellow blossoms the texture and colour of egg. Hawks and eagles bask in wind currents, high above mountains that soar up from the lake's shores. Virtually no humans – houses are miles apart. The occasional fishermen in punts, the odd curved ends of which are peculiar to Skadar. We reach a village after a couple of hours: the only time in Yugoslavia I see real poverty. Most of the cottages are in ruins, and though

74

the few that are inhabited have electric light and TV aerials, there is no road here – just a dirt track – and no fields, no cultivated plots; the land is all marsh and bog. Pigs and chickens wander about at will; there is shit everywhere, and a disgusting stench. No one tidies up: the gardens are thick with weeds. The expression on people's faces is of despair. In the cemetery three wizened old women in black are digging a grave.

Virpazar, at the western end of the lake, is a striking contrast. A sleepy, beautiful village with a good hotel, prosperity, and the laughing, chatty Montenegrins I've become used to.

Miločer, my headquarters this trip, is the nicest place on the Montenegrin coast; no more than a handful of old stone houses with terracotta roofs, at the gates of what was once the summer palace of King Alexander. (He who was assassinated at Marseilles in 1934.) The palace is now a hotel, but the grounds – huge and overgrown; it would need an army of gardeners and all the miracles of St Tryphon to restore their splendours – are public domain, open day and night. Most evenings I stroll through here in the dusk or dark, and out the other side to the causeway that joins Sveti Stefan to the mainland. Sveti Stefan is a Yugoslav version of St Michael's Mount; it appears on the covers of all the tourist brochures, but, like that place, it's more attractive in photographs than in reality. It was once a fishing village, but thirty years ago its inhabitants were moved into new houses on the mainland – pleasant houses with big gardens, but who would enjoy being forced to leave? The island's cottages have been turned into a hotel complex: an *extremely* expensive hotel for film stars, tycoons, and minor royals. You can visit Sveti Stefan (the entrance fee is outrageous) and be disappointed: it's so rebuilt, so designed to look 'pretty' it's utterly false – the Yugoslavia of a film set.

The palace grounds at night ought to be ideal for gay trolling, but on only one occasion do I spot another man also on the look-out. I suppose it is *miles* from any big city

. . . He's from Hercegovina, thirty-six, a professional soldier, and – in the moonlight – very handsome. I decide not to ask him to my hotel: we could both be disappointed. He's an expert on Bogomil ste čaks (tombstones), which are to be found in Bosnia and Hercegovina; there are none in Montenegro. The Bogomils – later, in France, called Cathars or Albigensians – believed that everything in this world was created by the Devil and should be rejected: 'God is perfect,' says an old Cathar syllogism; 'Nothing in the world is perfect; therefore nothing in the world was made by God.' They were vegetarians (vegans in fact); they drank no alcohol; they disapproved of procreation and regarded marriage as the ultimate sin. This led the Inquisition in France to accuse them of being homosexual, but, apart from the word 'bugger' being a corruption of 'Bogomil', there is, alas, no evidence to suggest that they were or were not. There was much about the Cathars to admire (the weirdness of their beliefs is no odder than any other religious beliefs): their integrity, effective organisation, their piety and devotion to a life of the spirit, the simplicity of their religious services. They persecuted no one. Catharism was the most powerful and widespread heresy in Europe until Luther; it lasted for four hundred years. In France its adherents were jailed and burned; no trace of them is left, apart from some documents, one tombstone, and one of their strongholds, the castle of Montségur: but in Yugoslavia they were more or less tolerated. When the Turks arrived, they seem to have been quite willing converts to Islam.

King Tvrtko the First of Bosnia was a Bogomil, which perhaps is why the heresy took root there so strongly; but it began in Bulgaria and Macedonia. It's a variant on the most common of all heresies, Manichaeism, which was of Persian origin: the Magus Zoroaster; in one form or another it has spread through Christian Europe in almost every century since the death of Christ. Gnostic, Bogomil, Cathar, Paulician, Waldensian, Swedenborgian, Manichaean, David Icke – they're much the same. Bogomil tombs, my army officer tells me, come in all shapes and sizes – there's no set pattern – and they are interesting for their strange pictorial decoration and carving, and for their inscriptions. I quote him: 'I cut this stone when I was alive;' 'I'm not as you are, but you will be as I am;' 'When I wanted to exist I ceased to exist;' 'I was praying to God, no evil thoughts, when lightning struck me dead.'

I do not spend all my time with this man discussing Bogomil funerary art. Despite the Montenegrin taunt, at least one Hercegovinan, I discover, has an entirely satisfactory cock.

After Bogomils, Serbian Orthodox monks. There are two monasteries near Miločer, one – Praskvica – has a fine, early nineteenth-century iconostasis, and is a short walk from my hotel; the other, Rezěvići, is a bus ride away, six miles down the coast. A helpful Montenegrin has written on a piece of paper 'When does the next bus for Miločer depart?' in Serbo-Croat; I'm to give it to one of the monks who'll write down the answer for me. Rezěvići has two churches, the smaller with seventeenth-century frescoes, the larger with seventeenth-century ikons. Grave, un-smiling Byzantine faces: long Greek noses. Olive trees outside, and herb scents, choisia, new-mown grass, wild flowers, the sea mumbling to itself at the foot of the cliffs. But it hasn't always been so peaceful – Rezěvići was damaged by the Turks, and then by Napoleon's troops; in 1941 the Italians set it on fire. But it endures. In the cemetery more old women in black are digging graves.

I can hear a radio blaring from the kitchen, so I go there in search of a monk who'll read my message and write down the bus time. Three people – a young man and his girlfriend, and a black-robed, elderly monk with a huge grey beard are all dancing to *Do The Locomotion*. It isn't quite what I imagined. She returns to her task of grilling fish and kneading bread; the monk pours me a glass of grape brandy so strong it nearly blows my head off. Nobody knows the bus times – there's even some doubt that today there'll be *any* bus. (All in Serbo-Croat.) But I'm urged to sit and enjoy my drink. I do, but I wonder if my damaged leg muscles will be sufficient to transport me six miles. On one wall of the kitchen there's a phalanx of ikons. Another young man appears, the driver of a soft-drinks lorry. He has some business with the monk: two large bottles of dark yellow wine (or liqueur?) called Dioklecijan are wrapped up in old newspapers and exchanged for fifty dinars. My predicament is explained, loudly and with much waving of arms, to the lorry-driver. Who immediately gives me a lift back to Miločer.

And after the kindness of strangers and Serbian Orthodox monks, I explore Catholic churches: my one venture into Croatia is to Dubrovnik. Because of the political events of this week I expect hold-ups by armed militia at the Montenegro/Croatia border, but there's nothing; not even a road-sign to tell you you're crossing from one republic into another. The last road-sign in Montenegro says, in English, 'You are now leaving Herceg Novi. Have a nice trip.' Maybe there's some intended irony in that.

Over the centuries Dubrovnik has been given more enthusiastic praise – 'the pearl of the Adriatic' – than any other city in Yugoslavia, and it indeed merits such encomiums: another ancient town behind stout walls, but bigger, more lived in, less of a museum-piece than many; spotlessly clean, and, as usual, a total ban on wheeled traffic. Venice reminders again, and Dubrovnik has always looked west rather than east – the Adriatic is a narrow sea; Italy, it seems to tell you, is not far away beyond the horizon. I'm in a very different world from Ulcinj. Dubrovnik's history is extraordinary. It was an independent republic for six hundred years called Ragusa (the word argosy is a corruption of Ragusa) that grew rich and powerful through its maritime trade; it maintained its independence by subtly negotiating a whole series of alliances with whoever happened to be the most powerful neighbouring state – the Byzantine Empire, Hungary, Venice, Serbia, Bosnia, Turkey, Austria. It lasted even longer than Venice, not succumbing to Napoleon until

1806. Its régime was an oligarchy of nobles, but they were much more civilised than their Venetian counterparts: by 1347 Ragusa had an old people's home; it was the first place in Europe to abolish the slave trade (1417); torture was unknown; and by 1432 it had an orphanage, an efficient health service and public assistance for the needy. The pharmacy, the oldest in Europe, opened in 1317 – and is still functioning. It was one of the most enlightened city-states that has ever existed. After Napoleon, Ragusa was annexed for a century to the Austro-Hungarian Empire. The Austrians behaved as badly here as they did in all their conquered territories – the Governor had the cathedral's baptistery destroyed because, he said, it blocked the view from his windows.

Presiding over Ragusa's nobles was a doge-like figure called the Rector; his appointment lasted only a month, during which time he lived in a palace and was not allowed out, except for ceremonial state occasions. 'Work for the public good' is a motto carved in Latin on the stone above the doorway of his study – during his month of office he was not even permitted to see members of his family. The Rector's Palace is a modest building compared with the Venetian doges': but everything in Dubrovnik is modest. Its cathedral, its churches and public buildings are all worth seeing, though none is of outstanding architectural or artistic merit, and the main street – the famous Placa – is unexceptional. Nevertheless: Titians can be seen in the most unlikely churches; the cloisters of the two monasteries, filled with shrubs and flowers, are beautiful; every house, fountain, statue, street corner deserves a glance. It's a marvellous city for unhurried pottering – absorbing atmosphere.

I had hoped I'd see, among all the English tourists in Yugoslavia, somebody who would resemble my idea of our ambassador at His Majesty's Legation in Cetinje; but I'm disappointed until my last evening, when the absolute personification of Our Man in Montenegro (and his wife) appears in the dining room of the hotel at Miločer: he a prelude in fawn, she a concerto in beige – he, florid, damp, balding, she with a face like a horse and a fixed smile of tombstone teeth. Their accents are impeccably upper-crust. Waiters float round them, a colony of penguins brandishing soups and hors d' oeuvres. I'm delighted to find, among all the working-class Brits and Communist Montenegrins, one little reminder of imperial glory; a scene that would not have been out of place in the eighteen eighties at that superb pink villa a brief stroll away from the Royal Palace in Cetinje.

I can go home now, quite satisfied.

May 1991

That's how it seemed at the time. No one could have guessed that a bunch of power-mad Serbian generals would want to smash everything to bits. What has happened to medieval Dubrovnik? Is my Hercegovinan soldier still alive? This isn't a civil war – it's old-fashioned, imperialist expansionism by Serbia, Europe's last remaining bastion of Communist nasties.

Spars of purposes – countries that used to exist – was one of my themes in the travel pieces in *Dog Days, White Nights*: Estonia, Latvia, Lithuania; Normandy; Scotland. But no spar of purpose succeeded so well then failed so spectacularly as Languedoc (as it came to be known), which in its heyday was Le Toulousain, the Comté de Toulouse. For three hundred years – from the tenth to the beginning of the thirteenth century – it was the most civilised country in Europe. Its people were enlightened and cultured; its merchants were rich; it had an urban bourgeoisie when such a concept was unknown elsewhere; it was the land of the troubadours, of poetry and music, individualism, courtly love. Its people were free: there was no feudalism, for the Counts of Toulouse, the rulers of Languedoc, behaved with a liberality and a tolerance centuries ahead of their time. It had its own language, Occitan, and it considered its northern French-speaking neighbours as barbaric. It was the ideal place for Catharism, a religion that practised what it preached, to take root, particularly as the power and the corruption of the medieval Church was universally resented. The Cathars flourished in the towns and villages on or near what is still Languedoc's main highway, the road from the Mediterranean city of Béziers to Narbonne, Carcassone, Toulouse itself, and Bordeaux. Much of this road traverses the southern part of the diocese of Albi, which is why the Cathars became known as les Albigeois, though the city of Albi was never a Cathar stronghold.

None of the Counts of Toulouse, it's thought, was a Cathar, but they permitted the heresy to spread and gave protection to its adherents. Various popes tried – rather feebly – to win Languedoc back to the Faith by dispatching high-ranking emissaries to preach the Catholic idea of the Gospels, but all their efforts met with total failure. What changed things was the election to the Papacy in 1198 of Innocent the Third, and the murder in 1208 of his legate to Languedoc – the murder happened the day after the legate had quarrelled violently with the Count, Raymond the Sixth. Innocent ordered a crusade to exterminate the Cathars. He should have known better: this most intellectual of popes, the ablest politician in Europe and a sincere Christian, was quite well aware that crusaders were thugs and vandals who needed little excuse to loot, burn, rape and kill indiscriminately. Only five years before he had been horrified that the Fourth Crusade, instead of freeing the Holy Land from the Infidels, had sacked Constantinople. The Albigensian Crusade, nevertheless, was launched; and for twenty appalling years Languedoc was ravaged by foreign armies besieging castles, cutting down olive trees and vineyards, burning Cathars at the stake, destroying towns, and generally reducing the whole country to uninhabitable misery. When it was too weak to resist any longer, Languedoc was annexed by the French; it ceased to be a separate entity, and the Inquisition completed the work by hunting down and burning the last remaining Cathars.

From a modern standpoint one can only pity them all, on both sides; but the role of the Church and Innocent (what an ironic name!) can still produce strong feelings. To think of this story, and at the same time be in Languedoc looking at the interior of a Catholic church stuffed with the usual tawdry plaster saints and virgins, the tenth-rate pictures no gallery would ever display, the old women in black muttering meaningless mumbo-jumbo, fills me with anger: a desire to smash it all to bits. The ultimate irony, I suppose, is that Lourdes – an obscene monument to superstition and bad taste – is in Languedoc.

Thirty years ago there were few signs that the Counts or the Cathars had ever existed; Le Toulousain was merely a part of France where people spoke with a strange accent. Today Counts and Cathars are big business. The shops in Toulouse sell books, in English, German, Italian and Spanish, as well as French, on the history of Languedoc, the Cathar religion, the Cathar sites; the insignia of the Counts is to be seen everywhere; you can stay at a Hotel des Cathares, drink in a Café des Cathares, eat at a

Restaurant des Cathares, though none of these places has any specific connection with les Albigeois. Street names in Toulouse are in both French and Occitan, and Montségur, thirty years ago a neglected, dilapidated ruin, is now one of France's top half-dozen, most visited tourist attractions. The enormous interest, I suppose, comes from a world-wide change in attitudes: the contemporary enthusiasm for alternative religions, the divisions in the Catholic Church since John the Twenty-third, the growth of regionalism, the desire to preserve rather than suppress minority languages and cultures. One sees parallels in the break-up of the Soviet Union, the power of independence movements in the Baltic States, Croatia, Slovenia, the Basque territories, Catalonia, Scotland, and so on. Not that Languedoc is likely to secede from France; but an Occitan 'identity' that draws notice to its history, Count and Cathar, certainly brings in the tourists. Even the language is beginning to revive. I heard three women in a Toulouse restaurant speaking Occitan.

But sightseers looking for relics of Counts and Cathars in Toulouse will be disappointed; none of the Counts, for example, is buried here. Some of them died on crusades in Palestine, Raymond the Fifth at Nîmes, and Raymond the Sixth, who did happen to die at Toulouse, wasn't allowed a Christian burial because the Pope – Honorius the Third – said he was a Cathar. (Honorius in fact knew he was not.) His coffin was left outside the city walls for so long that wind and weather caused it to disintegrate; the bones were scattered and disappeared. No house in Toulouse is as old as the eleventh or twelfth centuries, though the city centre is an attractive warren of medieval streets, albeit ineffectively semi-piétonné. (Nothing will ever persuade the French to relinquish their belief that the car must always take precedence over the pedestrian, even on street-crossings controlled by lights.) Not a stone is left of the Counts' palace, the Château Narbonnais; the site is now the local jardin des plantes. It was considered by medieval travellers to be the gloomiest, most uncomfortable palace in Europe; the Counts themselves disliked it, and they rarely lived there – they preferred their castle at Saint-Gilles in the Camargue – so maybe its loss is not to be mourned.

Some of the churches in Toulouse, however, the Counts would recognise: the basilique Saint-Sernin, the world's largest Romanesque structure, has not changed since the eleventh century. It's a massive red-brick edifice – there's no building stone in Languedoc; so most of Toulouse is brick, and it's therefore known as la ville rose, which is also a comment on its political affiliations. One of the doors, the Porte des Comtes de Toulouse, which was used only by the Raymonds and their families, is a very ornate affair. Inside there are five aisles, a superb forest of pillars: but it seems empty and cold – for once there is a *lack* of furniture, of decoration. St Sernin is another obscure character. He arrived in Toulouse in the year 250, and tried to convert its inhabitants to Christianity; they were singularly unpersuaded, for they killed him by allowing a very ferocious bull to gore him to death. The city's dislike of alien preachers also showed itself in the Middle Ages: no papal legate diverted Toulouse from Catharism by the power of oratory, though such persons were treated with more politeness than in 250 – argument, no bulls, was used to get rid of them.

The most interesting church in Toulouse is the Eglise des Jacobins (*not* a reference to the French Revolution, but a nickname for the Dominicans); it's thirteenth-century, built during the reign of Rayond the Seventh, and is a unique piece of ecclesiastical architecture – a single row of pillars, running along the centre of its interior, supports a vault like palm fronds in stone. It contains the tomb of that ideological expert, the Dominican St Thomas Aquinas, perhaps the only medieval Catholic authority for whom one can feel respect; a man of first-class intelligence and width of reading, whose devotion to the Church did not prevent him from understanding and properly evaluating the worth of Aristotle and other pagan philosophers. Five hundred years before Blake Aquinas was thinking heterodoxies most unmedieval; people who suppress their

84

natural desires, he wrote, destroy themselves: happiness comes from the harmony of body *and* soul. We should recruit him, by proxy as it were, to the gay cause. Aquinas had absolutely no connection with Toulouse – he never came to the city; he did not die here. Gregory the Tenth, pope when Aquinas died in 1274, ordered that he should be buried in Les Jacobins because it was a Dominican monastery of international renown; but the real reason, I think, was symbolic: to entomb this most brilliant of theologians in a city that was still Cathar in thought if not in fact, smouldering with resentment against the Papacy, was a warning. As if the Puritans had decreed that Cromwell should be buried in Dublin.

Modern Toulouse is a large, provincial city. Its imposing main square, the Place du Capitole (Plaça del Capitoul in Occitan) with its huge hôtel de ville, conveys no feeling of having once been the centre of a thriving, independent state. Its restaurants and cafés are very French, which means one can't eat badly (though I'm not thrilled by the local dish, cassoulet – a lot of old bones stewed up in a concoction of fart-making butter beans); the chicness and style of people's clothes are also très français; and after a football match, as in any French city, the young men sound their car-horns in a raucous din of discords, regardless of whether their team has won or lost. It's a prosperous city: France's aerospace industry is here. But I'm struck by the numbers of beggars on the streets, something I haven't noticed since the nineteen fifties; the opposite side of the coin, I imagine, of material wealth: the unacceptable face of Mitterrandisme.

The trains are on strike. 'Grève très grave,' says one newspaper, and another screams more melodramatically: 'Toute la France est *paralysée*!' I'm relying on trains to get me to Castres, Carcassonne and Albi, then over the Pyrenees to Barcelona – the SNCF is usually much superior to dirty, perpetually late British Rail. In any country the frustrations and hassles of a train strike are enormous, but in France they seem worse than elsewhere. People become very bad-tempered, unhelpful and rude; the roads are chock-a-block with traffic; the blasting of car-horns goes on all day; and in the summer heat a great deal of Latin, particularly Midi, temperament flares up. I go to Castres and Albi by bus, but the journeys are twice as long as by train, and exceedingly uncomfortable. At Lavour the bus driver gets into an argument with a policeman; the bus is obstructing a pedestrian crossing. The driver refuses to move – a car is parked by the bus stop. "If you don't move this old crate immediately," the gendarme says, "I shall stuff my truncheon right up your arse!" The driver is furious, leaps out of the bus, grabs the gendarme by the lapels, seizes the truncheon, and threatens to stick it up the gendarme's arse. Meanwhile, the cacophony of car horns rises to a climax of Wagnerian volume and Shostako-vichian dissonance. "J'ai mon travail," says the policeman, breaking away and turning his attention to the traffic, for the centre of Lavour is indeed now paralysée. The driver hands back the truncheon, and we continue, with immense slowness, towards Castres. The countryside is superb: rich, lush farmland; wide, sluggish rivers, willow trees trailing in the water; beautiful, ancient villages; all the flowers of summer.

Castres, on the banks of the Agout, is more attractive than Albi or Carcassonne, though it has nothing to compare with Albi's extraordinary cathedral or Carcassonne's ramparts and towers. It's simply an interesting mélange of sleepy old streets, like Dubrovnik ideal for pottering; every corner, every twist and turn, unfolds a pleasing group of houses, a worthwhile view. Windows look down from both banks into the river: I'm reminded of Florence. I'm here for the Musée Goya, which has the biggest collection of Spanish works of art outside Spain, including almost the whole of Goya's etchings – Los Proverbios, Los Caprichos, La Tauromaquia, and finest of all, Los Desastres de la Guerra (The Horrors of War). There are paintings by Goya too, and Velazquez, Ribera, Murillo, Zurbarán and so on. An enterprising citizen of Castres bought them during the last century and gave them to the town: it's as if Newbury had a fascinating collection of Degas, or Okehampton a museum devoted to Rubens. *The Horrors of War* is not for the squeamish: 'They'll serve again' is the title of a print that shows some appallingly mutilated soldiers being carted off on stretchers; and the evils that accompany war – torture, rape, executions, looting, the suffering of children – are drawn unsparingly. A horse crumpled and on its knees Picasso reproduced almost exactly in *Guernica*: he was clearly paying homage. Not only to Goya – a work of Miró's that predates *Guernica* by three years portrays a woman screaming, face upturned – Picasso includes this face, this scream. It's as if all such art leads to *Guernica*, though *No More*, the most memorable, the most terrifying of Goya's, is not used by Picasso. It shows a man being hanged. His trousers have fallen grotesquely to his ankles. A soldier, lounging against a balustrade, looks at him, grinning. Humans are shit, Goya is saying, more bestial than beasts, random and meaningless in their violence to one another. I'm not repelled by his vision. I agree with him.

The collection is housed in what was the Bishop's palace (Castres has an extremely uninteresting eighteenth-century cathedral); outside it is a well-kept knot garden where I stroll in the Sunday sun. It's also, I soon realise, the local gay trolling-ground, and I remember that nearly every city in France has such meeting-places; 'les facilités' French gays call them. In Quimper, ten years ago, it was the Place de la Tourbie – it was *rampant*. I watch, for a while, men pursuing men; illusion, delusion, doubtless to be followed by disillusion. No one looks at me – my hair's too white. If I dyed it black, then they would look. Illusion, delusion, disillusion. On the bus I find myself observing four young people, undergraduates returning to Toulouse after a weekend at home in Castres. One is a girl with her boyfriend (a gorgeous, sexy Arab with huge, dark eyes and curly hair); behind them sit her brother and *his* boyfriend (a bearded Jesus.) Definitely boyfriend: I can understand every word they're saying. At the bus station they were seen off by the parents of the brother and sister, well-to-do middle-class types driving a big Citröen. What on *earth*, I ask myself, does this provincial, middle-aged couple know of their children's lives? Everything, and their blessing on it, I hope. (But don't quite believe.)

It's a beautiful late afternoon: the countryside seems richer, riper, more fruitful even than this morning. Utterly at peace. Rounding a bend, the bus pulls up sharply – there has been a crash; one car in the ditch the other in the middle of the road upside down. Bodies, inert, horribly blood-soaked, are dead or dying. The police, beginning to sort it out, wave us on. A few yards up the road an old man and his wife, on the veranda of their house, are drinking an aperitif, completely unaware of what has occurred.

The strike is over! The booking-clerk at Toulouse's Gare Matabiau is now all smiles; "Of course monsieur can go by train!" And it's true; I'm whizzed down to Carcassonne in less than an hour. Snow-capped Pyrenees decorate the distant horizon. By ten a.m. I'm exploring the medieval, hill-top city, a quite distinct and separate place from la ville basse of Carcassonne, on the other side of the River Aude, though this is also medieval in origin. Of haute Carcassonne the architect, Viollet-le-Duc, said, "I don't know anywhere in Europe more interesting and more picturesque than this sensational ensemble of towers and walls, which were built in the fifth, twelfth, and thirteenth centuries." Three decades ago I agreed with him, but now, having experienced in the interim a great many other medieval cities, I'm not so sure. Is it superior to Durham, Salamanca, Siena, Florence? I doubt it. It's certainly over-restored and not as we would do that kind of thing (Viollet-le-Duc, a nineteenth-century French equivalent of Pugin or Gilbert Scott, was responsible); but it is, with its fifty-two towers, perhaps the grand-daddy of them all.

The basilica of Saint-Nazaire, once upon a time the cathedral, is much more attractive than the dull elephant in la ville basse that is today the cathedral. It has sumptuous fourteenth-century windows; the only gravestone in existence of a known Cathar, one Sans Morlane (the fact that it is in what was the *cathedral* shows the extraordinary tolerance of Languedoc's rulers); and a superbly sculpted slab that was the top of Simon de Montfort's tomb: it depicts the unsuccessful siege of Toulouse in 1218, in which de Montfort was killed. Nearby is the castle, once the home of the Counts of Béziers, vassals and allies of the Counts of Toulouse – one of the crusade's initial crimes was to kill the young Count of Béziers (he was twenty-four), who was a neutral in the conflict. Though the views from its windows are magnificent, the castle is not impressionnant; its neatly arranged artefacts are worth only a moment's pause – except for some curious tombstones that are probably Cathar in shape and design: they resemble what I was told of bogomil stečaks in Yugoslavia.

The streets of this old city irritate in a way that those of Durham or Dubrovnik do not: too much tourist tat, not enough real life. It's a pleasure to get away from them, and walk along les lices, the wide, grassy expanse between the outer and inner ramparts. Nobody else seems to think of doing this, I'm glad to say: I'm alone with the sunlight and the wind, marvellous vistas in every direction – only here do I get any real feeling of what it was like as a citizen in medieval Carcassonne, of the battles between crusader and Albigeois: under the grass a large number of the dead seem to communicate with the living.

By mid-day I've had enough; I'll return to Toulouse. But the strike has started again. There won't be a train for five and a half hours. And there really is *nothing* to do or see in la ville basse: it's a totally boring, second-rate place. I want to scream, like the gendarme and the bus-driver, "La belle France – you can stuff *yourself* up your arse!" But it's impossible to be angry with the French for long: I'm safely in Toulouse before nightfall, and another good dinner, another excellent bottle of wine – all very cheap compared with dining out in England – restore my good temper.

A more dramatic warning to the Cathars than burying

Thomas Aquinas in Toulouse was the building of the cathedral at Albi. It's the most impressive piece of architecture in Languedoc, a red-brick stronghold rising up from a hill-summit, its walls grim and impossible to scale, its windows the narrowest of slits – as if the thirteenth-century Catholic authorities were expecting a siege requiring defence by an army of bowmen – and its roof is completely flat: good, I suppose, for standing on and hurling barrels of boiling oil at the enemy. No cathedral is so uncompromising, so severe and stark: devoid, it seems, of any concept of Christian charity, of 'Come unto Me.' At a distance it looks like a liner stranded miles from the ocean. You enter its portals with trepidation, and see a characteristic Languedoc medieval interior – aisleless, with no division between nave and choir, a gigantic barn. To begin with it must have been utterly gaunt: but succeeding centuries, the Cathar threat having disappeared, brought about a softening of the austerity – in 1485 the choir was given inner walls, which are an amazing contrast: as flamboyant and ornate as Gothic architecture can ever be, the beautifully carved statues still perfect, unmarked by any ravages of time. At the end of the fifteenth century a huge Last Judgement was painted on the back wall; and finally, in 1512, the whole of the rest of the interior was painted with murals which, like the statues, have never been spoiled, restored, or 'improved.' This cathedral is exactly as it was nearly five hundred years ago.

But I think the Cathars – or at any rate the Counts – had the last laugh. The tourists flock to Albi not so much for the mailed fist of medieval Catholic might, but for the Toulouse-Lautrec museum, which is next door in the Bishop's palace, a building as stern as the cathedral itself. After Raymond the Seventh there were no counts ruling an independent Languedoc, but the family did not disappear: Henri de Toulouse-Lautrec was a direct descendant of the Raymonds. His paintings are filled with the compassion and charity that typified Count and Cathar, and which Innocent and his crusading thugs so obviously lacked. Compassion, in particular, for the plight of women – that whole cortège of beggars, can-can girls and prostitutes who almost shriek with the pain of exploitation and of poverty; here they all are, in Albi, Lautrec's birthplace. It's the largest collection of Lautrec in the world: one explores, in room after room, his entire life – the immensely privileged childhood and adolescence; the youthful drawings and paintings (his parents, his dogs, his horses); until, in the final two rooms, all the great posters: overwhelming, this, for there cannot be many rooms anywhere which contain such masterpieces; grisettes, danseuses, old men at the Moulin Rouge, May Milton, Aristide Bruant arrogantly swathed in his red scarf, Jane Avril, La Goulue, Chocolat – the black cabaret artist – camping it up, M. Caudiaux striding like Groucho. An infinitely more rewarding experience than that unchristian cathedral.

The strike has definitely ended, and I'm en route for Spain: a single-track railway winding up thousands of feet into the Pyrenees. Above the snow-line. No lush, opulent landscape here – soaring mountains, fir forests, Alpine flowers in bloom. Castles on so many peaks, all with Cathar associations, and very attractive towns with romantic names; Foix, Tarascon-sur-Ariège, Ax-les-Thermes. "I've always wanted to wander in the Pyrenees," Estragon says in *Waiting for Godot*, and Ax-les-Thermes looks so seductive, so sweet, and the train stops there so long I'm tempted to get out, find a room, wander . . . But I don't. The railway skirts the frontier with Andorra; I can see the customs post. At La Tour de Carol (or La Tor de Querol) we change trains, a Spanish train now, and it's downhill into Catalunya. The scenery is much the same, a little more arid perhaps, but the villages are decidedly un-French and the smells are so different . . .

June 1991

Barcelona Days

The most memorable line in *Fawlty Towers*, so good it's become a catch-phrase, occurred during the episode in which Manuel lost his pet rat. The foyer of the hotel was in a state of siege – guests angered beyond breaking-point by Basil – and Sybil was trying to calm them down. Enter the rat, Manuel in hot pursuit. Summoning up her most reassuring smile, and speaking in tones that suggested her words would explain the entire cause of such chaos, Sybil said, "He's from *Barcelona*!" Two or three strolls up and down Las Ramblas, Barcelona's busiest street, confirm that Sybil really did know what she was talking about; there is something a bit mad about this marvellous city – a cultivation of the deliberately outrageous, a delight in being different. Like San Francisco's Castro, Las Ramblas is a perpetual circus: street entertainment of all sorts (mime artists, Tarot-card experts, jugglers, dancers, singers, strippers, and so on); sellers of anything and everything from flowers to caged birds, from the whole of Europe's newspapers to *extremely* pornographic magazines; the odd prostitute of either sex; open-air cafés; a snake-charmer on the Miró pavement; palm-reading gipsies in the Rambla dels Caputxins; gay men (check macho shirts, Queens with poodles, pretty boys fluttering come-to-bed eyes); and, most of all, men and women of every class, race, age and sex who simply like walking from the Plaça de Catalunya to the Columbus Monument and back to see – and be seen.

It's wonderful, except for the caged birds, which should be banned by law. If Sydney is the city in the Southern Hemisphere where the party really is, then Barcelona is the Northern Hemisphere's equivalent. Impossible not to love it, to find it totally exhilarating. Even the Metro is enjoyable (one of the most efficient in Europe, and a book of ten tickets means your journey – any distance – is twenty pence a time) and also a bit mad: foreign Metro stations frequently seem to us British to have the weirdest names, but Barcelona's are excessively weird, Penitence for example, and Diagonal and Paral.lel. The most peculiar is

John the Twenty-third Provisional. What can it imply? Some ridiculous quarrel between Church and State, Catholic conservatism confronting Red anarchy, an echo of the Civil War? Barcelona's architecture, as everyone knows, is famous for being quite mad; it is the Modernist city par excellence, the only place in the world that gave immense financial backing to the Art Nouveau fantasies of Josep Puig i Cadafalch, Lluís Domènech i Montaner, and Antoní Gaudí. Tourists are easy to spot – they're the ones standing still on the pavements, craning their necks as they stare at yet another bizarre house-front or roof-top decorated like an upturned loo or a wedding-cake.

These buildings are easy to miss, for they're often sandwiched between perfectly ordinary nineteenth- or twentieth-century façades in some narrow lane; though not perhaps in the Eixample district, where the Passeig de Gràcia, Barcelona's widest street, has the Manzana de la Discòrdia (the Block of Discord) with houses, several storeys high, of all three architects jostling next to each other, like an illustration by Randall Jarrell of a Grimm fairy-tale brought to life in three dimensions of stone. And there's Parc Güell, designed by Gaudí, a public park not remarkable for its flowers, shrubs and trees, but for its strange entrance pavilions with chimneys like fairground hats or pepper-pots, fountains masquerading as giant iguanas, and Gaudí's own house, another fairy-tale, gingerbread creation, a witch's cottage in the woods. Most famous of all, and Barcelona's – indeed Catalonia's – most well-known symbol, is Gaudí's unfinished cathedral, La Sagrada Família.

At no time do I see it at a distance; thus, coming out of the Metro, I'm right beside it: the effect of it suddenly being there is astonishing, for no picture postcard or photograph I've seen of it has done it justice. If it's possible for a building – and this one, being unfinished, resembles a bomb site; I think, incongruously, of St Mark's church in Surbiton, destroyed by a Nazi oil bomb during my wartime childhood – to inspire emotions of sheer joy, then La Sagrada Família more than any other does so for me:

just gazing at it makes me dance with excitement. It doesn't have that effect on everybody – George Orwell hated it; its spires, he sneered, resemble hock bottles. Well . . . they do. But *I'm* not sneering. Vast Arizona cactuses would be a better description, with wheels on top like the fly-wheels in cigarette lighters. The whole thing is a dreamscape in stone as was Beckford's Fonthill, and I'm thrilled that one genius, for once in the history of the world, was permitted to make a reality out of such a colossally expensive, but beautiful, private vision.

The old cathedral (fourteenth-century) in the Barri Gòtic is a flat, dispiriting experience after Gaudí: dark inside, as are nearly all Spanish cathedrals, lit only by the dim, religious light of votive candles; a trashy clutter of grilles, statues, reliquaries and Baroque reredoses; and that suffocating, airless smell, uniquely Spanish Catholic, of dead flowers and stale Jesuit breath. Outside, though, is an example of one of the most appealing aspects of Spain – an old house built round a patio, fountain in its middle, geraniums in pots, tiled walls. An echo of the Moors, the Emirate of Córdova: grace, stillness, sweet fresh air. Nearby is Catalonia's parliament building, the Palau de la Generalitat, about which there is nothing of any particular note; but I remember its role in the Civil War, and photographs of President Companys on its balcony, his henchman, Tarradellas, beside him. Companys went to France when Barcelona fell to the fascists, but in 1940 the Nazis handed him over to Franco, who had him shot. Tarradellas was luckier – he spent nearly four decades in exile, returning to Spain after Franco died; when Catalonia was allowed a parliament again, he was elected President. He stood on that balcony and announced to the crowds, "So . . . here I am." As if Civil War and forty years were nothing. The laconic, throwaway remark is typically Spanish: a professor at Salamanca was arrested in mid-lecture by the Inquisition, and was thrown in jail for five years; when he was released he resumed the unfinished lecture exactly where he'd left off, prefacing it with "As I was saying . . ."

I keep using the word Spanish, but Barcelona is Catalan first, Spanish second. The Catalan language, full of 'x's and peculiar double 'l's, I can barely make head or tail of – just enough to ask for a room or a direction, to decipher a menu. I eat well here: Catalan cuisine is more varied than Spanish, not so much oil, more vegetables. One dinner – asparagus, veal escallope, strawberries, and Penedés rosé – is delicious. Catalans laugh and smile more than Castillians. I've never found an unpleasant, unhelpful, discourteous man or woman anywhere in Spain, but Catalans have less gravitas, a greater sense of humour.

There's nothing specifically Catalan about Picasso, though he lived here as a teenager and a young man; he obviously felt, however, some considerable affection for the city – he gave Barcelona so many of his paintings that a whole museum was needed to house them. It has one nice touch that only Barcelona would think of; the men's toilet is decorated in the same shade of blue as the Blue Period pictures – I imagine the women's is Rose Period pink . . . The canvases in the Museu Picasso are, almost all of them, Pablo's acceptable face; that side of him the public likes – his earliest work, very post-Impressionist, à la Toulouse-Lautrec. One is amazed by what a prodigy he was, the Mozart of paint: there is a magnificent portrait of his mother, done when he was fifteen; several pictures of his father, who has an uncanny resemblance to Kirk Douglas; an enormous room entirely devoted to the Blue Period; another to the Rose, the latter containing the beautiful *Harlequin*; and some violent landscapes painted at Horta when, aged seventeen, he was living with a gipsy, whom he said was the greatest love of his life – but, curiously, there's no portrait of this man. Horta – I don't know if it's the same Horta – is the terminus of one of Barcelona's Metro lines: it may have been out in the wilds in Picasso's youth, but I guess today it's a Catalan equivalent of Cockfosters. The strangest feature of this museum is that there is almost no example of Picasso's work from his mid-twenties until his mid-seventies; a fifty-year gaping hole. The last rooms contain the entire *Las Meninas* series, a set of variations, as it were, on a theme by Velazquez; the extraordinary talent revealed is undoubtedly impressive, and there is also a certain serenity of old age – but, finally one says, they're remarkably arid, devoid of emotional impact. I prefer, in a nearby room, the *Las Palomas* series, painted at Cannes in 1957: much more serene, and filled with a brilliance of Mediterranean colour – dazzling yellow beach, intense blue of sea and sky; so sensuous you can feel the hot sun, the cool of the water.

Another fascinating museum is the Fundació Joan Miró, in the hills of Parc Montjuïc, but I have two problems here – the first is that I don't really understand what Miró is trying to do; I can't read him, as I can Lautrec or Goya or Picasso. I can only appreciate his work as blobs of interesting colour, though the fifty or so paintings of the *Barcelona Series*, his comment on the Civil War, do say something that is similar to Goya's *Horrors of War*; brutal, bitter, ironic – unnecessary. Miró, I suppose, had Goya's series in mind, and Picasso's *Guernica*. The second problem is in my eyes: I've it had for months now; it's called 'a posterior vitreous detachment.' Seborrhoeic dermatitis that has bothered my hair, face, and ears is causing some solidification – or at least jellification – of the eye fluids in the right eye. This means, particularly in strong sunlight, that all outlines are blurred, and viewed through a veil of black lace or a snowstorm of black dots. In the evening, or in artificial light, the problem is less of a nuisance. The chief restriction it's put on how I live is that I can no longer drive very far; I can get about town to do my chores (bank, shopping, library) or visit friends, but I doubt I will ever again be able to drive to London, or even the North Devon coast. There is no cure. There's not even anything I can do to alleviate it. It may get worse; it may not; it may – *very* small chance of this – clear up by itself: the gunge may shoot itself out of the areas of vision. One compensation is that I now have an orange sticker, a disabled badge, on the windscreen of my car, and I enjoy parking, quite legally, on double yellow lines. (I try to find where a traffic warden is standing; parking under his stare of disapproval and walking off, knowing he can do nothing about it, is a pleasure.)

The Fundació Joan Miró, inside and out, is a brilliant white, and today the summer sun is exceptionally strong: the lace, the snowstorm, therefore, are more distressing than usual. I can't tell if these dots are in my eyes or on Miró's canvases. I make my way down to the city (the Funicular to Avinguda del Paral.lel), and in the Barri Gòtic I sit for a while in the church of Santa Maria del Mar, which is fourteenth-century and much more pleasing than the old cathedral: spacious, airy, totally without ornamentation. Lovely stained glass. I can focus as I cannot in the Miró museum: the stained glass helps. And I try, as I sit, to count my blessings, which are indeed many – one of them is being able to see Barcelona while I still can. Quand même . . .

Antoní Gaudí's death is a chilling story. In 1926, aged seventy-four, he was crushed under the wheels of a passing tram; he was taken to the nearest hospital and died there two days later. Inert on his hospital bed, this most famous of Barcelona's sons was visited by nobody. Nobody knew who he was. When Barcelona did find out what had happened, it was horrified, and he was given a magnificent funeral. (He's buried in the crypt of La Sagrada Família.) The reason why nobody knew who he was is that in the last twenty years of his life he was a virtual recluse; he stayed in his house in Parc Guëll, working on the designs of his cathedral, and he only left it occasionally, to see how the building was getting on.

I fear something similar will happen to me, though I doubt that Exeter will be horrified into giving me a magnificent funeral. I'm not Antoní Gaudí. But I have become a recluse – willingly, and also not. The willing part is I can no longer endure pubs, parties, crowded restaurants – though I don't automatically refuse invitations. The unwilling is that most people I know can't deal with Aids. (Or cancer, TB, any life-threatening illness; or an obvious disability such as Down's syndrome, quadriplegia, blindness . . . whatever.) So the invitations are fewer than they were, once. It isn't that people, gay or straight, imagine I'll deposit Aids viruses all over their drinking glasses, lavatory seats and door-knobs; I don't know anyone as stupid as that – it's more, I think, a kind of embarrassment: what do we say or do if Rees starts talking about Kaposi's Sarcoma or AZT, or speculates on whether X or Y is positive? They haven't, somehow, arranged their emotions, their reactions to disease in a proper pattern. Few people ever do. They'd much rather forget about Aids, and, in particular, friends of theirs who have it. It reminds them of their own mortality. Their own risks. They'd rather discuss *Coronation Street*.

On a TV programme I was watching recently a blind man said his lack of vision made him both an isolate and, paradoxically, cocooned in a charity he neither needed nor wanted. With his dark glasses on and his white stick in hand he is left alone on trains or in pubs; an awkwardness people ignore because they don't know what to say – they don't even know what to think or feel, as if there were somehow a 'correct' way to think about blindness that is different, and unknown, instead of just treating him as he wishes to be treated: as they'd treat anybody else. But if he stands up and walks to the door, there are instantly seven or eight pairs of arms helping him, directing him; he doesn't need that kind of assistance, he says – he's perfectly capable of finding his own way to the door. It's the same with Aids. I have a friend – all PWAs know someone like him – who rings me up from time to time and asks how I am; he's also the first to visit me when I'm in hospital. If I really want anything, he'll do it for me. But when I'm well – which, so far, has been the norm – he makes no effort to see me. The fact that this leaves me very cross has also made me, in the past, feel guilty.

But I no longer experience any guilt. About a month ago I had to spend a few days in hospital for the removal of a growth from my tongue, a smoking-related cancer I suspected, but it was not; it was a wart that had become virulent and developed into a tumour. It's a little-known fact that those who are HIV positive have no ability to resist wart viruses, and though on certain areas of the body, such as up one's arse, warts can be controlled, they can't be removed – as they can with people who have a properly functioning immune system – except by surgery. If any readers think that having a lump cut out of the tongue is extremely painful, they are absolutely right. I had a general anaesthetic of course, but . . . *afterwards*! For days I lived on soups, fruit juice, and liquidised casseroles. The only reassuring side of it was that my tongue healed with remarkable speed – in just over a fortnight there wasn't any pain, not even a twinge. The mouth, I suppose, is a superb cleansing agent, and it's good to know that one part of my body at least still has its healing abilities intact.

I was just coming round from the anaesthetic when I noticed this friend of mine standing at the door of the hospital ward. I felt terribly annoyed that he was there: a cold, unreasoning fury. Why the *fuck*, I said to myself, can't he be bothered to see me when I'm well, come to my house for a drink, a good laugh? I closed my eyes and pretended I was still unconscious until he went away. And – for the first time – I felt no guilt. Like the blind man, I neither want nor need people's charity. I don't think people should feel they've been very good to me. What I do want is that they and I regard the hours we spend together as a period of mutual, selfish enjoyment – that is what friendship, first and foremost, is about.

Gay men and women should stop congratulating them-selves on how brilliantly they deal with the Aids dying and deal a bit more often with the Aids living: spend as much time with us as they used to do – no, more time because we may not be around for long. Instead of the phoned enquiry concerning our health, or being prepared to rush to the hospital bedside, why not have dinner with us? Take a holiday together, laugh and bitch with us, go to the opera . . . anything. I guess I won't be crushed, like Gaudí, under the wheels of a tram, but I don't want to be found, stiff and cold, a week after I'm dead. Obviously I shan't be aware of that – but . . . well . . . it doesn't seem right.

Meanwhile, I'm in Barcelona, and alone, and enjoying myself, even if I'm calling this piece *Barcelona Days*.

Barcelona nights I know nothing of; all I'm fit for in the evenings is to eat, have a drink, take a constitutional, read a while, then go to bed. Las Ramblas at night will have to do whatever it does without me: I don't mind that – not at all. But I think I'd be enjoying the days more if one of my so-called friends had felt he – or she – could have decided it would be no hassle and come and shared them.

June 1991 . . .

From Nero's Bath to the Popemobile

Rome, 1991, is not a pleasant city: like New York it seems to be on the point of collapse, though in different ways and for different reasons. Its public transport makes London's look superb; Rome has a mere two Metro lines, and no bus that displays its destination. Unless you've opted for sightseeing on a tour bus, you have to explore on foot – not impossible as the city centre is fairly compact – but walking about Rome is a trip through Hell. None of its narrow medieval streets is pedestrianised; you can't walk on the pavements as they are littered with abandoned cars; few crossings are controlled by lights, and the traffic never gives way to people. It's choking to death with cars and the thousands of motor-cycles young Italians are so fond of; it's unbelievably polluted and noisy. It's also one of the most expensive cities in Europe. Hotel prices are astronomical, and so is the cost of eating out – fast disappearing from restaurants is the idea of table d'hôte, the menu del giorno. Which does at least mean it's not over-run by tourists; St Peter's is surprisingly uncrowded. Only in the Sistine Chapel are there vast mobs: all craning their necks to view the restored Michelangelo ceiling.

Rome has never got its act in gear. It has never possessed a concert hall, nor a symphony orchestra of international repute. Concerts, such as there were, until recently were held in the larger churches, but that has stopped – an edict from on high has ordained that only sacred music can now be performed in church, and all tickets must be free. Rumour says the edict comes from Giovanni Paolo Secondo himself, old Red-socks as Ian Paisley calls him; the two hundred and sixty-fourth Pontifex Maximus, whom from now on, for reasons of space, I shall refer to as J-P Two. Rome has no municipal art museum: Italy has no National Gallery. Rome, of course, is stuffed full of works of art – nowhere in the world has so much or so many visible signs of history – but its paintings and sculpture are scattered about all over the place in one palazzo or another, or in some dark corner of a church where they are difficult to see, badly cared for, and prime targets for theft. All these palaces and churches have different opening hours that are constantly being altered, or they are 'temporarily' closed for repairs that have lasted for as long as a Northern Line escalator has ceased to work – indefinitely. And museum charges have recently doubled ... I want to shout, as did Mark Antony, 'Let Rome in Tiber melt and the wide arch of the rang'd Empire fall!'

If you can set aside this hassle, blot it out, concentrate on the art and history beneath, then Rome is a culture vulture's orgy, though it's never treated its past with reverence – one era's buildings have always been the stone quarries of the next. Its history reveals itself like the layers of an onion. San Clemente, for example, is at first sight another identikit Renaissance church, but the mosaics in its apse are Byzantine and the marble panels of its floor date from the fourth century; underneath it is an entire fourth-century church, and underneath *that* a second-century Temple of Mithras and an Ancient Roman apartment building (a huge rabbit-warren of rooms); you stand where nothing much has changed in more than two thousand years and above your head roars the traffic in the Via San Giovanni in Laterano. It's easy to get distracted in Rome. On my way to the Forum (yes, funny things *do* happen on one's way to the Forum) I find, more or less by chance, a church with a Caravaggio – the *Madonna dei Pellegrini* – then another church with *three* Caravaggios, a third church with Fra Angelico's grave and Michelangelo's statue of *The Risen Christ*, a fourth, Sant' Ivo alla Sapienza, with a dramatic Art Nouveau spire, or rather spiral, that predates Gaudí by three hundred years (it was built by that most original of Baroque architects, Borromini); and then, turning a corner, I discover the Pantheon, the only building of Ancient Rome to survive intact. A *vast* building, designed by the Emperor Hadrian, who confused the world for two millennia by placing above its façade an inscription that says Agrippa built it. The inscription came from something else: in 1892 archaeologists found that every brick of the Pantheon is date-stamped A.D. 120, by which time Agrippa was long since dead. The Pantheon has the world's biggest dome, bigger than St Peter's or Santa Sophia – it is quite beautiful. Buried in here are Rafael, and two Italian kings, Umberto the First and Victor Emmanuel the Second.

But I do at last reach the Forum. Some years since I visited a major ancient site: Ephesus, in Turkey, which couldn't be more different – Ephesus has been thoroughly excavated, labelled, and in part rebuilt; Rome is almost exactly as the seventeenth century would have seen it, or as wrecked buildings appear in the pictures of Claude and Turner. Almost nothing has been excavated, labelled, rebuilt: it is a fantastic jumble of weed-filled ruins, mar-vellously atmospheric and ghostly – Septimus Severus's crumbling triumphal arch, broken columns, headless marble torsos, the remains of houses and temples, the Palatine Hill in particular with its quiet, shady streets (yes, one of the few quiet places in Rome) and what's left of Domitian's palace and stadium, acanthus and poppy in flower, sweet smells on the air instead of car exhaust. The sixteenth-century gardens, the Orti Farnesiani, laid out in the ruins of Tiberius's palace, are another delight: grottos, fountains, flowers, streams – deliciously melancholic. At the foot of the Capitoline Hill is Trajan's Column, a Bayeux Tapestry in stone, and the same Emperor's market, so intact and well-built I can't understand why it's not still used for its original purpose. And it's a pretty exciting sensation to stand on the spot where Julius Caesar was cremated, and on the Rostra where Mark Antony altered the course of history; 'Friends, Romans, countrymen . . .'

Trajan's Column and Market are separated from the rest of the site by the Via dei Fori Imperiali, a busy main road that Mussolini – one in a long line of Roman vandals – blasted through the ancient ruins from the Colosseum to the Capitoline Hill; another of his dubious bequests is the featureless, Fascist Monumental Via della Conciliazione that links Castel Sant' Angelo to St Peter's Square. Nothing, however, spoils brooding, sombre Sant' Angelo, which like everything old in Rome, has had many uses in the two thousand years of its existence. It was originally the world's biggest tomb, that of Hadrian; the popes subsequently turned it into a fortress (much of the work was done by the Borgia pope, Alexander the Sixth, who doubtless needed some protection when his children began murdering each other); later it was a jail for political prisoners. A raised walkway, the Passetto, runs from here to the Vatican; its purpose is to make it easy for popes in troubled times to flee from St Peter's and shut themselves up in Sant' Angelo. It was used by Clement the Seventh in 1527 when German soldiers sacked Rome. A frequent problem for Rome, being sacked by marauding Huns: Ostrogoths, Nazis. Sant' Angelo is now perhaps most famous for its roof, off which Tosca so spectacularly hurled herself. I stand on the roof and, with other tourists, sing a few commemorative bars of *Vissi d'arte, vissi d'amore* . . . She certainly had a magnificent view of Rome as she made the final leap . . .

Maybe it doesn't matter that the Via della Conciliazione is so soulless, for its end, St Peter's Square, is also very soulless (Bernini's gargantuan columns, built for the Chigi pope, Alexander the Seventh, surrounding an obelisk brought from Egypt by, of all people, Caligula) and St Peter's itself is . . . well, Fascist Monumental. What can one say about St Peter's other than it's very large *indeed*? Its Renaissance splendour is that of a palace, of power; not that of a church, of holiness. I don't find it beautiful, or moving, or exciting; but, I suppose, the papacy has nearly always been an institution more involved in power politics than spirituality. "Size isn't everything, Mostyn," I find myself saying as I observe on the floor of the nave the various inscriptions that tell you how far short of St Peter's is the length of the world's other big cathedrals; and I begin to understand how it was that Mussolini and Pius the Eleventh got on so well. The enormous bronze statue of Pius inside St Peter's makes him look as majestic as a Roman emperor; pope, emperor, fascist or Communist dictator, Tsar – they're all much the same. Yet, in abolishing an old order, Christ was founding something very different. Or so I thought.

Opposite Pius is another huge bronze statue, of his successor, Pius the Twelfth: it particularly emphasises his glasses, making him look incredibly sinister, a sort of ecclesiastical Tonton Macoute. John the Twenty-third is also very strange: a row of bishops behind him, their mitres like a bunch of clothes-pegs, and a woman holding a child seems to be recoiling from in horror. (I don't think this was the intention; John, originally a papa di passaggio, became the most revolutionary and most loved of popes. I admire him.) The nineteenth-century popes get a raw deal in their monuments – a shortage of good sculptors, perhaps. The best are of an earlier date – Canova's anxious Clement the Thirteenth, and some superbly effective memorials from the Baroque era, Paul the Third, Alexander the Seventh, and the Barberini pope, Urban the Eighth. Paul's monument had a nude figure on it representing Justice; his sister was the model. Four hundred years later it was all too much for Pius the Ninth who, alas, had her covered in marble drapery, which is still there. Urban's sumptuous tomb was carved by Bernini; Death, a skeleton, is writing Urban's name on a stone slab. All very camp, as is the bronze baldacchino over the altar at the crossing, another Art Nouveau piece three hundred years prior, a weird edifice like twisted barley sugar, also built by Bernini for Pope Urban. It's covered with the Barberini family symbols – bees – of such colossal size that they look like mutant insects from a space-age film. Urban, another vandal, had the bronze taken from the Pantheon to build this curious object, but he was a man of sophistication, wit and intelligence who did much to beautify Rome, building fountains (also covered with giant bees) and assembling in the Palazzo Barberini a large collection of paintings. He refused, despite immense pressure from his blinkered cardinals, to have Galileo tortured; his only concession to the cardinals, according to Brecht, was 'Let him see the instruments – Signor Galilei is an expert on instruments.'

Down in the crypt are more papal tombs including John Paul the First, the nice Luciani pope who died three weeks after his election, poisoned by a nun, maybe, with fox-gloves; and what Pius the Twelfth said was the tomb of St Peter – another 'maybe' in my opinion: not proven. The oddest memorial is in the nave, Canova's monument to three kings of England who never became kings: James the Third, Charles the Third, and Henry the Ninth – the last members of the House of Stuart. But the most beautiful work of art is Michelangelo's *Pietà*, which, since it was attacked by a madman with a hammer in 1972, is kept behind a shatter-proof glass screen. I think it's the most beautiful work of art in the whole of Rome: one returns to it again and again – the dead weight of the dead Christ, the restrained grief in his mother's eyes. Nowadays Michelangelo and Caravaggio are the artists who pull in the crowds – it used to be Michelangelo and Rafael. Which is strange, for Michelangelo and Caravaggio are the most overtly gay of Renaissance artists, whereas there's definitely nothing queer about Rafael. His portrait of his mistress, *La Fornarina*, is in the Palazzo Barberini; probably the first great painting ever that is filled with unashamedly rampant sexuality, of straight man's appreciation of big, voluptuous boobs. But I'm alone in the Palazzo Barberini looking at it. And in Santa Maria del Popolo it's the Caravaggios, not the Rafael frescoes, the tourists have come for. And what is it everyone is staring at on the Sistine Chapel ceiling? Twenty utterly gorgeous naked young men, all the more gorgeous since they've had the grime of centuries – the candle-soot of protracted papal conclaves – stripped off.

Caravaggio, says my guide-book, provided the Church with homosexual pornography, which is yet another heterosexist put-down that angers me: would anyone say *La Fornarina* is straight pornography? The word is ridiculous to use of either artist. Thirty years ago Caravaggio was not considered important, just a mildly interesting villain who did some unusual things with light and shade; it's another gay artist, Derek Jarman, who, more than anyone, is responsible for the shift in our sensibilities – the effect of his film, *Caravaggio*. My reading this trip is

Jarman's *Modern Nature*, not yet published; this is a proof copy I have for review purposes. I don't find it easy to be critically objective about this book as he and I are so similar – isolates who love flowers and gardens, who pepper their work with quotations; cultural omnivores from the educated middle class, gents of public school and university background, more or less the same age (he's the younger), the same values and the same beliefs, even sharing some of the same friends; the only two public or semi-public Britons, as Peter Burton said, who have come out in print as PWAs. I have no problems in understanding why Derek loves Caravaggio so much . . .

The Vatican is Europe's biggest palace, bigger even than the Winter Palace in Leningrad, but it doesn't have quite the same mind-boggling grandeur – whole rooms don't drip with porphyry, lapis lazuli, crystal and gold. J-P Two and his staff occupy only a minute corner of it; the remainder is open to the public who flock to the Sistine Chapel, but, curiously, ignore almost everything else. Pope Julius the Second moved his own collection of sculpture into the Vatican and it's still here, in a pleasing, eight-sided courtyard that has a fountain in its middle. It just so happened that Julius owned, among a hundred or so other priceless objects, the *Laocoon* and the *Apollo Belvedere* . . . We have a lot to thank him for, as we do other popes like Leo the Tenth who weren't the least bit religious, but who loved great art. "Since God has given us the Papacy," Leo said, "it is up to us to enjoy it." Julius, I'm certain, would have agreed. It was he who commissioned Michelangelo to paint the Sistine Chapel ceiling, and to sculpt the splendid tomb he ordered for himself in the church of San Pietro in Vincoli: Michelangelo never finished it – the *Slaves* in Florence were meant to be included – but it does have the marvellous statues of Moses, Rachel and Leah. Julius and Michelangelo didn't get on: a clash of mega-size wills. Michelangelo, the pope said, had 'terribilità,' was 'frightening' (he was); Julius, Michelangelo said, was 'annoying and vexatious' (also true.)

Julius disliked the papal suite because his predecessor,

the Borgia Alexander the Sixth, had lived in it and allowed a whole series of atrocities to be committed there: it was a wonderful excuse to have new rooms built, and to get Rafael to decorate them. Nothing religious about these superb frescoes: this is the Renaissance celebrating life – man and woman as the most beautiful of God's creations, capable of organising the universe. Quite absent is the tortured soul of a Michelangelo – Rafael wholeheartedly enjoys everything. There are paintings of his, too, in the Vatican's art gallery, all quite magnificent; but most memorable there is the one Caravaggio: an intensely moving *Deposition from the Cross* that recalls Michelangelo's *Pietà*. Elsewhere in the Vatican one can see Nero's bath, a huge round tub of porphyry; and the first popemobile, an extremely uncomfortable rattletrap built for Paul the Sixth – Nero's bath (why on earth is it in the Vatican?) looks much more fun. Down in the basement J-P Two's kitchen does good coffee and an excellent hamburger and French fries. I'd envisaged a more Polish cuisine, but . . . all highly necessary after so much culture. This café is decorated with photographs – J-P Two kissing babies, and a selection of his exotic taste in footwear. He seems in these pictures to be as he always is – a charismatic, but reactionary, old fart. I think of Nostradamus's prophecy that the two hundred and sixty-fourth Pontifex Maximus would be a non-Italian and the *last* pope. Well . . . we'll see . . .

Urban's, Paul's, and Alexander's tombs have given me a taste for the Baroque, and I'm beginning to enjoy, indeed love, its outrageousness, its transformation of everything into pure theatre (what, after all, is *Tosca*, or a Derek Jarman film, if not Baroque?), its obvious link with the architectural fantasies in Barcelona of Gaudí, Puig and Domènech – the mental and emotional straight line from the Trevi fountain, Bernini's *St Theresa*, and Borromini's spiral spire to la Manzana de la Discòrdia and La Sagrada Família. I hunt round Rome, looking for everything I can find of Bernini and Borromini. Other relics from other ages that could be called Baroque just in the sense of 'excessive' don't please: the Colosseum, for instance (too many awful

things happened there), the Arch of Constantine (grandiloquent and clumsily sculpted), the Vittorio Emanuele
Monument (pointless bad taste, part wedding-cake, part
absurd Victorian typewriter, all in cheap and nasty white
marble.) Except for the baldacchino in St Peter's, Bernini
did not do his finest work to order; the same with
Borromini: Rome's cathedral – San Giovanni in Laterano,
commissioned by Innocent the Tenth – is a cold, dull
rectangle, very imposing, very 'civic.' The twelve vast
statues of the apostles show Borromini a little less uptight,
enjoying himself a bit; that of St Simon is particularly eye-
catching – a defeated, dishevelled peasant trying to lift a
colossal hack-saw.

But the two little churches outside the Quirinale Palace
are masterpieces; Bernini's is Sant' Andrea al Quirinale,
Borromini's San Carlino alle Quattro Fontane. Architecturally they're the two most interesting in Rome, though
neither has much purpose: Bernini and Borromini (as
Gaudí later) built them simply because they wanted to do
so, and, also like Gaudí, they found wealthy financial
backers who let them do as they pleased. Both churches are
ovals, though Borromini's oval has ripples in its curves: a
piece of geometric perfection with a coffered dome,
decorated quite sparsely so as not to distract from the
building's beautiful and original form. The cloister outside
is another delight. Bernini's oval is more conventional, but
a lovely shell for the sculpture and painting he created on
the theme of the life and death of St Andrew. (He always
puts more emphasis than does Borromini on the interplay
of architecture, statuary and painting; whereas Borromini
is obsessive about new structural shapes, how stone can
suggest movement.) Bernini considered Sant' Andrea his
chef d'oeuvre – long after it was completed he would sit in
it for hours on end, just staring at it. Nice to be able to do
that . . . But in Santa Maria della Vittoria he produced his
most extravagant and most bizarre combination of building, painting and sculpture, the Cornaro Chapel with its
Ecstasy of St Theresa. She's lying on her side, robes and
limbs quivering fervently; standing above her is an angel –

111

in fact Cupid with a bow and arrows. Nothing religious about this: it's orgasm in marble. Meanwhile, the Cornaro family, also in stone, observes the performance, framed in what looks like a box at a theatre; one of them, a woman, appears to be reading a programme. How, one wonders, did Bernini get away with it? Religion has become a night at the opera, divine love sexual love; we (and the Cornaros) are prurient voyeurs.

Rome undoubtedly benefited from the childish tantrums of those rich, upper-class families who provided many of the popes. The Borghese pope, Paul the Fifth, annoyed by the Baroque splendour of the chapel in Santa Maria Maggiore that the Peretti pope, Sixtus the Fifth, had constructed, built an even more Baroque chapel in the opposite aisle for himself and another Borghese pope, Clement the Eighth. The Pamphili pope, Innocent the Tenth, jealous of the fountains Barberini Urban the Eighth so liberally scattered about the city, devised the Piazza Navona: it is still one of Rome's most pleasant squares, thanks to Borromini and Bernini, whom Innocent called in – Borromini did the church (Sant' Agnese), while Bernini concentrated on the fountains, which are another con-glomeration of high camp, over-the-top statuary. One could stroll about Rome just looking at fountains – they seem to be papal equivalents of the emperors' triumphal arches: luxurious toys that symbolise power and largesse, though somewhat more useful to the city's inhabitants. The Trevi is the most famous (unfortunately not working just now; switched off, for the usual duration I suppose, while it's being 'restored'), but the Piazza della Republica has a fountain almost as outré – four strapping, naked women with huge thighs and arses, wrestling vigorously with sea-monsters. It caused a scandal when it was built – the women were modelled on musical comedy stars of the day. The weirdest fountain is the Barcaccia at the bottom of the Spanish Steps, another Bernini/Urban creation, in which the water spouts from a sunken marble boat; but my favourite is the little-known, sixteenth-century Fontana della Tartarughe in the Piazza Mattei: four luscious nude youths brandishing turtles and happily prancing on the backs of dolphins – the water spews from the dolphins' and the turtles' mouths. Talk about queenery . . .

The air traffic control people are on strike: my flight has been postponed for twenty-four hours. The Alitalia officials are rude and unhelpful; "Nothing to do with *us*," they reiterate. Trains in France, planes in Italy: echoing Cleopatra, I say to myself, "Sink Rome!" and a lot of other thoughts more abusive. I do *not* wish to spend another twenty-four hours in this noisy, dirty city. But I have to. The cost, the insurance claims and so on . . . *Fuck!* But, as with the French, one can't be very annoyed with Italians for too long. Another bottle of wine, another good meal – Italian food is second only to French, and tonight I eat pizza napoletana of the utmost delicacy: one should eat pizza only in Italy, for in no other country does anyone know how to cook it. This, at a pavement restaurant – a hot summer night – in the Campo dei Fiori, a bustling, lively piazza that is now Rome's flower market, but which in 1599 was the scene of the execution of Beatrice Cenci. (Her portrait, Guido Reni's masterpiece, hangs in the Palazzo Barberini.) In the evening sun Rome's buildings exude a warmth, a reddish glow – I've noticed it on previous evenings too, eating in the Trastevere – that is exactly the colour of these buildings in eighteenth-century pictures; and, on my way back to the hotel, I discover at last a *quiet* street, the Via Giulia (built – again – by good old Julius the Second), a beautiful street, vines near the Palazzo Farnese hanging down from a foot-bridge.

I conclude the evening by seeing Pavarotti in *Tosca*. Not, alas, in the flesh – it's on the hotel's TV – but wonderful all the same. There's a large party of working-class French tourists at the hotel (the men look like railway porters, the women, solid as tanks, Mesdames Defarge taking time off from knitting and guillotine-watching), but I warm to them when they return from their dinner out, for they fall silent and listen to the divine Luciano as intently as I do; at the end of *Recondita armonia* they applaud and shout "Bravo!

Bravo! Ça, c'est quelque *chose!*" Later, in bed, I think of
what I've seen and done this week: despite Aids, despite a
creaking, painful back (again) that slows me to the speed of
a snail, a lot. A lot. Thoughts continually revert to the
popes; to Catholicism in general, the highjacking it is of
Christian ideals. I suppose, in particular, it's a decision of
Constantine's – to transfer the Empire's capital to Constantinople. It produced a power vacuum, which, in the
short term, left Rome too weak to resist the barbarian
hordes: but the barbarian hordes came, vandalised, then
disappeared. Veni, vidi, disparui. In the long term pope
simply replaced emperor. From Nero's bath to the popemobile. The early Church had five archdioceses (Rome,
Constantinople, Antioch, Alexandria, Jerusalem) of equal
importance, a structure that still holds good in the
Orthodox East – the Serbian, Rumanian, Russian and
Bulgarian hierarchies do not kow-tow to the Patriarch of
Constantinople. Rome's supremacy, the idea of 'Pontifex
Maximus' is a corruption. An error, a heresy.

But I'm glad the popes built fountains; employed Rafael,
Michelangelo, Caravaggio, Bernini, Borromini and so on;
and collected Greek sculpture. J-P Two and I were born on
the same day, though not in the same year; *he's* the elder.
(By sixteen years.) Will I outlive him? I guess not . . .

July 1991

is the grandfather of botanical gardens: if it's not at Kew one's unlikely to see it. But it's not somewhere to go for a superb display of spring, summer or autumn flowers (the reason why most people visit most gardens); its point is, as the guide-book says, 'an ordered collection of plants, assembled primarily for scientific and educational purposes . . . an encyclopedia of living and preserved plants . . . a green laboratory.' By the luck of the seasons there may be a superb display – the bluebells in the woods near Queen Charlotte's Cottage, the million and a half crocuses by the Temple of Bellona – but not always the riot of colour at Giverny, or Wellington or Christchurch, that comes from plants which are grown to dazzle, to have 'the look of flowers that are looked at.' Not that Kew is a disappointment; *absolutely* not. I've never seen all of it. Entering as I invariably do at the Victoria Gate, the intention I have in mind wavers, for I can't miss the Palm House, the Temperate House, the Order Beds, the Water Garden, the Pagoda, the Princess of Wales Conservatory, the avenues of trees; though I've seen them many, many times. So I never get as far as the Rhododendron Dell or the Bamboo Garden, because after two or three hours my brain can't take anything else in and I'm physically exhausted.

I love the conservatories, those beautiful nineteenth-century structures of iron and glass that served as models for the Crystal Palace; the architecture is as fascinating as the plants: tranquil, harmonious casings for green thoughts in a green shade. I'm in Sydney again – eucalyptus, banksia, Moreton Bay chestnut – or New Zealand rain-forest as wet as the Haast Pass, the Franz Josef Glacier; the Yugoslavia of white acacias, the San Francisco of yellow acacias; the Mojave Desert (cactuses and Joshua trees); pittosporum on Tresco; the grottos of Rome's Orti Farnesiani; and I'm in touch with feelings and mental processes of past bits of myself: who I was with or what I was doing, even the pop songs of the time. To visit Kew is to uncover buried layers of my life, for the plants and flowers of the places I've seen are as important – perhaps more important; I don't know – as the churches, the art galleries, the museums. And Kew also provides the experience of what I haven't seen, as a novel may give a sense of lives quite unlike my own (different place, different period, different values); the exotica of mandrakes (they don't shriek, alas, when you pull them up), lotuses, loofahs, quaking grass, myrrh, squirting cucumbers, flesh-eating fly-traps, desert plants one would imagine were stones, giant South American water-lilies with leaves more than six feet in diameter. The trees are another distraction: though many were lost in the October 1987 hurricane, there are scores of majestic, ancient trees that make one stop and stare. Not surprising I haven't yet discovered the Rhododendron Dell.

It's July and I'm looking at the Order Beds – oblongs of herbaceous plants laid out family by family, not for show, but to teach students of botany how to identify things. The rudbeckias are just beginning to bloom, more species of them than I could ever acquire: some dwarf, some giant, their daisy-like petals yellow or orange, though there are red, purple, even pink, each with its striking green or black central cone. I have six varieties in my garden, including the purple and the rare pink, and the most common but best of all, the black-eyed Susan. Rudbeckias and all daisy-like flowers are my chief source of pleasure in summer and autumn gardens – helenium, heliopsis, helianthemum, shasta daisies. They outvy even globe thistles, sea holly, zinnias, geraniums, cornflower, mallow, nicotiana, verbena, hollyhocks, every one of which is in the Order Beds: and in my own garden, though numbers and varieties in mine are miniscule compared with the richness here.

But my garden earns me compliments from friends, neighbours, even passers-by in the street. It takes time, love, money and hours with a hose-pipe; in recent years I've been able to give more of all four to it, though the work becomes increasingly difficult – Aids or AZT (perhaps both) slow me down – I need a week to recover from a day's hard graft. Yet I'm doing so well, they've said this morning at St Mary's. Ten years (probably) with the virus, and no major opportunistic infections. Lifestyle, I suggest: cast of mind. I'm very privileged. I have money; I love my work; I'm beholden to nobody. I can't be sacked or thrown out of my house. Yes, they say; *that's* when people start going downhill – losing their jobs, their homes. It's the biggest killer – more than ks, pcp. But my thigh muscles, though not useless, are wasting away. I have to adjust each year – each month – to doing less in the garden than I would like in a given amount of time; however . . . I get there in the end. So the compliments please rather more than if gardening were child's play, particularly "It looks exactly as a cottage garden should look." I've always considered June, July and August in my garden inferior to the spring – it's probably true of most English gardens – and I've tried to concentrate therefore on summer flowers, spent a lot of money on buying them: and this July, at last, I'm reasonably satisfied. The shasta daisies are superb, and the Jackmanii clematis, the late-flowering ceanothus, the penstemon, the dark brown Moerheim helenium, the golden coreopsis, the red, white, pink and purple phlox. I *love* phlox: the richest and most satisfying of flower scents.

June, however, despite aruncus (turrets and spires of white) is still a problem: a betwixt and between period; irises, geum, pyrethrum, foxgloves past their best, though pansies I bought three years ago still flourish, some of them in June a marvellously deep velvet black. There would be more colour if I stocked up on roses – I have barely a dozen; I'm not a rose freak: all that greenfly, black spot, mildew, and their smell doesn't convince. May is the most beautiful month; the flowers then seem to look after themselves with almost no assistance – Shirley poppies (forty blooms on one plant this year, an effect like Flanders fields), a zillion columbines of every possible hue that seed themselves like mad (as does the love-in-a-mist), red-hot poker (though I have to watch out for snails), tulips, irises: the latter blue, yellow, white, black, brown – this autumn I shall invest in the pink variety. September and October are also good: what's flowering then seems to last and last, sometimes into November, even December. Kaffir lilies, belladonna lilies, yellow jasmine, anemone japonica, montbretia, chrysanthemums – though I can't persuade chrysanthemums to survive the winter; I have to buy fresh each spring. As I do lupins – the Russell lupin, in contrast to its spread in New Zealand, is in southern England very difficult now to think of as a perennial. Disease or frost; I'm not sure which. Frost last January killed my agapanthus except for one plant: but I'm maybe foolish to expect agapanthus to enjoy our winters. If, however, it could hold out for a year or two, become established . . .

From the Order Beds I stroll to the Orangery and the Palace, stopping to admire a swathe of scarlet verbena: it is the daintiest of flowers, clusters of tiny blossoms – I must put my own in groups like this; among other plants solitary specimens do not stand out. Kew's most attractive piece of architecture, the Orangery, ceased functioning as such in the mid-nineteenth century (the wet the trees required was damaging the building), though it again housed orange trees, I remember, in the nineteen sixties –but, as modern technology is no more able than Victorian to cope with the damp, it is now a shop and a restaurant. Prosaic fate. The Palace, built in 1631, was bought by Queen Charlotte in 1728, and was the home of her son, Frederick, the Prince of Wales, and his wife, Augusta: he never became King as his father, George the Second, outlived him. Pope, a neighbour at nearby Twickenham, gave him a dog and wrote an epigram that had inscribed on its collar:

> I am his Highness' dog at Kew;
> Pray tell me, sir, whose dog are *you*?

Augusta stayed on after Frederick's death; it was her idea to lay out the grounds as a botanical garden. (She planted the maidenhair tree in the Broad Walk.) George the Third and Queen Caroline lived here from 1802 until her death in 1818 – the only time Kew has been the chief home of the royal family. It's hard to decide which of these two sovereigns was the more mad: he, suffering from porphyria and chatting to the trees, she virtually incarcerating her daughters to stop them finding husbands. (There weren't, in her opinion, any princes around in Europe who were suitable; Napoleon had got rid of them all.) It's an ugly palace – minute, inconvenient, and architecturally a cross between a prison and a school. It has bad vibes – not astonishing when one thinks of George, Caroline, and those frustrated daughters. The Queen's Garden, at the rear, is full of herbs, and is kept almost exactly as she would have known it: a living horticultural monument.

I depart as I arrived, by the Victoria Gate (the nearest to the District Line); the houses in the roads that lead to the station are expressions of a philosophy similar to that of the gardens: order, graciousness – early nineteenth-century and beautiful. Behind their windows I see full-size grand pianos, old rocking-horses, and huge cheese-plants. The whole area is an oasis in the stressfulness that is London. The afternoon is hot and humid, presaging a storm: typical London July. Much as I like Kew, I shall be glad to be back in my own garden in Exeter this evening, looking at the look of flowers that are looked at, and deciding the phlox and the coreopsis are as decorative as their upper-crust relations at Kew. With a glass of vodka and orange in one hand and a hose-pipe in the other, I shall revitalise both them and myself with our usual summer evening drinks.

July 1991

A La Ronde

Exmouth is not the most exciting resort on Devon's Costa
Geriatrica – a dull place with seaweedy beaches that looks
as if it has enjoyed better days. Tucked into a spit of land
between the Exe estuary and the sea, it's not even somewhere to drive through: a terminus that provides just one
reward – the oddest and indubitably one of the most
interesting houses in England, A La Ronde; and for that
Exmouth is worth visiting again and again. Originally
thatched and limewashed, A La Ronde was built in the
seventeen nineties by two eccentric spinster cousins, Jane
and Mary Parminter; it's a cross "between a house and a
temple of a circular shape," one visitor said in 1866, "with
a fantastic Chinese-looking ornamental roof." Jane
Parminter designed it herself, inspired to do so by having
see the octagonal basilica of San Vitale at Ravenna.

Her father, a Barnstaple man, owned a cement factory in
Lisbon, where in 1747 Jane was born; he died in 1784 and
left her a very wealthy woman. She immediately set out to
'do' Europe, taking along with her her ailing sister
Elizabeth, her cousin Mary who was twenty years her
junior, and a friend, a Miss Colville. Though it was not
unique for women at that time to travel abroad without
male protection, it wasn't exactly commonplace; but what
is unique about this particular Grand Tour is that it lasted
ten years. The four women inspected France, Switzerland,
Germany, Italy, Portugal and Spain, buying up en route an
incredible quantity of knick-knacks and souvenirs which
they carted home to Devon; most of these objects can still
be seen today inside A La Ronde. For the first few months
of the tour Jane kept a diary. Extracts from it were published in 1902 – fortunately, for the diary was destroyed,
together with the greater part of the West Country's
historical documents, by the Germans in the 1942 air-raid
that smashed the centre of Exeter to bits. The diary shows
that the women were indefatigable sight-seers, visiting –
for example – in Paris dozens of churches in a single day,
and taking themselves off to the theatre every evening. The

purpose of the tour, Jane said, was to improve her sister's health; but the hectic pace and the problems of eighteenth-century travel – 'a very dirty inn and poor accommodation, did not sleep for the bugs' – were too much for poor Elizabeth, who, soon after they returned to England, breathed her last.

The diary is not great literature, but, like any diary, it gives the reader a vivid portrait of the writer's character; and Jane emerges as a breathless, opinionated enthusiast, with a fatal preference for quantity rather than quality. In Abbeville she noticed 'one hundred carriages kept by private families, thirteen bridges, thirteen parishes, thirteen chantries, one handsome cathedral, a large manufacture of cloth and dyed wool and they sell cheap cambric, seven gates, thirteen nunneries,' but she does not stop for a second to describe any of it. At Versailles she saw Louis the Sixteenth and Marie Antoinette in the Galerie des Glaces (how on earth she succeeded in getting herself inside the palace she doesn't say); 'the Queen is tall and elegant,' she tells us, but Louis is 'a corpulent man, not strikingly agreeable.' At Saint-Cloud she does reveal, at last, a touch of sensibility; she is admiring a fountain – 'but I had rather see a natural stream dripp from a natural rock in its own wild meandering gushings.' Wild meandering gushings is a suitable epitaph for her prose style.

And so to Dijon, where they 'slept all four in a room at the Prince of Condé's Hotel.' That is also interesting, for it's impossible not to speculate on what kind of women they were. Jane and Mary, on their return to England, set up house together, an arrangement that continued till Jane's death in 1811. Mary survived, alone at A La Ronde, dying there in 1849. She made a will of extraordinary length and complexity (it takes an hour and a half to read), the main terms of which are that A La Ronde can never be let, and can only be inherited by unmarried women. Over the years there has been a liberal supply of such persons, and in consequence A La Ronde was owned entirely by women, with one exception – Stella Reichel Tudor, the niece of the cousin who inherited from Mary, was allowed by changes in the conveyancing laws to bequeath the house to her brother. After his death in 1923 it returned to female ownership until 1990, when Ursula Tudor Perkins sold it to the National Trust.

Jane and Mary Parminter didn't like men; that's obvious – but why is not so clear. One more little bit of gay history may be lost, buried beneath the words of that diary and that peculiar will. What of the friend, the mysterious Miss Colville, whose portrait still hangs in the drawing-room at A La Ronde, but about whom we know absolutely nothing? And what held Jane and Mary together, apart from a common desire to build a very weird house and to spend the rest of their lives decorating and furnishing it in equally weird fashion? With Mary so much younger (she was only seventeen at the start of the Grand Tour) and Jane both so bossy and so rich, one imagines a stereotypical butch/femme relationship, Mary the meek, submissive half; but her will contradicts that – she's clearly as strong-minded and quirky as her cousin. The will is an attempt to rule people from beyond the grave. Nothing in A La Ronde was to be sold, or even moved; there are pages of instructions to the legatee about keeping everything exactly as it was: though Mary says the house is to be 'enjoyed as a convenient and delightful residence for a gentlewoman,' she had decided it would be a mausoleum, a monument, to herself and her 'late dear cousin Jane.' In a codicil, she requires that 'the funeral remembrance of my dear friend and cousin which I wear round my neck,' be placed 'into the cabinet in the middle room at A La Ronde.' None of the trees outside is to be cut down; the shrubberies, green-houses, hothouses, fountains and 'the urn obelisk' are not to be disturbed; the only changes permitted are for necessary repairs. One nice touch, however, is that each owner is ordered to buy two cows and fourteen sheep 'to be left on the grounds at A La Ronde for the use and enjoyment of the person next in succession.'

Her demands, of course, were not obeyed; though much of the house is as she would know it, and many of her precious gewgaws are in the places where she left them, each succeeding proprietor made changes. The most extensive and the most regrettable of these were carried out, as one might guess, by the sole male owner, the Reverend Oswald Reichel, who replaced the thatch with tiles, lit the first floor with dormer windows, and built an exterior cat-walk around the roof. Inside, he enlarged some of the rooms by knocking down walls; he erected stair-cases, and had the whole house centrally heated: a gargantuan, Victorian heating-system, most of which, one's glad to say, has now been removed. And, one's also glad to say, the National Trust intends to restore the house to what it originally was: thatched, with no dormers and no cat-walk.

Virtually nothing remains in the grounds of the shrubberies, greenhouses, hot-houses and fountains; there are no sheep or cows, nor an 'urn obelisk.' But not much has altered in the chapel, called Point-in-View, that Mary and Jane built; though the little school attached to it long ago became a vestry. The almshouse, also attached, still exists: it was for the use of 'four single women, having never been married;' they must be 'of approved character . . . and over fifty years of age.' The trust deeds of the school say that boys cannot be educated there and – another quirk – preference in both places must be given to 'a Jewess who shall have embraced Christianity.' The almshouse has two old women living in it today. Jane and Mary were deeply interested in the conversion of the Jews. Mary gave money to a number of organisations devoted to that end – the Temporary Relief Fund for Converted Jewesses, for example, and the London Society for Promoting Christianity Among the Jews (but, to earn it, the latter organisation had to preach a sermon, once a year, at Exmouth.) Jane Parminter, in *her* will, said of the trees at A La Ronde, 'These oaks shall remain standing, and the hand of man shall not be lifted against them, till Israel returns and is restored to the Land of Promise,' words which, according to a pamphlet published in 1881 by some missionary institution, had so fired a well-known London barrister, Lewis Way, that he spent the rest of his life and all

124

his vast wealth turning Jews into Christians. Jane, the pamphlet says, is totally forgotten, but her words have had enormous consequences; in the late twentieth century, however, the reverse is the case: thousands of people visit A La Ronde every year and discover the two eccentric cousins, but no one these days goes around manufacturing Christians out of Jews.

Mary, who inherited Jane's fortune, made bequests to literally scores of distant relatives scattered up and down the length of Devon, and to innumerable charities; none of these bequests, she says, can be paid in kind (she was determined that nothing at A La Ronde should be sold); cash only. She had bought a great deal of property in various parts of England, most of it in London; she even owned a pub, the Angel at Islington. From the sale of all this, one assumes, the money was raised to pay the legacies. It sounds a bit like Monopoly: and had Monopoly existed when she was alive, her will shows she would have thoroughly enjoyed the game, and been very good at it.

The National Trust's purchase of A La Ronde was timely: the house and its contents needed major restoration; but something has been lost in the transfer – the atmosphere of rooms that were lived in, and loved and cared for by the same family for two centuries. It has been open to the public since 1935 (Margaret Tudor's idea); to be shown round by Ursula Tudor Perkins, a colourful and forthright character (one always felt the Parminter single-mindedness was in her genes), was an experience in itself. In the basement are the boilers of Oswald Reichel's elephantine heating-system, and a tea-room that served excellent Devon teas – scones, home-made jam, and lashings of clotted cream; appallingly calorific – and on a hot summer day one could eat outside, looking at the superb view of the Exe estuary and the Haldon Hills, Ursula Tudor Perkins regaling the assembled company with yet more enthusiastic anecdotes about Jane and Mary. But she's gone, and A La Ronde is the poorer.

The house, as its name suggests, would seem to be a round house, but that is a trompe l'oeil; it has sixteen sides.

The entrance-hall leads into the main room, the ballroom, which is octagonal, with apparently vast walls that stretch up to the roof: another trompe l'oeil – as in some Baroque churches in Rome, the dome of the ceiling is flat, painted. The walls are only thirty-five feet high. There are eight doors in the ballroom; they lead into the eight principal rooms, which are rectangular and interconnecting, so it's possible – or was – to walk round the entire inside of the house, often through lobbies no bigger than cupboards and shaped like triangles. Jane's and Mary's bedrooms (next to each other) were on this floor, but Oswald Reichel turned Mary's into a music room and Jane's into a study. In the doorways of the ballroom are hinged panels which can be lowered and used as benches – presumably for spectators at dances – and five of Mary's chairs, unique objects: the seats are octagonal, the backs triangular and surmounted by octagons painted with flowers.

The objets d'art and souvenirs the cousins collected are in these rooms: family portraits; furniture; prints and pictures from the ten-year Grand Tour; Jane's square piano; more pictures, sculptures and figurines made by Jane and Mary from shells, straw, sand, seaweed, paper, tin, semi-precious stones, beads, wool, and silk; an eighteenth-century perpetual calendar; an invitation to the coronation of William the Fourth; books acquired over two hundred years, including an eighteenth-century collection of children's books and miniature text-books; urns; ceramics; a musical-box disguised as a glass decanter – it's a veritable Aladdin's cave of antiques and oddities. Much exists, too, of the original decoration of the rooms: friezes and borders made of feathers, the green paint the cousins were particularly fond of, architraves marbled to look like porphyry.

The first floor, pre-Reichel, had no windows; it was one huge, dark space encircling the central drum of the ball-room: its purpose, I guess, was storage. Above it a minute, back-breaking staircase leads to the top of the house and its most impressive room, the Shell Gallery, 'a Gothic fantasy of painted vaults and pointed arches,' says the National

Trust guide-book, 'encrusted with bands of shells.' Up here, Jane and Mary worked for years like Michelangelo in the Sistine Chapel – and without the help of the balustrade, a Reichel addition, to stop them plunging thirty-five feet to the ballroom floor – sticking shells, mirrors, quartz, lichen, paper, bones, stones, feathers, pottery and glass onto the walls and ceiling: the result is an illusion of being inside some bizarre cave or grotto, like Waitomo, stuffed with glittering gems. The scale of the project was enormous, and it's astonishing that work so fragile has survived: it has decayed and is presently being restored, but most eighteenth-century and early nineteenth-century art of this kind has vanished, unable to withstand dust, wind, people, the years.

I can sympathise with Mary Parminter's wish to preserve À La Ronde as a mausoleum of herself and her cousin; I suppose we all harbour such self-indulgent whims – but it's vanity to assume that people and time won't change everything. I look at the interior of my own house, and think it would be nice to preserve it as it is, a Rees museum; my books (first editions, some of them, including Virginia Woolf's *Orlando* which has photographs of Vita Sackville West in a variety of period costumes), *my* collection of children's books (some trash, but many given to me and signed by their authors), paintings of four generations of my family, and *my* souvenirs of a life that also contains tours abroad – the ikon from Budapest, the Spanish waterpot, the jade vase from Turkey, my Leningrad opera-glasses, my Bernard Leach bowl, the Red Indian totem grateful librarians gave me in Vancouver, my glass and alabaster paper-weights, the mug for drinking the waters in Carlsbad . . . etcetera, etcetera. But, as Sir Thomas Browne said in *Urn Burial*, 'The iniquity of oblivion blindly scattereth her poppy;' the world wants Mary Parminter's seaweed, but I doubt it will want my Hungarian ikon.

Better to concentrate on how to survive: a thought that must have frequently crossed the minds of Jane, Mary, Elizabeth, and Miss Colville as they wandered round

Europe in a decade of chaos without previous parallel – while they were travelling the French executed their King, that 'corpulent man, not strikingly agreeable,' and plunged the whole continent into war of unprecedented magnitude. Apart from that, Mrs Lincoln, how was the play? Ten years of 'did not sleep for the bugs,' of 'a very dirty inn indeed, the staircase shaking, the maids bold and impertinent, the treatment sparing and the charge extravagant.' We may not now have to brave the dirt and the bugs – except in Russia – but the treatment can still be sparing, the charge extravagant – and the trains motionless, the aeroplanes grounded. The pleasures and problems of travel are different, but they still exist. How did these women cope when one of them became ill, which must have occurred – simply by the law of averages – at some time or another during ten years? Particularly poor Elizabeth, in bad health before she even left England.

Much, I suppose, as I would – and do. Apothecaries were available, as doctors and chemists now, in all the civilised corners of Europe, though the drugs and methods of cure might seem to us barbaric; and if the worst was likely to happen, the four of them could have made full speed for home. They probably took a medicine-chest of pills with them, as I do. AZT, omeprazole, dapsone, pyrimethamine: if they don't work, I'll drag myself to the nearest airport and onto the first plane to London. If I die abroad, it's of no significance – one six-foot depth of earth is as apt as any other – or someone can stick my corpse in a box and send it home: before I've started I've usually paid my return fare. Jane may have taken similar precautions. My T-cell count invariably goes up when I'm travelling, which means, I guess, that despite the physical exhaustions and hassles, the mind is stimulated, the spirit enriched: *that* is the most effective method of dealing with Aids. Pleasure is the best of drugs. So, too, for Jane, Mary, Elizabeth and Miss Colville: if she hadn't embarked on that ten-year holiday, Elizabeth might well have expired all the sooner. Keep on going – church-crawls and nights at the theatre (opera, concert, whatever) postpone illness and death.

Were they lesbian? They probably were – what clinches it for me is the grave, inside Point-in-View, in which both cousins are buried. When Jane died, Mary had the following words inscribed on the gravestone:

> Here sleep: no noise shall break thy rest,
> Till the last trump proclaim thee wholly blest;
> Then shall thy former partner claim each dust
> And both in one made perfect join the just.

August 1991

Other Local Oddities

A La Ronde is not the only eccentricity in my patch of Devon. Exeter abounds in oddities – a street that has no-entry signs at *both* ends; a cathedral with a statue of St Peter in the nude, full frontal; a station from which you can travel to London by one of two railways, but the trains leave in *opposite* directions; Major Cheese, who lives in a house called *The Mousetrap*; a damp-proofing firm, Damplast, which rather defeats the object I would think; and an estate agent, Force, who is responsible for notices outside some Exeter houses – SOLD BY FORCE. Two nearby hamlets called Peamore and Pocombe ... But in the surrounding countryside the eccentricities are on a somewhat grander scale – Castle Drogo, for instance, England's newest castle, built by Edwin Lutyens in the early years of this century for Julius Drew. The Parminters were miniaturists, creating a world that resembles Lilliput, but Julius Drew would have been at home in Brobdingnag: his ideas were gargantuan. In 1883 he opened a shop in London, the Home and Colonial Stores; six years later there were more than a hundred branches of it in various parts of England, and Julius was a millionaire. His success came from tea: he aroused in the British a desire for Indian tea – we had, in the past, always drunk China tea – and the Home and Colonial stocked the Indian brand. At the age of thirty-two he retired and set about giving himself all the airs and trappings of a country gent.

The first job was to find some ancestry more romantic than his clergyman father and tea-merchant grandfather. He employed a genealogist who convinced him that he was related to the Drewes of Broadhembury in East Devon, and whose original ancestor was the improbable-sounding Drogo de Teigne, a Norman baron of the village of Drewsteignton, some twelve miles west of Exeter. The genealogist may have told Julius simply what he wanted to hear; the wording in the National Trust guide-book is circumspect: 'The pedigree *contrived* to show the family

131

descent from Drogo,' and Julius *'assumed* a relationship' with Drogo. Whatever . . . he instantly changed his name by deed poll from Drew to Drewe, bought fifteen hundred acres of land at Drewsteignton (a place with which his only connection was quite fortuitous – the vicar happened to be his mother's cousin), and commissioned Lutyens to begin work on an enormous mock-medieval castle that would suit his newly 'contrived' status.

It all sounds utterly absurd, and indeed it is; a tale of rampant snobbery and vast sums of money that could have been devoted to more philanthropic ends. Lutyens's designs were at first for a castle three times bigger than the one that was eventually built – it would have had keeps, barbicans, moats, gatehouses, and a colossal dining hall – but even Julius found this prohibitively expensive. He reminds me of Thomas Love Peacock's Mr Chainmail, the mad enthusiast who also built a mock-medieval castle, and who thought that nothing before or after the twelfth century was worth a moment's consideration. I doubt, however, that Julius Drewe had read Peacock; his library is not that of a literary man – encyclopedias, bound copies of *The Gentleman's Magazine*, and fourteen probably unread and unreadable volumes of his father's theological effusions.

Because Castle Drogo now belongs to the National Trust it is frequently visited – the National Trust gives places, whatever their merit or lack of it, a kind of imprimatur – but there's nothing at Drogo of any historical or artistic interest. It was, and is, a folly, a folie de grandeur. The views from its windows, of Dartmoor and the gorge of the River Teign, are magnificent, but one can see all that without paying to go inside. The gardens are pleasant, and huge of course, but unremarkable: there's scarcely a flower or a shrub I don't have in my own little garden. Inside the castle Lutyens did manage to achieve something: a satisfactory balance between the appearance of medievalism and the necessary mod cons of gracious living circa 1920. But the Drewes' tastes add nothing. The furniture is mostly a job lot Julius bought from a bankrupt Spanish tycoon, and the pictures – family portraits – are insipid. A gigantic, mud-coloured portrait of Julius dominates the staircase: he looks ill-at-ease – an actor dressed up in country gent's clothes, with a very dead-looking salmon. His wife, also on the staircase, is in white and surrounded by roses; so ethereal one imagines she's about to fade like a ghost into the empyrean. One wonders what she thought of it all, dragged off in the name of Drogo de Teigne to a bogus castle on the edge of Dartmoor. Visitors to these rooms – Mr Drewe's study, Mrs Drewe's boudoir – displaying the same reverence as they would in the apartments of Louis the Sixteenth and Marie Antoinette, are to me another symptom of human folly and absurdity. One would respect Julius – and them – much more if he was merely remembered as the man who gave us Indian tea.

There's a fully operational portcullis in the vast entrance-tower, crenellations, castellations, slits for firing off arrows, coats of arms and – as at A La Ronde – a chapel, with font, stained glass, family pews, and an organ. Why, one wonders, did all these people who had more money than sense, need chapels on their estates? Not because of a deficiency in the West Country of religious edifices of all persuasions: status symbols, I suppose. At least the Parminters had charity in mind, with their little school and their housing for indigent, middle-aged, unmarried, converted Jewesses; but there's nothing at Drogo that indicates charity – just vain expense. Nor any sign that it made Julius happy: he never got over the death of his eldest son (killed, aged twenty-six, at Ypres in 1917), and the castle took so long to erect – it was begun in 1911 and delayed for years because the workmen went off to fight in the 1914-18 War – that Julius was dying when it was completed in 1931. He had only two months left to enjoy it.

The vanity of human wishes . . .

At the other end of the Costa Geriatrica from A La Ronde is a nudist beach, Weston Mouth, and in the fields on the cliffs above it is the Donkey Sanctuary, the creation of Elisabeth Svendsen, who has devoted her life to travelling about the world in order to rescue ill-treated donkeys: she brings them back to what is in effect an Eventide Home for Distressed Gentledonkeys in the acres above the beach where people prance about with nothing on. An eccentricity indeed, and one that is peculiarly British. Why donkeys, one says; why not cows (we ill-treat cows with pesticides and scrapie-infected animal feed) – or rattlesnakes? Donkeys – it's true, alas – are abused in many countries, though I doubt more so than any other creature; but they are marketable – cows and rattlesnakes are not. They're cute, and seem patient – they can in fact sometimes be very ill-tempered – and children can stroke them, ride on them: they arouse sentimental feelings in a great number of people. Particularly, to be more specific, British maiden ladies. At the Donkey Sanctuary huge wall plaques that resemble war memorials list the names of donors, of whom about ninety per cent are unmarried women of, one guesses from their Christian names, a certain age and class: Maud, Gladys, Elsie, Doris, Irene, Vera, Florence, Beatrix – Doris Mabel Shaw, Beatrix Constance Dowd, Irene May Whitsitt, Gladys Irene Rundle, Rose Maud Rabbage. Women who, because of their experience of life (*they've* been ill-treated?) perhaps prefer to give money to animal welfare organisations rather than charities for humans.

The sanctuary began in a small way in 1969, then in 1974 a Miss Violet Philpin of Reading bequeathed to it over two hundred donkeys; and to house them a farm and fifty-four acres of grazing land were purchased at Weston, the money coming from private sources and the Charity Commissioners. Today, four thousand nine hundred donkeys later, the sanctuary looks like big business, though its information office is littered with appeals for money. It's open to the public – one can walk about and see the animals; children can ride on some of them: it's a popular tourist attraction, but – and this is odd – it charges no admission fee. In the shop one can buy postcards, posters and Christmas cards, all with pictures of donkeys, and books (*Eeyore, the Naughtiest Donkey in the Sanctuary, Collected Poems and Stories of Donkeys*); there's a video room, and all sorts of propaganda about the persecution of donkeys – Spain and Mexico seem to be the chief villains. One poster shows a donkey on a Mexican rubbish-tip: 'Starving and worm-ridden, this donkey competes for the meagre food supply with the other scavengers' – vultures – but the biggest scavengers of all on such rubbish-tips are not in this photograph: people.

There's a donkey hospital at the sanctuary, with an intensive care unit and an isolation ward, an 'Oldies' barn and yard,' and the farmhouse is now the Slade Centre, where physically and mentally handicapped children come to ride on the animals. (They mustn't be more than eight stone in weight.) The sanctuary has six full-time inspectors and fifty-two voluntary staff who work all over Britain, following up complaints and looking after the welfare of donkeys; in Mexico it has an ambulance to transport vets to remote places where mistreatment is particularly bad; and it recently gave two thousand pounds to an animal charity in Spain in order to protect a donkey that's persecuted during the fiesta at Villaneuva de la Vera – the wretched burro is dragged through the streets, a rope knotted round its neck fifty times, then ritually killed. Mrs Svendsen organised a petition – one million, six hundred thousand people signed it – to protest about the goings-on at Villaneuva de la Vera; she sent it to the Spanish Ambassador in London, to King Juan Carlos, and to the Pope: apparently without success.

There are scores of memorial tablets at the sanctuary – a stable, for instance, 'in loving memory of Bertha McCarthy of Claygate and Winifred Galloway of Esher,' and rustic seats – 'Happy memories of Ivan Lockyer from his friends and colleagues at Calor Gas.' As if donkey rest-home was somehow combined with human graveyard. And there's a Donkey Charter:

'This charter grants to every donkey admitted to the sanctuary the right of life, regardless of age or health, and to the best possible treatment, care and drugs to preserve its life to the maximum. It grants permanent peace and freedom, the care and protection of the sanctuary and the right to return if rehabilitated to a new home. When the time comes, it grants a dignified, peaceful death, this only being induced in the event of extreme suffering and as agreed by the veterinary advisors' (sic) 'and sanctuary staff.'

All the high-flown language of a Bill of Rights or a Declaration of Independence, but I doubt it's read by the donkeys. It's another piece of useful propaganda, designed to make people donate.

Mrs Svendsen, like the Parminters and Julius Drewe, is someone with an over-riding idée fixe. I don't know what to think of it. It's such an obviously worthy cause – preventing cruelty to animals, delighting children, helping the disabled: but it poses the same question as Castle Drogo – wouldn't the money, the energy, the time, be better spent on *human* philanthropy?

The donkeys, I say to myself as I lean on a gate and look at one moth-eaten, smelly specimen hee-hawing its head off, have a superb view of the sea. And the naked humans are tucked away below the cliffs, out of sight.

Exeter's most interesting oddity of all is its best-known landmark: looking up from nearly every street in the city, one can see it on the hills to the south – Lawrence Castle, or as it's sometimes called, Haldon Belvedere. It's eighteenth-century and triangular, and it stands on the highest point of the Haldon Hills, nearly a thousand feet above sea-level. On a clear day the view from its roof is one of the most spectacular in Europe – the Bristol Channel to the north, the English Channel to the south, the Quantocks, the Brendons, the Blackdowns, Dartmoor, Exmoor, the whole coast as far east as Portland. It was built in 1788 by Sir Robert Palk as a memorial to his friend, General Stringer Lawrence, and it's another relic, I think, of gay history. Though it is open to the public and admission is a mere thirty pence, it's very rarely visited, unlike Castle Drogo and the Donkey Sanctuary, for it has no National Trust to promote it, nor the sentimental allure of cute animals. It's owned by a man who has lived in it since 1932 – originally with his brother and their bed-ridden parent – but Mother died in 1978 and the brother in 1990. Not married, and I guess in his late seventies, this old man now lives in quite extraordinary, almost breath-taking isolation.

Lawrence Castle has three storeys, each consisting of one large, triangular room, with, on the ground floor, two smaller rooms in the north and south-west towers. In the ground-floor room is a rather ludicrous statue of Lawrence, strutting in a Roman toga, and on each of the three walls lengthy inscriptions: 'To the memory of Major-General Stringer Lawrence, who for the space of twenty years commanded the British armies in India; and by his superior genius, consummate skill, and unremitted' (sic) 'exertion, with an inferior force extinguished the power of France . . . nor were his talents in war more eminent than his milder virtues; he aspired to, and attained, a name more glorious than that of conqueror: he was the deliverer of India, at his approach every village poured forth its inhabitants; every eye was riveted with attention on his person . . .' And so on. Palk mentions his friend's 'integrity,' 'modest manner of writing,' his 'singular diffidence in speaking of himself' and quotes the Nabob Wallajah Ameer al Hind, 'Prince of the Carnatic and ally of His Britannic Majesty,' as saying that Lawrence was 'the first founder of the English power in Hindustan.'

Lawrence and Palk met in 1755 in India, where Sir Robert, who was an official of the East India Company and Governor of Madras, made a considerable fortune. In 1767 Lawrence, whose star had been eclipsed by that of Clive, left the army and returned to England with Palk, who bought Haldon House and twelve thousand acres of land from the Earl of Chudleigh; the two friends moved in together, Lawrence dying eight years later, having bequeathed all his money to Palk. He was buried nearby, in the village church at Dunchideock – the plaque that Sir Robert put in its nave says 'this frail memorial friendship rears.' Apart from its stables, which are now a hotel, Haldon House no longer exists: the estate in 1892 was giving the then Lord Palk an income of a hundred and nine thousand pounds per annum, but he was so profligate that in 1901 he was declared bankrupt – the estate was sold, and in 1923 the house, because no buyer could be found, was demolished, its stone subsequently being used as hard core for road construction. Again . . . the vanity of human wishes. Sir Robert, however, is not quite forgotten, for, as well as Lawrence Castle, the village of Hennock – a few miles away – has a pub called the Palk Arms, which was run for many years (it seems apt) by two gay men.

Lawrence Castle is disintegrating – its owner clearly has no money to spend on repairs. The plaster on its outside walls is peeling off; its windows, smashed in the hurricane of January 1990, are boarded up; the wind whistles through huge gaps under its shrunken doors, the handles of which are broken. The driveway is so overgrown no car can use it, and the grounds are out of control – a wilderness of brambles, ferns, shrubs and wild flowers, the air on a summer day heady with the scent of peppermint, a smell I haven't detected since childhood. There seems to be no phone in the castle, and the only heating is from oil stoves. The old man said to me that, during a cold snap last winter, ice on the water in a glass beside his bed was by morning half an inch thick. How he survives is difficult to imagine. Hunched and shuffling, even on a warm August afternoon he looks cold: ancient brown jacket and trousers, shabby sweater, muffler knotted round his throat, a pair of spoon-shaped shoes of a style forty years out of fashion. The whole castle smells of damp dog. He spends much of his time dusting and polishing the furniture – the ground floor is full of tables and chairs, as if it was a café: maybe it was, once. Upstairs, in the so-called ballroom, there are friezes by Adam, mahogany flooring Sir Robert shipped from Madras, and the stairs are cuddapah, a native Indian wood; all invaluable I guess, but no source of income for the old man.

I don't have to strain my neck, he says, writing down the inscriptions: they are printed in the guide-book – I can work more easily from that, sitting at one of the numerous tables. But I can't buy the guide-book – he has only a single copy. Price fourpence, I see on its cover, and published in 1932. Visitors so infrequent there was never a need to reprint – or the family just couldn't afford the cost? When I've done, I thank and say good-bye to a man as eccentric as the Parminters, Mrs Svendsen or Julius Drewe, then I stroll about in the one bit of the grounds that isn't a hopeless tangle: it's marvellous up here on the roof of Devon, utterly silent apart from the wind. Below me is Exeter Forest, much in the news a decade ago for the Headless Torso Murder – the body of Mrs Zumsteg-Telling, one of the world's richest women, was found here by a man walking his dog. A classic Joe Orton scenario: she was minus her head, which was discovered later in a disused sauna in Derbyshire.

I much prefer Lawrence Castle to the Donkey Sanctuary or Castle Drogo; if ever an appeal was launched for funds to repair it I'd willingly give – I can resist donating to the upkeep of donkeys or Julius Drewe's megalomania, but Sir Robert Palk's memorial to his life-long companion is another matter entirely. Its owner, I suppose, will one morning be found dead in his bed – frozen rigid. Then what will be the fate of Lawrence Castle? The National Trust should buy it *now*.

August 1991

Sunk Lyonesse

I'm standing on the top of an uninhabited island. It isn't particularly high – perhaps a hundred feet above sea level – nor is it large; it takes less than an hour to walk the whole circuit of its shoreline. Nor is it very interesting: though cattle once grazed here (the ruins of a cow-shed and a cottage ivy has buried are the only indications of people and their animals), the life that flourishes now is bracken and deadly night-shade; nothing else. Walking is slow and uncomfortable, for the wind blows sand off the beaches, smothering paths, ferns, weeds.

The sea is an exceptionally rich, deep blue, bluer it is claimed than elsewhere in the British Isles because of an almost complete absence of plankton; but it is a fertile sea, for there are swathes of tangleweed and kelp, a marvellous copper colour. And fish. This island is called Tean. To the north there is another island, also uninhabited but more interesting, St Helen's, where monks lived (the few remains of their primitive monastery attract the tourist, including an altar which may be as old as the fifth century) and from the summit of which there are spectacular views of more uninhabited islands – Round Island with its light-house, Northwethel, and Men-a-vaur, the latter so eroded by the sea that only rock remains, three great peaks of it shaped like volcanoes. It has to withstand the full blast of the Atlantic which this morning is in magnificent disarray, white and furious as it crashes into the granite, flinging huge columns and clouds of spray into the air. Over the thunder of the ocean I can hear the cries of sea-birds: black-backed gulls, oyster-catchers, and a surprising number of gannets – gannets are majestic, solitary creatures, not usually so gregarious.

In the opposite direction the sea is as flat as a lake, and a mere few yards across the sound St Martin's – on which people do live – is enjoying a sweet, soft, late summer day, and in the distance are the Easter Isles, inhabited only by seals and birds: the two Ganinicks, the two Ganillys, Great

Arthur, Nornour and Hanjague. Superb names! To the south is St Mary's and its little port with boats and hotels and restaurants and Harold Wilson and helicopters and every comfort of civilised life, and I shall be returning to all that when the sun goes down. Meanwhile I'm perfectly happy this September day to sit, a convenient piece of granite supporting my back, on the summit of Tean, uninteresting though this island is: and think, meditate.

For it is one of those rare places that sets the imagination soaring – like Sir Thomas Browne's field of urns. Or Troy. Not that anything Homeric, in a mythical or a real past, happened here, nor are there burial sites to make one speculate on what sort of existence was the lot of our neolithic ancestors; no, the imagination flares because Tean is disappearing more rapidly than any other of the Scilly Isles. The sea is eroding them all, and will eventually destroy them all, but Tean is its number one target. Scilly's white sand is so fine (in the days before blotting-paper it was exported in vast amounts to dry the ink on our letters) that the wind has no problem in lifting it off the beaches, drifting it, shifting it, so that the sea can cut a channel here, a passage there, and so chop the land up into miniature archipelagos, and then it will undermine the little cliffs it has revealed, which are only earth and stone – a good winter storm can slice out whole acres – and suck away the top-soil that falls in consequence. Eventually Tean will be like Men-a-vaur: jagged peaks of rock colonised by sea-birds. It won't happen in my lifetime, but well before the year 3000 it will have become bare rock. I can see from where I'm sitting the place the ocean will attack next, and after that, and after that, and after that.

Off the west of Tean is a very small island, the Old Man of Tean; it is joined to its larger neighbour at low tide by a sand-bar – it's not exactly what the French mean by a presqu'île, but, literally, it is an almost-island. Not a rare phenomenon on Scilly: Gugh is another, more impressive example, linked at low tide to St Agnes. But soon it will be a real island. More impressive still is the bar that links the two bits of St Mary's (though the tide, except in freak conditions, does not cover it at all – yet), for Hugh Town is built on this fragile and impermanent neck of sand. An absurd place for Scilly's one port and the houses of most of its people, but it was the only land – still is the only land – in the islands that is freehold. The Godolphins owned all the rest, and, after them, the Duchy of Cornwall. The sea at the moment, fortunately, is not bothering Hugh Town. Tean is its priority, and what interests me about the Old Man of Tean is that its status as an almost-island is very recent; it isn't even a century old – it became what it is during my lifetime. So if I sit here long enough . . .

The slow inevitability of it all, the massive forces at work, make me feel utterly insignificant, not even a dot, a speck on what is in fact a mere dot or speck in the universe; make Troy or urn burials equally insignificant. Slow inevitability – I can't actually see it happening – but the process, taking into account the time that has elapsed since Britain formed its present shape, has been incredibly quick. The Romans knew Scilly as an archipelago – Insulae Solis, the Sun Isles, the Cassiterides – where the Phoenicians bartered for a much-prized commodity, tin; but in the Stone Age these islands were all joined up. Densely populated it was then, for though there are no prehistoric remains on Tean, there are more burial chambers, neolithic villages, and other stone relics per square yard in Scilly than anywhere else in Britain: indeed *huge* numbers of burial chambers. The romantically inclined have thought the quantity so in excess of the population Scilly could hold that the dead were brought here from other places for special rites and ceremonies, but the only evidence for this is Pliny the Elder writing down what he had heard from somebody else. (This presumably gave rise to the myth of the dying King Arthur being carried off to Avalon, the distant Isles of the Blessed.)

In Scilly legend and truth are extraordinarily hard to disentangle, for records are almost non-existent, and the artefacts of what might have been are buried under sand and sea. (That Sir Cloudesley Shovel's flagship, the *Association*, wrecked on the Gilstone in 1707, was only discovered in the nineteen sixties and has still not been properly explored, and that two of the other three ships wrecked at the same time have never been found, shows how difficult – indeed almost impossible – under-sea excavation is in these parts.) The absence, of course, of records and artefacts makes us speculate, our imaginations flare – creates myth and legend. But the Scillys were undoubtedly once all one island. The sea between them is very shallow, mostly no deeper than five fathoms, and, if our eyes follow the ten-fathom line on the ordnance map, we can see the shape of the land as it was three thousand years ago. If the sea would drop a mere five fathoms, all the islands – except for St Agnes – that are inhabited now, St Mary's, St Martin's, Tresco, Bryher, would be joined up, together with the Easter Isles, the Northern Isles, Samson and the Norrard Rocks. At very low tides it is possible to walk from Tresco to Bryher, and to wade from Tresco to Samson. The oldest map of the Scillys (early seventeenth-century) shows St Mary's and St Martin's linked by a causeway; a road, it's believed of stones placed on the sand. No trace of it is visible now except at Par Beach on St Martins when the tide is at its lowest; all the stones further out and at the St Mary's end have been washed away long since. The sand remains, however; it is called the Crow Bar and is a treacherous hazard to shipping.

Today is the lowest tide of the year. I can see from my eyrie on Tean men standing miles out in the ocean, knee-deep in the water, fishing for shrimps. I shan't attempt to paddle on Samson Flats or the Crow Bar, or stroll from Bryher to Tresco: it's nicer here – sun, wind, heat, salt.

That island one can observe on the map at the ten-fathom line has a vague resemblance to Antarctica, or a fish, and St Mary's – a curious coincidence – has almost exactly the same shape, as if the sea in its scourings and gnawings knew precisely what it was about, had learned from experience, was attacking just as it did millenia ago. But I assume it's merely a local law of geography: the sea erodes from the west; the tide sweeps in from the west, as do the prevailing winds – and maybe, too, the land's

144

weakest points have always been in that quarter.

What was the island's name? Nobody knows, but tradition is that it was Lyonesse, and it was even bigger than what is revealed on the map at the ten-fathom mark – it was joined up to Cornwall. Certainly it was once joined up to Cornwall, but when humans first came to Britain it had long been separate. It is said that a hundred and fifty churches lie buried between Land's End and Scilly, but that is nonsense, and nonsense too is the story that Lyons, the capital city of Lyonesse, was situated near the group of rocks called the Seven Stones. An eighteenth-century travel writer, Heath, said a marble pillar was found there and taken away to Cornwall, where it could still be seen in the porch of Sennen church, that pieces of leaded glass had been discovered too, and that the tops of buildings were visible under the water. Nobody else has ever confirmed this tale, and if Lyons existed at all I'm sure it was not eight miles north-east of Scilly across a sea of a much greater depth than five or ten fathoms. Maybe the island did have a capital city – though capital and city are not appropriate words for the addresses of our Stone Age and Celtic forebears – and maybe it was called Lyons. But it really could not have been built at the Seven Stones. Archaeological research indicates that the centre of population on Lyonesse – I have to call it something – was in what are now the Northern Isles, St Helen's in particular yielding the richest finds. I'm quite happy to think that Lyons may have existed on or near St Helen's.

What we do know is that this island was wooded and fertile, that a great many people lived here, that they had a curiously large number of graves, that they sometimes cremated their dead and sometimes buried them sitting up, that they farmed and fished, that they ate food we would consider most unpalatable (limpets, seals, and puffins), that they mined tin, and that they were sophisticated enough in their technology to have drainage and sewage systems. Pliny says they wore long, black, frock-like garments (dress that lasted on Scilly into the Christian era.) But most of what they left behind the sea has long since

145

entombed, destroyed, or washed away.

Nevertheless . . . this beautiful morning as I lie on the summit of Tean, gazing out over the azure water to dozens of gentle islands and tooth-like rocks, listening to the cries of gulls and the Atlantic battering itself on Men-a-vaur, smelling the bracken and the salt in the wind, enjoying the sun's heat on my skin, I wish it were all true: all still joined up and Arthur buried here, the hundred and fifty churches, and not Hugh Town to which I shall be returning for tonight's dinner and sleep, but the fabulous, unique city of Lyons.

I slowly become aware that the elderly couple eating in a corner of the restaurant are Harold and Mary Wilson. I can't hear what he's saying; his voice scrunches like gravel, but hers is loud: "For a man who said he hadn't an appetite, you've licked that plate bloody clean!"

Mumble mumble mumble.

The bill arrives. *She* looks at it; *she* pays for their dinner. They have to pass by me on their way out – she floats on; he pauses, looks at the shirt I'm wearing – horizontal green and white stripes – and says, "Tell me . . . what football team does that represent?"

How on earth should I reply? It isn't every day of the year that an ex-prime minister stops to ask me a question (indeed it's never happened before) and *Harold Wilson* to boot! It's like being suddenly addressed by God. I remember Marian Robinson describing an occasion when E.B. White spoke to her; she reacted, she says, with nervous giggles like a blushing teenager – her children, then quite young, had considerably more presence of mind, and pulled out of their bags their copies of *Charlotte's Web* for the great man to autograph.

"Oh . . . I wish I knew," I say to Earl Wilson of Rievaulx, absurdly. And giggle.

"Well . . . my team's Huddersfield Town," he says.

"Yes. I remember that."

The face is as interesting as it always was: the rabbit teeth and the shifty eyes that, chameleon-like, transform in

146

a second to a look of distinction and acute intelligence. My mother-in-law, watching on TV the famous 'Prime minister – think again' speech during the Rhodesia crisis, said, "I would do anything for Harold! *Anything!*" I can understand that.

Mary gives him a 'Come *on*, Harold!' glance, and they've disappeared into the night. Weeks later I discover that my shirt is identical with Glasgow Celtic's – perhaps he wonders, therefore, if I'm Irish (I am) and Catholic (I was) and have come to the Scillys with an IRA bomb (I haven't.) Or, even in old age, he's unable to stop recruiting a would-be supporter. Or is just rambling.

This incident is of the utmost triviality, not for one second worth preserving. But my mind and my eyes and my ears are still full of the day on Tean, occupied – after that contemplation of sea, of eons of erosion, of what clues may be buried beneath sand and water – with human insignificance. Did the Lord of Lyonesse speak thus to a toiling, neolithic peasant?

At Bant's Carn, on the north-east cliffs of St Mary's, are the extensive remains of a Stone-age village: houses with garden plots, field systems, a little street with the foundations of walls – it reminds me of similar streets in Troy. And, also like Troy, a superb view of the sea: except that the inhabitants of this village would not have been looking at water, but over corn-fields, other villages, and dense woods to the hills that are now the islands of St Martin's, Tresco and Bryher. There's no kiosk, no entrance money to pay, no crowds of tourists: just me. No discouraging awareness of an outdoor museum, thank God; so I'm able to *enjoy* the atmosphere of this marvellous place.

Dominating the village is its largest structure, a tomb – a communal tomb, I guess; their equivalent of a country churchyard. I sit on the great stone slabs of its roof and wonder what their lives could have been like. Eating puffins. Roast puffin, so I've read, is a very tasty dish, a bit like duck, though somewhat more salty. So much of a delicacy was it considered in the Middle Ages that the annual rent the people of Scilly had to pay was calculated in puffins. We, I suppose, would rather see puffins alive and well and nesting on cliffs, and the decline in their numbers is not caused by us, or our pollution of the environment, but by black-backed gulls who delight in pecking baby puffins to death.

Were any of these people gay? The word, with its nineteen-nineties connotations, when applied to Stone-Agers, is ridiculous, and so is the Victorian invention, homosexual. Were they loved and respected by Stone Age straights . . . or cast out, walled up alive, perhaps, in this tomb? No. These people revered the dead, so maybe they also revered the living. Life itself. I'd like to think that, to think they had virtues modern man has abandoned. For how long did this civilisation last? There's no evidence, until Viking times, of invading hordes of barbarians. The Phoenicians came, but that was to trade; the Romans came – to maroon people they didn't want to execute, recalcitrant governors, I imagine, or generals too ambitious – and Irish saints and hermits. The latter busied themselves converting anybody they found to Christianity. Like Jehovah's Witnesses and Mormons. St Warna, the patron saint of shipwrecks, rowed from Ireland to St Agnes – if, by her date, the sea had encroached to what is now the five-fathom line, St Agnes and Gugh would have been separate from Lyonesse, one island about as large as present-day Tresco – in a flimsy, wicker-work coracle. 'Persons of an uncanonised status,' the guide-book says, 'are *not* advised to use this method when voyaging to St Agnes.' Of the Dark Ages in Scilly nothing is known: then Vikings, quite early in their quest for territorial expansion, plundered and pillaged here and – I assume – raped too; the end of a continuous, unbroken line of civilisation.

Scilly is extremely vulnerable to marauders and pirates: flat, open, defenceless. Elizabeth the First, fearing its capture during the long years of hostility with Spain, built a castle at Hugh Town, an elegant fortress shaped like a star. It is now a hotel and restaurant – meals are served in the dungeons. Spain didn't bother with Scilly; the

Germans, however, were very interested during World War Two: they frequently bombed here, but caused almost no damage, except to shift slightly a logan-stone on Peninnis Head so that it no longer rocks. Spoilsports . . .

The three big islands I can see from Bant's Carn though so close together are amazingly different from one another. St Martin's is soft and pretty, and though it is the most sheltered of the three from the westerly winds, it has problems with sand, even the briefest of sand-storms will cut to ribbons the flower crop on which the islanders depend for their income. So the daffodil fields are made to be as small as possible, and planted around them are huge hedges of eronica, pittosporum and escallonia. Tresco, despite its abbey and famous tropical gardens, is dark and gloomy. It has more trees than any other island, but they are dark and gloomy too, and the north end is dull, brown tundra. I don't like Tresco. St Martin's people may battle with sand, but it is no difficulty on Bryher – here they fight the sea. The north-west coast – Hell Bay – faces the whole uproar of the open Atlantic; there's nothing between here and Massachusetts: its cliffs are as dramatic and shattered as any in Britain, and even on the calmest and bluest summer day the sea churns and tosses, bashing the rocks with such force that immense fountains of frothing spray are hurled skywards. Yet the south end of Bryher has a beach of dazzlingly white shell-sand where not a ripple disturbs the surface of the water.

On each of these islands is a tiny church, attractive and worth a visit. St Martin's has an excellent stained-glass window, and its light-bulbs are covered by British Home Stores paper lanterns, the kind we buy for our bedrooms and living rooms. These churches have interesting grave-yards: sagas inscribed on stone of shipwreck and drowning, of heroic efforts to save men from the sea, of widows who outlived their dead husbands by half a century or more.

> The wave cry, the wind cry, the vast waters
> Of the petrel and the porpoise.
> In my end is my beginning.

The saddest story is of what happened to the people of Samson. The young men sailed away to fight Napoleon, and they all died in battle. Not one returned. Samson became a grieving community of the middle-aged and the old. Eventually, unable to look after themselves, they were evacuated and resettled on St Mary's and Tresco. No one since has lived on Samson – not for a hundred and fifty years.

Sir Cloudesley Shovel also haunts these islands. The boatmen will take you to the rocks that destroyed his ships; the museum in Hugh Town has some of his personal possessions; at Porth Hellick on St Mary's a stone marks the place where he was washed up and buried. Washed up alive, it is said. But totally exhausted. He escaped from the wreck in a small boat with his treasure chest and his favourite greyhound, and was strangled at Porth Hellick by a woman greedy for the gold rings she saw he was wearing. When he was disinterred for a more lavish funeral in Westminster Abbey it was noticed that his rings were missing; the marks they had made on his fingers could still be seen. On her death-bed the woman confessed to her crime . . . but what happened to the treasure and the greyhound is not recorded. 'Oh, God,' states an old Scillonian prayer, 'let there not be shipwrecks. But if it is Thy will that there shall be, direct them to Scilly so we may not be deprived of our livelihoods.'

By helicopter to Penzance, to England I feel like saying, for Scilly is so different – its history and geography, its climate, its flowers, the colour of its sea, its legends: not English. Penzance is a depressing reminder of what is English and mercifully lacking in Scilly – crowds and cars and bustle and ugliness, the mish-mash of a town that is docks, end of the railway, and seaside resort; candyfloss, fish and chips, McDonalds, take-away pizzas, and tacky, tacky souvenirs. There is nothing to see in Penzance. The neighbouring fishing-harbour village, Newlyn, was once an attractive place where a colony of artists seeking quiet sketched and painted, but Penzance has grown, sprawled, gobbled it up.

On the train I sit with three very old ladies, Jean, Rene and Beat, sisters who are going home to Wolverhampton; they are drinking endless gins and tonics, and playing cards for money. Thick Black Country voices. They remind me of the gannets I saw.

As at the finale of any journey . . . I have to adjust.

September 1990

"Nobody goes to Belgium ... If it's Tuesday, perhaps ... Do you have a meeting of some kind in Brussels? A committee of Euro-gays? ... What on earth *for*?" Thus, the comments of friends; but the last question reminds me of what I'd like to answer – why does it exist, this artificially created country of two races, Dutch and French (Flemish and Walloon to be specific), who despise each other to the point of total non-cooperation? Roman Catholicism – again – is the snake in the grass, the cause of the two bourgeois, conservative revolutions that led to independence in 1830: the Catholic Flemish refusing to accept the idea of tolerance for all religions that the Dutch monarch, William the First, wished to introduce in his short-lived Kingdom of the Netherlands (now Holland, Belgium, and Luxembourg.) Absurd, but a lot of Belgium is absurd – the awful cuisine of its average restaurants: menus typical of Britain circa 1948, soup of the day, steak and chips, ice cream – chips, chips, chips, fatty and squashy, with everything; a mean stinginess (ten francs every time you need a public loo, ten francs for the carte de ville which, at tourist offices in every other country, is given away, forty francs to go into the very few churches in Antwerp that aren't locked up all week, hotels that offer very little to justify their ridiculously high prices, restaurants that say they'll accept the usual credit cards, but won't unless you pay far more than you want to spend); this supposedly bilingual country in which neither race will speak the language of the other; where, except on the language boundary, no direction sign, no street, no shop, no newspaper – nothing – is written in French *and* Flemish.

But nobody, it seems, would have it any different. "I'm certainly not *French*!" a French-speaking woman says to me; she thinks of herself as Belgian – she can't bear the chauvinism of France. I understand exactly what she means – that ludicrous belief in France that nowhere else is civilised: "Oh, you can get walnuts in England? And Dijon mustard? Que c'est extraordinaire!" Yes, I feel like answering, we have hot water too, and wine, and drains – and a musical life in London infinitely superior to anything Paris has ever known. But enough grumbles: the Belgian public transport system is marvellous; you can go almost anywhere, at any hour of the day or night, quickly and cheaply – how appalling the British equivalent is! What must foreigners say to themselves when they get to Heathrow and find there's no fast railway to London. The countryside these still, misty September mornings is beautiful: not quite as flat as Holland and more wooded; a few windmills; gardens a blaze of flowers. And the art galleries.

The Musée des Beaux Arts in Brussels and the Koninklijk Museum in Antwerp are two of the most rewarding galleries in Europe, as fine as the Quai d'Orsay, the Uffizi, the Prado, the Pushkin, the Winter Palace; and as soon as I arrive in Brussels I head for the Musée des Beaux Arts – to see, above everything else, *Landscape with the Fall of Icarus*. I know it so well from postcards and copies and one of the most moving of twentieth-century poems, Auden's 'About suffering they were never wrong, the Old Masters . . .' It's in a room with all the other great Breughels – *The Census at Bethlehem*, *The Adoration of the Magi*, *The Massacre of the Innocents* and so on – as overwhelming as the room in the Uffizi that has all the great Botticellis, the *Primavera*, *The Birth of Venus*, *The Madonna of the Pomegranate*. I've seen those Botticellis twice and on each occasion – the only times it's happened to me with paintings – I was moved to tears; now, as I repeat Auden's words in my head, there's a third time. But . . . is it Auden or Breughel who is doing this? Both.

Auden must have stood exactly where I am, and, turning from *Landscape with the Fall of Icarus*, noted various details in the other paintings which he subsequently referred to; for in *The Census at Bethlehem* the aged are 'reverently, passionately waiting for the miraculous birth' with children 'skating on a pond at the edge of the wood,' and in *The Massacre of the Innocents* martyrdoms do run their course 'anyhow in a corner' where 'dogs go on with their doggy life.' The only detail missing is the torturer's horse

154

that 'scratches its innocent behind on a tree.' He's so right about Icarus: everything does turn away quite leisurely from the disaster, the ploughman:

> . . . and the expensive delicate ship that must have seen
> Something amazing, a boy falling out of the sky,
> Had somewhere to get to and sailed calmly on.

The 'human position' of suffering: yes – 'someone else is eating or opening a window.' Aids dying, but people have to get to their next appointment, their bus, their dinner. Nobody can expect the world to stop and say there is no sorrow like unto my sorrow. Even if we wish it would.

In these galleries at Brussels and Antwerp, and at Ghent and Bruges, I learn a great deal about Flemish painting; artists I've always been aware of but not thought much about, simply because outside Belgium one sees very few examples of their work – Van Eyck, Memling, Van der Weyden, Gerard David, Jordaens. Memling and Van der Weyden are superb: the triptych of Memling's, *Angels Playing Musical Instruments*, at Antwerp, his *Reliquary of St Ursula* at Bruges (a sculpture in wood of a Gothic cathedral, everything painted in miniature), and the detail in Van der Weyden's portraits – the troubled eyes of the Duke of Burgundy's illegitimate son; Philip the Good at prayer, earth in his fingernails as if he's just been digging the garden. Van Dyck, I discover, is a much more interesting painter than I'd imagined, but the Van Eyck brothers – this is heresy – do little for me. The fathers of painting (like Bach for music, Chaucer for English literature), but even the hugely famous *Adoration of the Lamb* at Ghent doesn't stir, doesn't excite: very well done, I say to myself, but . . . so what? Bosch, as ever, is fascinating, a medieval surrealist with a penchant for arseholes, from which crowds of weird and wonderful demons fart in immense profusion, but Jordaens is *awful* (colossal naked women with disgusting rolls of fat), and so is Frans Hals – cheap, shoddy, shallow. Rubens at his finest is magnificent, *The Adoration of the Magi* at Antwerp for example; but he often succumbs to the same elephantiasis that affected sixteenth-century Venetians, Tintoretto, Veronese: vast, swirling mythological or Christian subjects in which detail is ignored and nothing is ever still. One painting, alas, that sticks in the mind is Gerard David's *Judgement of Cambyses* at Bruges: a terrifying, nightmarish scenario that depicts with monstrous realism a man being skinned alive.

Not all, of course, in these galleries is Flemish: deliciously coy nudes by Cranach (they're always wearing *one* article of clothing, a glove, a slipper, an absurdly sumptuous hat); a Bonnard nude that reminds one of Cranach (she's about to get into the bath, but is still wearing a pair of elegant blue shoes); Jacques-Louis David's wonderful picture of Marat, very dead and in *his* bath, clutching Charlotte Corday's letter ... But one turns back to the Flemish primitives, most often to Pieter Breughel the Elder: his knowledge of life, his irony, his scepticism. And, one adds, how cold Flemish winters must have been in the sixteenth century! Or was it just his own passion for ice, snow, frost, thin wintry light?

The great Gothic churches of Belgium should also be a rewarding experience, the cathedrals at Brussels and Antwerp in particular, but they are not: the Belgian authorities seem to have realised later than those in other countries that these buildings have been falling to bits for years because of pollution and age – so almost everything is wrapped in the scaffolds of restorers. The choir at Brussels is sealed off and invisible, and so are the choir *and* transepts at Antwerp (they've been working on this cathedral since 1963 and won't finish it in my lifetime; its famous Rubens canvases are also being restored and can't be seen properly; yet you have to *pay* to go in!) St Nicholas's in Ghent, which, to judge from the outside, is superb, is completely closed because of restoration, as is the Eglise de la Chappelle in Brussels ... etcetera. Also, and no guide-book tells you this, many functioning churches are locked except at Mass times; St Charles Borromeo and St Andrew – two of the most interesting in Antwerp – are open to the tourist only on Wednesday afternoons and for one hour. Why, for God's sake? Do the bishops of Belgium think some member of the public will run away with the statue in St Andrew's of Mary, Queen of Scots?

Another absurdity. However . . . in Brussels cathedral, a beautiful stained-glass window portrays that busiest of Eurocrats, the Emperor Charles the Fifth, whose writ included Austria, Belgium, Holland, Spain, *and* the Holy Roman Empire (he got so bored with commuting he eventually abdicated and went to live in a Spanish monastery.) In Bruges, the Onze Lieve Vrouwekerk contains a Caravaggio and an exquisite Michelangelo *Virgin and Child,* the only sculpture of his that adorned a church outside Italy in his lifetime; and, again in Bruges, an amazing fourteenth-century church built as an exact copy in miniature of Jerusalem's Church of the Holy Sepulchre – in the crypt a sarcophagus with a sculpted dead Christ. There's another Caravaggio in St Paul's, Antwerp, and various Rubenses and Van Dycks – all rescued, unharmed, by the local prostitutes when the church caught on fire. The cathedrals at Ghent and Bruges are not being restored, but they're in a lower league, architecturally, than Brussels or Antwerp. Antwerp, if I could see the whole thing, I'd probably judge one of the world's greatest . . .

Charles the Fifth, who was born at Ghent (son of the Queen of Spain, Joanna the Mad), was not the only ruler of Belgium to cause a raised eyebrow. More modern kings, Albert and Leopold the Third, were marked by paradoxes peculiar to this countr, that are inexplicably odd. Albert reigned from 1909 to 1934 and was immensely popular, the charismatic soldier-prince who refused to surrender to the Germans in the First World War; he chose to see the remaining bit of Belgium not in enemy hands, the Ypres salient, razed to the ground rather than give in. Yet he died in mysterious circumstances – falling over a cliff he'd just climbed. What was a monarch aged nearly sixty doing, climbing up a cliff? His son, Leopold the Third, the father of the present king, is even more of a puzzle. In 1940, against his government's wishes and without informing his allies, he told his army to stop fighting Hitler's troops: thus immediately creating the debacle at Dunkirk (which the British, most sophistically, like to imagine was not a defeat) and the collapse of France. His reason, he said, was that by surrender and staying in Belgium he could mitigate the horrors of a second German conquest, and he did manage to stop half a million Belgians being deported to concentration camps and slave labour in German factories. But for him, the decision was entirely disastrous. He spent much of the war in an Austrian jail, and when he was released his own countrymen regarded him a a coward and a collaborator. Nor have the British and the French – it's hardly surprising – ever forgiven him. In 1950 he was more or less forced to abdicate: leaving his son, Baudouin, to patch up the wounds. A second Icarus, Leopold.

There's much in these ancient Flemish towns to please the eye: in every one a medieval stadhuis; an old hall that was the headquarters of a guild; a belfry that stands on its own, unattached to a church, in the main square – the top of Ghent's has a golden dragon crusaders nicked from Constantinople in 1204, Bruges's a carillon that plays Beethoven's *Ode to Joy* and, somewhat irritatingly, *Auld Lang Syne* – and delightful terraces of houses that once belonged to rich merchants, each unique, each with splendidly ornate gables, turrets and fol-de-rols. A bit like Amsterdam, yet not like Amsterdam: for this is Flanders. The language is Dutch, but not exactly Dutch (different dialect, different accent); if Dutch, I say to myself, is bastardised German, then Flemish is bastardised Dutch, and there's only one further degree of bastardisation – English. I can't speak a word of Flemish or understand a word of what people are saying, but it's the nearest language to English – I can read chunks of it. More Dutch, yet not quite Dutch, similarities are the canals: though Bruges has no echoes of Amsterdam. The city Bruges is most like is Cambridge; almost identical time-mellowed brick buildings 'whose walls the silent water laves,' bridges resembling Queens' or Clare or Trinity, huge willows on the banks trailing fronds, gorgeous still reflections. So like Cambridge is it that, in a boat on these canals, I'm back thirty years with Richard who, in white flannels and boater, fell out of a punt, with Keith, with William indolently poling us to Grantchester . . .

Bruges canals, like Cambridge's river, have no purpose: they're merely decorative. Five centuries ago it was the busiest port in Europe, but silt from the Schelde estuary completely dried up its outlet to the sea, the Zwin. In 1907 a canal was made to the coast and a port, Zeebrugge, which means Bruges-on-Sea, was constructed. But Bruges's industries had gone; Zeebrugge exists only as a ferry terminal. Just as well, for if Bruges had a purpose its almost excessive beauty would be spoiled – fine though it is, a great place for idle pottering. Ghent is different: though further inland it's a working port, so less attractive, less inundated with tourists. It's as gaunt as its name implies, a long, thin city in a zigzag of the River Leie, with tall, thin buildings. In the Abbey of St Baaf John of Gaunt was born (Edward the Third and Philippa of Hainault on vacation; summer hols for the infant Black Prince, for Edward a working break in which he successfully persuaded the Count of Flanders to help him bash up the French.) St Baafsabdij today is a ruin – Charles the Fifth provoked undying anger in Ghent's inhabitants by removing its stone to build a military fortress – and who St Baaf was no guide-book relates. Another obscure fanatic, I guess, who, like Tryphon and Sernin, probably had his head chopped off for interfering with the city's religious beliefs; perhaps in 250, that vintage year for beheading saints.

> Old Gaunt indeed; and gaunt in being old.
> Within me grief hath kept a tedious fast;
> And who abstains from meat that is not gaunt?

In Antwerp – 'hand werpen' is the Flemish for 'severed hand' – modern docks and medieval streets quite happily co-exist; after Bruges, it's the most beautiful Flanders city: an ancient castle, the Steen, dominating the Schelde; a (potentially) stunning cathedral; Rubens mementos; Plantin's , the Renaissance's most important publishing concern, now a museum of printing, full of priceless first editions; the marvellously preserved Vleeshuis, the butchers' guildhall; a main square almost as fine as the Burg at Bruges. Visiting Rubens's house is like stepping into a de Hooch painting of a Dutch interior, albeit on a grander scale – and there's a pleasant begijnhof at Antwerp: a community of Catholic women who withdraw from the world, but who do not want to be nuns. Originally founded for crusaders' widows and unmarried, dowry-less daughters, begijnhofs flourished all over Europe, but today they exist only in Flanders. The one at Bruges, which has a most attractive seventeenth-century church, is an enormous quadrangle of buildings: very like Trinity Great Court.

Antwerp grew rich from diamonds, spices and wool; but the Dutch, when they achieved their independence from Spain, closed the Schelde to all traffic, and Antwerp's decline was so total that grass covered its docks and streets. But the docks are once more some of Europe's busiest: though my first sight of the Schelde is a disappointment – smaller than I'd imagined. Not as wide as the Thames at Greenwich. The same feeling as in the Grand' Place at Brussels: curiously small. I discover the Grand' Place by accident, as I did the Old Town Hall Square in Prague; good God, so that's *it*! Fascinating, however, though the old houses and the Stadhuis in the Grand' Place are, they do not measure up to the Old Town Hall Square; Prague's is the most beautiful – absolutely no competition. Brussels, 'the capital of Europe,' full of those grey descendents of Charles the Fifth, the Eurocrats – grey-faced men in identikit grey suits, busy, busy, busy with meetings – is bland; it neither offends nor delights. Flanders architecture and French-speaking inhabitants, it's a frontier city, not a true capital. Prague is the centre of Europe, the obvious choice for 'capital,' and now that the

East is free, Communism dead, perhaps in time it will take on that function.

In the Parc de Bruxelles the revolution that gave Belgium its independence began, but I can find no monument that records it. At one end of the Parc is the graceful Parliament building, at the other the equally graceful Palais du Roi which is open to the public, even when King Baudouin is in residence – as is Queen Beatrix's palace, the Dam in Amsterdam. Bourgeois and democratic, thesePays Bas kingdoms; less aloof than ours. But devoid of ceremony, pomp and circumstance, pageant. And the Parc de Bruxelles is the dullest of gardens, not a flower to be seen.

Ypres is a totally different experience. Once the most important of all the Flanders cloth towns, with a population in the thirteenth century bigger than London's, it long ago became a sleepy backwater, the penultimate station on a single-track branch line that terminates at Poperinghe. No city in Europe – with the exception, perhaps, of Dresden and Stalingrad – has been squashed as flat as Ypres by the roller of war. The events of 1914-1918 destroyed all its public buildings, demolished every house and shop; it was a desert of stumps and rubble, a dreamscape, a nightmare-scape. Hundreds of thousands of men died here, or drowned just a few miles up the road in the mud of Passchendaele and Poperinghe. The full name of Bruges is Bruges-la-Morte, but la Morte is more appropriate for Ypres: Ypres is much possessed by death. On its outlying farms, ploughmen every year unearth vast quantities of spent shell-cases and live ammunition; it's surrounded by cemeteries; trenches, tunnels, parapets, and mine craters are still intact and much visited by tourists. Only the medieval ramparts survived the bombardments, though the ancient gates were ruined: in 1927 the Menin Gate was rebuilt as a memorial to the fifty-five thousand British soldiers who died here and who have no known graves. It's covered, from top to bottom, with their names. Every evening – still – Ypres's traffic is halted while buglers

161

from the local fire brigade, on silver bugles given to them by the British Legion, sound, at the Menin Gate, *The Last Post*.

The turrets and spires of Ypres rise up from the Flanders plain like those of Bruges or Ghent, and its streets are lined with the usual attractive houses: but they're modern imitations – Ypres was rebuilt to appear as it was. One can sense, looking at the cathedral or the enormous Cloth Hall, how magnificent its ancient architecture must have been; but, being now a copy, it's cold, clinical, dead. In the Cloth Hall a museum tells the story of 1914-1918: military artefacts, the proclamations and newspapers of the day (including the British *Wipers Times*), maps of the various battles, and – the most interesting and moving exhibits – a stunning photographic record of what occurred as it occurred.

In the cathedral the most famous of Ypres's bishops, Cornelius Jansen, who died in 1638, is buried; the tomb was smashed to bits in the war, but one can see the place in the chancel where his bones lie. Jansen's book, *Augustinus*, condemned by Pope Innocent the Tenth as heretical, argued that the grace of God, necessary for salvation, could not be earned: you either had it or you didn't have it. Such a belief is similar to Calvin's doctrine of predestination, and Jansen's followers were on the whole a dour, gloomy bunch. Pascal defended them in his *Lettres Provinciales*, and Racine was educated at the convent school of Port-Royal, a hotbed of Jansenism. The lasting effect of this strange heresy isn't doctrinal but in attitudes; Jansenist influence on Irish Catholicism is still all-pervasive – gloomy, fate-orientated, loathing the human body: the puritanical Catholicism I absorbed from my mother. It has, I suppose, dictated much of the course of my adult life, though I rejected, most happily, Catholicism and all its works decades ago. As I stare at the place where Cornelius Jansen is buried, I have a strong urge to spit. But I don't. One doesn't.

So, I say to myself, have I answered the question, what on earth for? I have not. I'm no nearer to understanding

why Belgium exists – but I wouldn't be immensely surprised to wake up one morning and discover it had ceased
to exist.

September 1991

Six Weeks After the Coup

I am observing a whole society, once the world's second super-power, slide gently, politely, almost humorously – into seeming chaos and collapse; a process that's been hastened during the six weeks since the abortive coup of August 1990 – the days of the fleeing Zils, the plotters forgetting to cut the telephone wires, John Major calling Boris Yeltsin: "Morning, Boris . . . everything OK?" Boris: "Morning, John . . . no, we're not dead yet!" Since the coup the institutions of the state have been impotent. President Gorbachev, whose achievements match those of the greatest twentieth-century statesmen, Churchill, de Gaulle, Tito, Roosevelt, and whose wheeler-dealer skills are superior even to LBJ's or Harold Wilson's, is an empty husk; on Moscow TV looking like Banquo's ghost, ashen, drawn, sick: for there is virtually no Soviet Union now. What's going to happen, everyone asks; what next? So it must have been in Germany at the beginning of the nineteen thirties when the currency disintegrated, but there's no Hitler in the wings. Nor any mad, bomb-throwing anarchists or Bolsheviks, no KGB, no army generals (though very disgruntled one's told) who want to seize power. God will help us; the West will help us. I doubt it. Carry on sliding I think is the future . . .

It *is* similar to the Weimar Republic, for the rouble is worthless; in 1987 the 'official' exchange rate was one pound for one rouble (but on the street one pound for two, even three roubles), now it's officially one pound for *fifty-five* roubles. So, if you can pay in roubles, Russia for us is absurdly, comically cheap, but you never know if they'll be accepted: my left-hand trouser pocket has roubles, the right-hand sterling – it seems more politically correct than the other way round – but some people won't take either; you can't in Moscow get a taxi without American dollars. It's a hassle even to buy a bottle of mineral water, and as for alcohol . . . some bars have no beer, some no vodka, some no change in any Western currency but they don't want roubles – in some a bottle of champagne is eight pounds, in others forty roubles (eighty pence!) It's so wearing. Outside the hotels, and at the places tourists visit such as the Kremlin, crowds of kids swarm round you like flies, as they do in Istanbul, wanting to sell you postcards, cheap and nasty imitations of ikons, Russian watches (ho-ho!), tins of caviare, Red Army uniforms, babushka dolls and the latest toy, the Gorby doll: the man with the mark of blood on his head, as Nostradamus predicted, with, inside him in decreasing order of size, Brezhnev, Stalin, Khruschev, Lenin, Nicholas the Second, and the mad monk Rasputin. I buy one of these baubles for seven pounds – all dealings with street urchins are in Western currencies; they only have to sell a few 'souvenirs' to be very well off when they exchange their pounds for roubles: they can then afford to buy the only food available, which is black or 'free' market. A few years ago the police would have arrested them (you could, in theory, be sent to Siberia for illegal currency dealings, though it didn't happen very often); now the police ignore them or are busy doing the same thing. A man wants to sell us champagne at fifty roubles a bottle – no, no, we answer, forty's the going black-market rate. He explains the problem to a nearby policeman – "Forty, fifty," says the policeman with a smile; "Split the difference."

There is very little food in the state shops – in Moscow almost none – and the queues to buy what is available are enormous. The queuing looks worse than it really is, for the system is a typically Russian farce: few people are allowed into a shop at any one time so they queue outside on the pavement, then they queue for what they want, queue again to pay for it, then join another queue to collect their purchases. Crazy ... In the West we think that Russian food shortages are the result of primitive distribution and storage, and allowing a third of the crops to rot in the fields; but it can't be so, for the distribution, storage and harvesting methods of the Russians have always been like that, and in the past they've more or less adequately fed themselves. Until 1917 they had surpluses which they exported. The problem stems from the collapse of the central government: Moldova and the Ukraine, for example, the 'bread-baskets,' don't now automatically send their produce elsewhere – the food is for Moldovans and Ukrainians (though some of it surfaces on the black and 'free' markets); what's left has to be paid for by Moscow or Leningrad or wherever. (No one calls it Leningrad now, and tourists who do are greeted with a pitying or withering look; it's St Petersburg.)

The state shops may be empty but there's no real shortage of food. In Kishinev I visit a market of gigantic size: it has immense quantities of every conceivable fruit and vegetable including delicacies like pomegranates, and the quality's superb; its meat hall is vast, and the cuts of meat excellent; there are innumerable kinds of cheese . . . But it's all private enterprise or 'black' and therefore beyond the ability of many people to pay, though for me absurdly cheap – I buy a bunch of delicious grapes for forty-five kopecks (one penny.) None of this produce finds its way into the hotels, for Intourist, a state organisation, is obliged to buy in the state shops and would prefer to, for everything there costs less; so hotel meals range from the very disgusting to the utterly disgusting – one wouldn't, in Britain, give the worst of this garbage to cats or dogs. Yet, when I was in Russia four years ago, the food, though not exciting, was perfectly adequate. Now, in Moscow, the chicken I eat looks as if it died of starvation; in Odessa there's no tea, the bread is a week old, and the butter is so rancid you can smell it as you come into the dining room.

The hotels are falling to bits. Curtains drop in a heap on the floor as you try to close them; door handles come off at a touch; bath plugs don't fit so, when you bath you have to keep the water running; and the bars and foyers are full of prostitutes. The police used to eject such people, but not now; at one St Petersburg bar where I'm drinking at seven p.m. the clientele consists of twenty-four female prostitutes, three male prostitutes and me. The males, Kazakhs, have youth on their side but are singularly unattractive; they keep smiling at me and blowing kisses despite my refusal to look straight at them. Some of the women ask me to buy them a drink: I tell them to fuck off. I find I'm getting very irritated, though I'm aware they have to earn a living; it's an invasion of one's privacy, one's space, as are the demands of the street urchins to buy souvenirs. The worst hotel for prostitutes is Moscow's Cosmos – the foyer is a heaving red-light district. This hotel, it's said, paid a tremendous sum of money to the local branch of the Mafia to ensure that it had a monopoly on the area's whores: it's much used by Westerners, so I wouldn't be amazed to hear that Intourist turned a blind eye. But someone informed the press, and the prostitutes vanished. Two weeks afterwards they were all back again.

In St Petersburg the waiters are more interested in flogging black-market caviare and champagne than in pouring out coffee or clearing tables. In Kishinev and Odessa the hotels are filthy and stinking; nobody's cleaned anything for months. Every room has cockroaches, and I think of Jane Parminter's 'could not sleep for the bugs': I sleep with the lights on. Lights! They're so dim (forty watts maximum, I guess) it's impossible to read. Black moulds grow on the bathroom ceiling; green moulds protrude from the plug-hole. Tiles are broken or missing. At Odessa there's no mattress on my bed, just three cushions; the hotel bank can't cash traveller's cheques, and the recep-tionist won't order a taxi: "There aren't any," she says. "We have a petrol shortage." There *is* a petrol shortage (the oil-producing republics are keeping it for themselves, or charging more than state-owned garages will pay); Aeroflot each week has to cancel thirty per cent of its internal flights. But there *are* taxis in Odessa – there's petrol if you have the money. Similarly with sugar: some people haven't been able to buy sugar all year, but it exists. Economic chaos is made worse by the black market and the activities of the Mafia – the state's income constantly decreases. Everyone has some connection with the black market; it's the only way to survive. A barman in Kishinev tells me he's just bought a smart, new, three-bedroomed flat, which cost him eighteen thousand roubles – and his monthly salary is a mere two hundred. For years he's been selling stolen TV sets: he's quite open and unashamed of how he's amassed a fortune.

It's not surprising that several people on our tour are affected by diarrhoea; I'm the first to suffer and the last to recuperate – also, considering my immune system, not surprising. Nor am I astonished that the little yellow pills I buy at a chemist for twelve kopecks don't work. They taste like sherbet. In Kiev, after sitting on the toilet eleven times in one afternoon, I decide to call a doctor. He arrives quite promptly with his mate, but now I am astonished: they're kids, teenagers (and very cute.) One of them is wearing a white coat and has a stethoscope around his neck. They speak no English, which is unusual in the Ukraine, and I no Ukrainian; I write DIARRHOEA in Cyrillic on a pad: still no comprehension, maybe because my Cyrillic is, to say the least, rudimentary. So I sit on the loo, point at my bum, then hold up my fingers, saying: "One! Two! Three! Four! Five!" At which point they guess and fall about, giggling. One of them goes off to look for an interpreter. So conversation is at last possible, and what the white-coated youth eventually tells me makes sense: he doesn't want to prescribe anything as he doesn't know what's causing the problem; drink plenty of bottled water, he says, and hot tea to avoid dehydration, and eat boiled rice. I stay in bed for the rest of the day, and a kind chambermaid brings me tea and bottles of water at frequent intervals. But I'm not cured until I return to England and swallow the correct drug, flagyl, which seems to be unknown in the Ukraine. The diarrhoea is caused by a parasite, giardia – it lives in the tap water and bad food. In 1987 the food and water were uncontaminated, but in 1989 visitors to St Petersburg began to contract giardiasis – the city's water supply was considered to be the culprit – and the bug was nicknamed the Leningrad fluke. That it's now endemic everywhere is yet another indication of the way all aspects of life have deteriorated. I ask the interpreter how old these young men are – the one in the white coat is twenty, his mate eighteen. Students at medical school, I suppose; the younger probably in the first week of his first term. What would have happened if I'd been suffering from a stroke or a heart attack?

Kishinev is the capital of what used to be Bessarabia, the north-east province of Rumania, which, in 1940, was annexed by Russia – Stalin wanted to control the mouth of the Danube, and amalgamated the province with a very small Soviet republic nearby, Moldavia, which, though it has never been part of Rumania, is also Rumanian-speaking. The whole region was then given the name of Moldavia: now it has severed its links with the USSR and is the self-proclaimed independent Republic of Moldova. It sounds confusing, and it is. In fact it's somewhat more confusing than I've suggested, for that small republic nearby (the one that was originally called Moldavia) won't have anything to do with an independent Moldova, and has seceded; it calls itself the Republic of Dniester, and wants to stay in the Soviet Union, even though the Soviet Union hardly exists. The majority of Moldova's inhabitants – dark-skinned, dark hair, olive-coloured eyes; Latins – desires reunification with Rumania. They even did in Ceausescu's time, which was insane, and since the execution of the mad dictator the clamour for reunification has grown. The Moldovan government, however, is not as keen on the idea as the people it governs: those in power have much to lose, for Kishinev would cease to be a 'capital' and would have to take its orders from Bucharest. Moldova has tried to stop Dniester seceding: it can't afford to lose the territory because most of its industries are there. In Tirsapol, Dniester's 'capital,' people have been killed, members of the administration whisked to Kishinev and jailed, buildings burned down. The housewives of Tirsapol have retaliated by blocking the railway; nothing from Dniester's factories can therefore be transported into Moldova. The women sit in relays, day and night, on the tracks. We see them as we drive from Benderi in Moldova, an ugly, depressing, Communist Monumental conurbation – the bridge on the Dniester River, which is guarded at either end by troops, is the 'frontier' – into Tirsapol, an attractive, well-preserved old city, where we stop for coffee and notice the statues of Lenin still in place and the Soviet flag flying from the 'parliament' building.

At Tirsapol everything is in Cyrillic: Stalin forced the Bessarabians to adopt Cyrillic too, but Moldova has now returned to the Latin alphabet; so in Kishinev, Rumanian name Chisinău, I can at least read the language (Rumanian's nearest cousin is Italian) even if I can't speak a word of it. The resumption of the Latin alphabet is one of many changes: Kishinev was the first town in the Soviet Union to demolish statues of Lenin, and since the coup some seventy street names have been altered – Lenin Prospekt is now the Avenue of King Stephen the Great, whoever he was – thus causing immense confusion for the inhabitants, particularly the postmen. Some of these changes are ridiculous: Pushkin Park is now Central Park. Pushkin has been demoted merely because he was Russian, though he lived in Kishinev as a young man. I ask myself, as he probably did, what on earth I'm doing in Kishinev – the capital of Bessarabia, once north-eastern Rumania, is a place as exotically remote, almost like Timbuctoo, as anywhere I've been; but it's a drab, uninteresting town, much knocked about in World War Two and rebuilt in the usual hideous fashion. 'A mixture of Eastern and Western architecture,' which 'reflects the turbulent history . . . including three hundred years of Turkish rule,' says the Intourist brochure, and Fodor recommends 'the Old City, with its picturesque winding alleys and streets;' but these statements are so totally false that I doubt whether any blurb-writer from Intourist or Fodor has ever been here. There's nothing Turkish in Kishinev, no picturesque winding alleys, no Old City, no mix of East and West. I don't think there ever was.

The cathedral, singled out for praise by Intourist and Fodor, is of no interest at all. But one tiny church, not mentioned by either – it's far from downtown and so hidden away it's very difficult to find; I discover it by accident – is a treasure-trove: its whole wall-space plastered with hundreds of beautiful miniature ikons, all

171

very ancient and painted with the utmost delicacy. Trees and flowers in Kishinev are pleasantly Mediterranean – acacias, succulents, cactuses; vines dangle everywhere – and the journey by road to Odessa passes through some attractive countryside: huge orchards, very well cultivated, on fertile flat land stretching to the horizon. It's remarkably like the Sacramento Valley in California. The villages look prosperous, with spacious, well-built houses, trees and large gardens; most of them, I'm told, are privately owned. As we cross from the Dniester Republic into the Ukraine we have to go through customs posts – another recent innovation.

The best way of avoiding the appalling hotel food is to eat in a privately owned restaurant, but finding one is a Herculean task. In Kishinev, however, the Latin alphabet is of great assistance, and on one occasion we do manage to eat quite well – hors d'oeuvres that are edible, a piping hot meat and potato stew, and some good Moldovan wine – but for me the chief pleasure of the evening is the entertainment, music played by a band of local gipsies dressed in folk costume. The instruments are a violin, balalaikas, an accordeon and a simbalom (the mixture, at last, of East and West that Intourist and Fodor promised), though I'm surprised and delighted to hear a cymbalom so far from Hungary. I recall, however, that I once heard cymbaloms in Czechoslovakia – in Bratislava – so maybe they're not, as one's told, just a Hungarian instrument. The music is absolutely fascinating, often wildly ferocious (I'm reminded of Bartók), exhilaratingly prestissimo, and of strange, polyglot origins: Greek, Zorba-like rhythms, Jewish intonations, Russian melancholia (Shostakovich – 'These are the steppes and there's nothing we can do about it') and Flamenco harmonics. I ask the cymbalom player for a solo, and he obliges (for twenty-five roubles – forty-something pence). He's brilliant, and I tell him so. The band, he says, has toured England, appearing twice at the Sidmouth Folk Festival. He's pleased with my enthusiasm, and really excited when he learns I'm familiar with the cymbalom part in Kodály's *Háry János*; at the end of the evening he allows me to have a go on the instrument. I'm thrilled: all my life I've wanted to play a cymbalom – the sound is *gorgeous* – and here I am, in the middle of Bessarabia of all places, doing just that!

We are even more successful at discovering a good meal in Odessa, despite the return to the Cyrillic alphabet. An Armenian restaurant near Primorsky Boulevard: delicious hors d'oeuvres of cooked meats and fish; tomatoes, cucumbers and spring onions of infinitely superior flavour to those from a British supermarket; caviare; an excellent main course of kebab-style lamb, chicken, and halibut; a basket of superb fruit; as much chocolate as we can eat; coffee; four bottles of champagne between seven of us; large brandies for everyone: all this, and a considerable tip, costs slightly under two pounds each – for the proprietor accepts roubles. Utterly ridiculous – and very, very nice. What on earth does Intourist do with the money we pay? Such holidays aren't cheap – over seven hundred pounds per head. The awful food and the abysmal accommodation cost next to nothing; the petrol for coaches and internal air flights also – a one-way ticket from Moscow to St Petersburg is eighteen roubles. Admittedly thirty per cent of what we are charged disappears into the state coffers as tax, but the rest? Into a bottomless pit, I wouldn't be surprised to hear, of backhanders and greased palms; somebody, somewhere, is doing very well at our expense. And there's nothing we can do about it.

As the republics, during the weeks since the coup, have followed each other in breaking away from the Union, people in Minsk, Kiev, Tbilisi, Samarkand, wherever – have inundated the switchboards of Government departments with phone calls asking what do we do now? What are we permitted to do? If we're no longer Soviets, then who are we? I cannot imagine that we in the West would require such information. If Scotland achieved independence the inhabitants of Kirkcaldy and Kyle of Lochalsh wouldn't phone London or Edinburgh to ask who they are. We are free to do what we like provided we don't break the law;

it's a principle on which we operate that is as natural to us as breathing. No Russian thinks like that – he says, I can't do anything unless I'm given permission. Above all else (better food distribution, the acquisition of Western technology and so on) such attitudes have to change. But it's very difficult for people to change not just seventy years but whole centuries of the way they think – life under the Tsars was as circumscribed by the need to obtain permission as it has been under the Communists. The Communist Party's head may be cut off, but its body still vigorously twitches; the vast and inefficient battalions of bureaucrats and functionaries continue to grind away at the work they have always done.

There are encouraging signs. It isn't all apathy and cynicism – three per cent of the land, for example, is now privately owned and it produces thirty per cent of the country's food. Land reform is clearly an immediate necessity and the politicians are aware of that: but the bureaucrats and functionaries are extremely unwilling to relinquish what they control for they would lose power and status; nobody anywhere ever wants to do that. Yet people are happier than they were, even though they view the short-term with alarm; they laugh about themselves in a way that's unprecedented. Brezhnev jokes in Moscow are as common as Reagan jokes were in America, and I'm amused by an Intourist guide telling us not to visit the Exhibition of Economic Achievements: "Russian economic achievements are like haemorrhoids," he says. "You can't see them yourself, and it's embarrassing to show them to others." Most Russians I talk to are delightful people: open, friendly, helpful, courteous, intelligent, immensely curious. There is hope.

But there's little that *we* can do, or should do. If we offered unlimited financial aid or enormous quantities of agricultural products, they would vanish down a vast hole of black-market, Mafia corruption. What has to be done can only be done by the Russians themselves. It shouldn't require Western finance or sophisticated expertise to dispose of cockroaches, hoover hotel carpets, clean public lavatories (which are for the most part utterly disgusting – animals get rid of their excreta more effectively), move loads of fruit and vegetables from Omsk to Tomsk, construct proper refrigeration and storage facilities. Russians have always been aware of this – Gogol, in his magnificent satire on provincial bureaucracy, *The Government Inspector*, was identifying the evils as long ago as 1836. Chekhov, too, was continually pressing the point:

> Our work-people are abominably fed and have to sleep . . . with bed-bugs, bad smells, damp, and immorality everywhere . . . Where are the crèches we're always talking about, where are the reading rooms? . . . There's nothing but dirt, bestiality, Asiatic customs . . . The Lord God has given us vast forests, immense fields, wide horizons; surely we should be giants, living in such a country.

Liubov Andreyevna's reply to this (I'm quoting *The Cherry Orchard*) is that of the standard, frightened Russian who needs permission:

> Whatever do you want giants for? They're all right in fairy tales; otherwise they're just terrifying.

But there are at last a few people who are beginning to think, like Trofimov in the same play, that 'The whole of Russia is our orchard.'

President Gorbachev asking the West for aid is in exactly the same position as Liubov Andreyevna and her brother Gayev begging for a loan to save the cherry trees. But it is just possible that the orchard won't have to be axed to solve the problem. Chaos, disintegration: maybe. But what happens afterwards is entirely up to the Russians themselves, not us. As I said, there *is* hope.

October 1991

Moscow, like Barcelona and Sydney, is one of those rare cities with buzz, with tremendous vibrancy; the party (and I don't mean the Communist Party) is *here*: to stroll in the Arbat, just people-watching, is as exciting as it is in King's Cross or Las Ramblas – you say to yourself, simply being here is *marvellous*! And I had forgotten how beautiful it is, particularly in this still, warm, autumn shirt-sleeves weather of slanting light, October colours as vivid and subtle as those of New England. No city has so many trees – I could happily spend my time just looking at them – now the most dazzling shades of yellow, red, orange, brown, copper; the sour smell of fallen leaves filling the streets. The dreary blocks of Communist Monumental flats on the outskirts (older than in most of Russia, so mellowed somewhat with age) seem almost attractive. Even Stalin's strange bequest to the inner city of seven vast towers (the University, the Foreign Office, etcetera), surmounted with so many spires and turrets that they look like an anthology of Mormon temples, seems to fit in, to have appeal. Fourmillante cité, cité pleine de rêves . . . ! The queue for McDonalds is twice the size of the queue for Lenin, though Lenin may soon become invisible: there are plans to give him a proper burial in St Petersburg. What then will be the focal point of Red Square? St Basil's, I suppose: one's eye constantly returns to its mountain of onion domes as vivid as a child's paint-box, though its interior is the most disappointing of cathedrals; more like a set of dungeons than a place for worship.

The Kremlin dominates the city. Again, the colours of a child's paint-box; though I discover the deep red of its walls is an outer casing of brick put there seventy years ago – it too may be removed. The Kremlin walls are built of limestone; they are supposed to be white. Combination of fortress and palace, it is unique, though its original function was similar to London's Tower; where it scores aesthetically over the Tower is that it has *five* cathedrals, all in one square: a magnificent riot of golden onion domes

177

and whitewashed walls, an overwhelming experience. Their interiors from floor to ceiling are decorated with murals and ikons so deliciously attractive one could almost eat them. In the Cathedral of St Michael are the tombs of the Tsars from 1533 to 1682 (in 1703 St Petersburg became the capital, so the later Tsars are buried there); the most elaborate and prominent is that of Dmitri, the ill-fated son of Ivan the Terrible, murdered, perhaps, by Boris Godunov – Boris ordered the tomb to be sumptuous so everyone could know that Dmitri was dead. He hoped to scotch rumours that the boy was still alive, but he didn't succeed; his years as Tsar were plagued by rebellions of 'false Dmitris,' Russian Perkin Warbecks and Lambert Simnells. Just outside Cathedral Square, on the pavement, is the world's biggest bell, intended for Ivan the Great's bell-tower, but it cracked when it was being cast and was left on the ground – had it been hung where it should be, the splendid sixteenth-century tower might have collapsed in ruins. Near to it is what was, until Saddam Hussein's super-gun, the world's biggest cannon; it was never used, for the balls it was supposed to fire were so heavy no one could lift them up.

The Kremlin's Armoury is not my kind of museum – costumes, thrones, carriages, regalia – but this collection is so stunning I find myself totally fascinated: gorgeously camp mitres and chasubles of medieval metropolitans and patriarchs; the Fabergé Easter eggs (one containing a model of the Trans-Siberian Express); Ivan the Terrible's ivory throne; the child Peter the Great's throne, a square cut out of its back so his sister, Sophia, concealed behind, could mutter the answers he was supposed to give to ambassadors and ministers; incredibly ornate royal carriages, the most resplendent of which was given to Boris Godunov by – of all people – our Elizabeth the First. (Though one cannot imagine Boris inside this fearfully unsprung, wooden-wheeled bone-shaker, fighting the mud and snow of a Russian winter.) There are also in the Armoury the usual boring, grandiloquent presents monarchs give each other – I'm reminded of the expensive junk in Istanbul's Topkapi

Palace – and, a curiosity: gold and silver ikon frames from which the ikons have been removed. They were the victims of the militant atheism of early Communist years, as was one of the city's most beautiful churches, the Cathedral of Christ the Saviour – destroyed to make way for a swimming-bath.

Now it's a different sort of ikon that's being destroyed. In Lubyanka Square on the plinth where the founder of the KGB, Dzerzhinsky, once stood, is the red, white and blue flag of the Russian Republic. Dzerzhinsky is lying face down in the mud in Gorky Park, together with Sverdlov, who signed the execution warrant of Nicholas the Second, and three Lenins. Children use them as they would objects in an adventure playground. All over what was the USSR the Communist ikons are disappearing, the cities and their streets reverting to their ancient names, though some people object – the new governments, they say, have got their priorities skew-whiff: pulling down statues and waving nationalist flags will not solve any problems. But it seems to me important to replace the symbols of a despised ancien régime with the symbols of change; it engenders confidence and hope. The iconoclasm has not been savage destruction by a revolutionary mob; it's been tightly, even amusingly, controlled. The statues in Moscow were removed by order of the Mayor, who asked a council demolition gang to do the job – and he paid them double time for being so efficient. The barricades erected outside the White House during the August coup have also gone, but one symbol of those dangerous days remains – the spot near Plochad Smolenskaya, where tanks killed three young men on August the twentieth, has become a shrine, a mass of wreaths and bunches of flowers. A monument is to be built there to commemorate what happened.
Even on the Metro people now chat, smile, laugh and joke. A daunting experience at first, the Moscow and Petersburg tubes, for they are filled with a seething crowd of humanity like Japanese bullet-trains, and on the stations there are very few direction signs. What signs there are of

179

course are in Cyrillic, so Western tourists venture in packs down the incredibly long escalators (you sometimes can't see the bottom – it's like descending into Hell); to be alone, one imagines, is an immediate recipe for getting lost. But this Underground is incomparably more efficient than London's, and the famous chandeliers are every bit as spectacular as the guide-books say they are. You can go any distance for fifteen kopecks, which means your journey costs about 0.3 of a penny. I survive by dint of counting on the map beforehand the number of stations to where I want to go, and reach the Novodevichy Convent and the Pushkin Museum without mishap, success-fully negotiating having to change at Turgenevskaya and Kirovskaya on both occasions: I feel I've *achieved* something!

The Pushkin has a first-rate collection of Impressionists and post-Impressionists: whole walls of Cézanne, a wonderful Pissarro of the Boulevard Montmartre on a wet day, some tremendous Utrillos and Dufys. Major Picasso Blue Period works, a large quantity of Gauguins – though as ever I find myself indifferent to Gauguin; his themes are monotonous, his colour-sense poor. The Monets and Bonnards here also do not – I'm surprised – thrill me; most of them painted in drab, muddy weather. But Marquet holds my attention – a much finer artist than I'd previously thought – and Matisse (several of them) makes me think about why he is so appealing: the simple pleasures of sunlight, deckchairs, domestic objects. The art of earlier centuries in the Pushkin is, all of it, worth looking at, but after an hour spent gazing at Impressionists, I find it difficult to adjust to seventeenth-century Spaniards or eighteenth-century Italians. Too rich a cocktail: and I think maybe it *is* a good idea that all the great Turners are in London, the Brueghels in Brussels, the Lautrecs in Albi, the Botticellis in Florence, even if it means looking at them for most of us can only be a rare experience. It costs one rouble and fifty kopecks to visit the Pushkin: three pence.

The Novodevichy Convent, built in the sixteenth

century, is a mini-Kremlin – a massive outside wall with twelve battle-towers, a very fine red-brick, octagonal bell-tower, and the huge Smolensky Cathedral: green walls and five golden onion domes glittering in the late afternoon light. The colours of the exteriors of Russian churches, I learn, are symbolic – gold means pleasing to God; green is life; blue (the sky) is hope for Heaven; white is joy. Inside, the ikonostasis is floor to ceiling and covered with beautiful, ancient ikons. Boris Godunov was elected Tsar in this cathedral. It's quiet, wonderfully atmospheric – as is the whole convent and its graveyard. A very fashionable graveyard: Sophia, Peter the Great's sister, and his first wife, Evdokya, Gogol, Chekhov, Mayakovsky, Scriabin, Prokofiev, Stanislavsky, Chaliapin and Eisenstein are all buried here. Two men somewhat out of place – Khruschev and Molotov. Molotov, perhaps, got in because he was Scriabin's nephew.

Four years ago almost every church in Russia had been shut for decades (though a few were functioning as museums); now they are open, and religious services are held all day long. Mass at ten a.m. and six p.m., christenings in the morning, weddings in the afternoon: the priests are working flat out. I haven't attended so many religious services since I was a teenager; curiosity about Orthodox ritual and enjoyment of the superb singing pull me in. Religion here isn't just for old ladies – children, teenagers, young men and women fill the churches; thousands of Russians every day are being baptised. The baptism ceremony is extraordinary – the participants, about twenty at a time, wear knickers, shoes and white sheets (they're expecting to become very damp, I suppose), and walk round the font intoning, waving lit candles (witchcraft rites, I guess, are like this); there's a great deal of anointing by the priest of ears, eyes, forehead, throat, hands and feet; much kissing of ikons, relics, bejewelled crucifixes and Bibles. Nobody seems to object to the tourists goggling – in the C. of E. vergers would throw us out – for a Russian Orthodox church isn't merely for ceremonies; it's a meeting-place. People come in to say a prayer in front of an ikon or light a candle, and ignore the service in progress; others remain in the narthex, where cakes and hot tea are sold, and use the church as a café in which to gossip with friends: in some you can even make telephone calls. I've never seen anything like it. The thin, beige-coloured candles fizz and sputter – a low, background noise, most pleasing, like gas-lamps, and the beauty of the music moves me to tears, as does the beauty of the ikons. I wouldn't, of course, but – at times – I find myself saying I could, for all the wrong reasons, be converted to Orthodoxy. The power, the mysteriousness, the gentleness! Far more attractive than Roman Catholicism.

To the New Moscow Arts Theatre (not the famous Arts Theatre that still puts on the plays of Chekhov exactly as Stanislavsky directed them) for a different kind of music: *Swan Lake*, danced by one of the many recent split-offs from the Bolshoi. The Bolshoi's future is very uncertain. Like other Soviet institutions it now has to go into the market-place to find its money, and apart from the enormous cost of staging opera and ballet, millions of roubles will have to be spent on its theatre, which is in danger of collapse due to subsidence. Many of the dancers have left to form companies like the one I see at the New Arts: the music is great; the dancing as technically proficient as ever; the choreography Petipa in aspic (the male dancers don't have anything like as strong a role as in Nureyev's version), and the theatre is ludicrously unsuitable. The stage is so small that a mere ten swans leaping about creates an instant traffic jam. I enjoy it, sure: *Swan Lake* in Moscow – who wouldn't? Afterwards, in the taxi to my hotel, the safety belt falls to pieces as I try to fasten it. "Don't vorry," says the driver, grinning like a hyena; "zees ees a *R-r-r-r-russian* taxi!"

I wonder where the men who cruise on the steps of the Bolshoi Theatre will go if it shuts, and I hope the Kirov (about to revert to its old name, the Marinsky) doesn't have to endure the same fate. Its corridors were *outrageous*, as was – I guess it still is – the Tsars' loo in the Winter Palace.

Kiev, a mere thirty miles from Chernobyl, is, I imagine, irredeemably poisoned: the food I eat, the streets I walk in, the buildings I enter are probably mega-dosed with radiation. But, I tell myself, radiation is not high on the list of illnesses that could speed me into a tomb. Kiev is the capital of the Ukraine, and the blue and yellow flags of this recently 'independent' country are flying everywhere; Lenin is wrapped in scaffolding, awaiting transport. It's a pleasant city of nineteenth-century houses, all painted in soft pastel colours – beige, yellow, maroon – on the banks of the Dnieper, one of the widest rivers in Europe. It isn't autumn yet; the leaves are still mostly green and the afternoons hot: St Luke's summer. It's the fiftieth anniversary of the massacre at Babi Yar – a ravine a few miles away, where in 1941 the Nazis shot three hundred thousand Jews – so a day of mourning, marked by a performance of Shostakovich's *Babi Yar* Symphony, his thirteenth; a song cycle, though labelled a symphony – a setting of poems by Yevtushenko. It's an interesting work (I've never heard it before) and an emotional experience: because I'm listening to it in Kiev and *today* of all days.

There's more food in the shops than in Moscow, but the new government is controversial – no Boris Yeltsin in charge and too nationalistic; Ukraine for the Ukrainians is not an idea that appeals to all. A BBC television crew is in town expecting trouble; but I see none, nor sense any brewing beneath the surface. Just six very angry policemen arguing with the driver of a corporation dustcart – he's dented the back of one of their vehicles – and several drunk, loud-mouthed Finns, whose football team has this evening been knocked out of the European Cup by Kiev Dynamo. Why are Finns abroad *always* drunk? St Petersburg, day and night, is full of them. (The break-up of the Soviet Union is causing problems for its football league. Kiev Dynamo – the current champions – and the other Ukrainian clubs, which, in the first division, include Dniepropetrovsk, Odessa Chernomorets, Zaparozhye Metallurg and Kharkov Metallist – what names! – are forming their own league. The Georgian clubs and those from the Baltics have already gone.)

Kiev is a city of great churches. Russian Christianity started here in 988, when Prince Vladimir, who married the sister of the Byzantine Emperor, Basil the Second, had his subjects baptised in the Dnieper. In 988 Kiev was already the capital of a flourishing principality – Moscow wasn't even a village. The cathedral of Santa Sophia, which dates from 1036, is the oldest building in all the Russias, and it is a miracle that it's survived – untouched by the Mongols, who sacked Kiev in 1240, the Bolshevik iconoclasts, and the Nazis, who destroyed a third of the city in World War Two. The appearance of the outside, green walls and golden domes, and the huge, detached bell-tower, is eighteenth-century (and no less attractive for that); but inside, apart from the strange, somewhat Moorish ikonostasis (another eighteenth-century addition), nothing has changed in a thousand years. It's absolutely stunning: not only much more advanced, architecturally, than any Western church a thousand years old, but it tells us almost exactly what Byzantine churches and cathedrals in Constantinople must have been like a millennium ago. The murals and mosaics are so fresh and glittering they look as if they've just been put there, and the tomb of Prince Yaroslav the Wise, who died in 1054, is sculpted with a beauty and sophistication unknown at that time in the West.

The Lavra Monastery is so big it's a walled city within a city, a vast complex of gold, green, white and blue buildings that include *forty-one* ancient churches; seen from the hill above, it looks like an improbable dreamscape of golden spires, towers, cupolas and turrets – mind-boggling. So old are these churches that they pre-date the invention of the onion dome (the idea of which is less than poetic – to stop huge accumulations of snow); the roofs of the Lavra are surmounted by piles of what look like golden Baroque hats, as do the towers of churches in Czechoslovakia, Austria and Slovenia. The real gem of the place, the Cathedral of the Assumption, was dynamited in 1941 by – it was always said – the Nazis; but since the demise of Communism the truth has emerged: it was blown up by the Resistance, who wanted to assassinate the commander-in-chief of the Ukraine's German troops. He had decided to visit the cathedral, but unfortunately he came – and left – twenty minutes earlier than scheduled, and so survived. It is, however, going to be reconstructed exactly as it was; it will be the first church in Russia to be built since the Tsars.

Another magnificent church is turquoise-coloured St Andrew's, designed in 1750 by the great Italian architect, Rastrelli, who also designed the Winter Palace, the Smolny Monastery, and most of the public buildings in St Petersburg. It's strange to see it in Kiev: it could be a Catholic church in Rome, Venice, Florence – Baroque, ornate and wholly Italian. The only concessions to Orthodoxy are the ikonostasis, which doesn't quite fit, the ground-plan of an Orthodox church not being the same as a Catholic church, and the onion domes. There's also a pulpit: *very* odd, as Orthodox priests don't use pulpits. The Vladimir Cathedral is interesting too; nineteenth-century – a period when Russian art had become so westernised that ikons almost ceased to be Russian. In this church the ikons are totally pre-Raphaelite; they could have been painted by Millais, Rossetti or Burne-Jones, and would not look out of place in the Tate Gallery.

Near Santa Sophia is the Golden Gate, not to be confused with the Great Gate of Kiev in Mussorgsky's *Pictures at an Exhibition*, which never got built. The Golden Gate was erected in 1037, but it's not particularly interesting despite its age. On the top of it is a church so minute you can hardly see it from the ground.

Odessa is a busy port on the Black Sea, not far from the Rumanian frontier: in Primorsky Boulevard shipping merchants and magnates, and well-to-do exiles from Greece and Revolutionary France built splendid houses which are still immaculately preserved. It was from here in 1918 that the aged Dowager Tsarina Marya Fyodorovna fled to London on one of the last boats. To go from Primorsky Boulevard to the port one takes the Odessa Steps, which, were it not for Eisenstein's *Battleship Potemkin*, nobody would every have heard of. The Odessa Steps sequence in *Potemkin* is perhaps the most famous single episode in the entire history of the cinema, and even those who've never seen the film will have seen the clip dozens of times – the crowd surging down to the mutineers and getting themselves shot by the Tsarist army; the broken spectacles and the pram, baby in it, bouncing out of control from top to bottom. It was all in fact, invented by Eisenstein; it never happened. The mutiny certainly happened (1905), and there are plans – ridiculous plans – to replace the statue commemorating the mutineers (who were heroic) with the statue originally here, of Catherine the Great (a nasty woman and decidedly not a heroine) who was the founder of Odessa. But such is the farce of present-day Russia that nobody knows where the statue of Catherine is . . .

There are a hundred and nine-two steps, and as one goes down their size increases; the bottom step is almost twice the width of the top. The purpose is a trompe l'oeil: the whole thing, a series of terraces, looks much bigger than it is. From the top one can see the terraces but not the steps – and from the bottom one can see only the steps. Another Italian, Boffo, designed this toy in 1837; he intended to put a triumphal arch at the summit, but, like the Great Gate of Kiev, it got no further than the drawing-board. There's a fine view of the port and the Black Sea, not so black today – dark blue and rough, wind whipping up the surf. It's hot, Mediterranean hot; high summer. Nearby stands the building that before the coup was the headquarters of the Communist Party: it's locked up, and about to be sold to an American business consortium. Also nearby is the opera house, a very grand affair, the work of the same Austrian architect who designed the Vienna Staatsoper – Odessa in its heyday was rich enough to afford such a status symbol. Caruso and Chaliapin sang here; Tchaikovsky, Rimsky-Korsakov and Glazunov were resident conductors. It's the campest opera house I've ever seen, positively dripping with gilt, silver, and red plush; its decor awash with statues, mirrors and the most *marvellous* grand staircase, fit for queens of every sex – I parade up and down several

186

times.

The opera company, however, is not in the same league. *Aida* is being performed (somewhat annoying; the only opera I've been to in Russia was also *Aida*, at the Kirov in 1987.) Admittedly Odessa's Amneris would succeed on any stage, and the orchestra is good, but the other principal singers wouldn't get jobs cleaning the loos at Sadler's Wells. The chorus is grotesque: a bunch of very old men and women, most of them – incredibly – without teeth, pottering on and off like blushing yokels in a village hall. They have, we're told, been dragged in at the last minute from the highways and byways; the usual chorus has downed tools and gone off to be extras in a film called *The Iron Curtain*. The producer may have gone with them, for production is non-existent, and, perhaps to lessen everyone's embarrassment, the second half is staged in almost total darkness with the chorus in the wings! Radames, in Act Two, has no soldiers with him to strut round in the Grand March; in their place we have four tenth-rate male dancers (nice legs however: *Aida* is a good opera for legs) cavorting – no, mincing – like pretty young creatures in the Bell. Weird . . .

Another indication of long-ago splendour is the art gallery, which has a sizeable collection of Italian, Dutch, Flemish and Spanish paintings, though only one really outstanding work: a superb Caravaggio, *The Arrest of Christ*. I'm sure Jarman doesn't know *that* one . . . Beneath the city is a vast warren of catacombs, which – so the story is – would reach, if laid end to end, from Rumania to Finland; they were the limestone quarries from which Odessa was built. They were used as air-raid shelters and classrooms for children during the war, and as the headquarters of the local Resistance. The Germans, well aware of what was going on, pumped poison gas into them, but succeeded in killing almost nobody – the Russians simply retreated further inside and blocked off the contaminated passages. I venture in (it's curiously warm; I'd assumed chill and damp) and I'm shown various relics the Resistance left behind – cooking pots, a stove, bath-tubs, beds, messages scribbled on the walls. The opera house, Odessa's heaviest building, is sinking into these catacombs.

There are no ancient churches, for the city was not conceived until the end of the eighteenth century. The onion domes are silver, which I haven't noticed elsewhere. But a rather grand edifice is the Odessa Hotel on Primorsky Boulevard, the best hotel in Russia the guide-books say, with an internationally famous cuisine. It closed in 1989 for refurbishment, and should be open again now, but it isn't: when inspectors from the Ministry of Tourism viewed the finished product, they found the builders had converted the restaurant, the kitchens and all the bars into bedrooms. Stalin would have had them shot . . .

I come to St Petersburg in reddish-gold, sunset light, mist at the edges of things: Paul the First's terra-cotta castle-palace; Decembrists Square and the astonishing Bronze Horseman (Peter the Great on a horse uprearing like Géricault's); the thin gold spires of the Admiralty and the Peter and Paul Fortress resembling those of Protestant cathedrals in Estonia or Latvia rather than Orthodox Russia; Rastrelli's Smolny Convent, harmonious blue and white walls and domes; the cruiser *Aurora* from which in 1917 the first bullet (a blank, ironically) was fired; it's all much lovelier and staggeringly bigger than the pictures in my mind of four years ago. The brain dwarfs the exceptional, the unique, to comprehend – The Grand Canyon, the Las Vegas strip . . . St Petersburg. The Neva, across which I stare at Rastrelli's ultimate fantasy in stone – the green, white and gold of the Winter Palace, and Palace Square with its Alexander Column surmounted by an angel – is vastly wider than I'd remembered. The Peter and Paul Fortress, lonely on its island, light glittering on its spire, a huge red sun on the horizon like a dazzling onion dome: the excitement of Nevsky Prospekt: the memorial to the six hundred and fifty thousand inhabitants who died of hunger in the Second World War: the Finland Station, modern and smart, where Lenin emerged from his sealed train, as Churchill said, "like a plague bacillus."

One of the world's magnificent set-pieces, this museum show-case; is it more beautiful than Prague? Everyone asks that question. It's grander, less provincial, but no . . . not *quite* so amazingly beautiful. Prague is number one, St Petersburg number two. And it lacks Moscow's buzz, 'fourmillante cité.' In dank February weather it can seem oppressive, I'm told, shut in on itself. Not now, not during October: Peter and Paul resplendent in early morning sun and mist, the colours of its trees like flames – though it's best seen at a distance, for its architecture is shoddy. St Petersburg's oldest building, Peter's proof that he now had 'a window on the West.' And indeed it's very un-Russian. Inside its cathedral are the tombs of all the Tsars from Peter the Great to Alexander the Third, except for Peter the Second, who died as a child in Moscow of smallpox, and the Tsar the world is more interested in than any other because of the events of his reign and the manner of his death – Nicholas the Second. Nicholas's body, and those of his wife, his daughters, and the haemophiliac tsarevich have recently been exhumed from the mineshaft at Ekaterinburg. If these bones really are Nicholas's and his family's, there may well be a last, colossal funeral in the Peter and Paul cathedral: the most sumptuous ever, I should think; the whole of St Petersburg and the world's TV cameras in attendance.

The Fortress was used as a prison. Those condemned to die arrived by boat through Death Gate, like their counter-parts through Traitors' Gate at London's Tower; today Death Gate is the haunt, even in October, of sun-wor-shippers, swimmers, and cruising men. The cells are grim, but curiously spacious. The Tsarevich Alexis (Peter's son), the Decembrists, Gorky, Trotsky, Lenin's elder brother, and the Kronstadt sailors were locked up here; outside the cell doors are photographs of some of the last prisoners. Across the Neva is the Winter Palace, from which the Tsar could stare at his jail. How to describe the Winter Palace, the most luxurious the world has ever seen, its millions of treasures and vast art gallery, the Hermitage? It's im-possible. Here the Romanovs lived in a splendour unequalled in human history, Catherine the Great eating roast nightingales' tongues, while outside their subjects experienced almost unimaginable squalor, dirt, poverty and disease. It still seems like that, when one looks at the hideous tower-blocks like gigantic ant-heaps of concrete with which St Petersburg is ringed. How can these be inhabited by *humans*? The depression they must cause, the psychological problems! While the Winter Palace is overflowing with gold, silver, bronze, marble, jasper, agate, porphyry, malachite, crystal, lapis lazuli; with dazzling chandeliers, gilt mirrors and magnificent staircases. The Pavilion of the Small Hermitage is an absolute Queen's dream, and the columns of the Throne Room are a Realm of Gold . . . The Hall of 1812 is fascinating: huge portraits of the architects of Napoleon's defeat – Kutuzov, Wellington, Barclay de Tolly, Frederick William the Third of Prussia, Alexander the First, Francis the First of Austria, most of them in full regalia dashing around on horseback. But no George the Third or Prince Regent. *Why not*? Nobody can tell me.

In the Hermitage there are more great Rembrandts than in Amsterdam, including the wonderful *Deposition from the Cross*, more Giorgiones than in Venice, two Leonardos (*The Benois Madonna* and *The Madonna Litta*), roomfuls of Claude, Watteau, Corot (much more interesting than any other French painter of the early nineteenth century), Goya, El Greco, Velazquez, Titian, Rubens, Van Dyck, and – what one wants to see more than anything else – the enormous collection of Impressionists and post-Impressionists. Great Cézannes (in particular *The Banks of the Marne, The Pipe-smoker*, and two still lives with apples); masses of Gauguin and Renoir (I don't like Renoir any more than I do Gauguin: sentimental and too many grossly fat women); another superb street-scene of Pissarro's; forty-five Matisses including the enigmatic *Dancers* and the equally enigmatic *Musicians*, both reminiscent of some joyous Stone Age rite; Picasso at his most cuboid, but some Blue Period masterpieces; Bonnard and Vuillard in sludge and mud mood; Monet, Van Gogh, Sisley, Degas . . . I totter out, satiated, aware of having merely scratched the surface, and sink down in a café for much-needed cake and tea. Late afternoon: the fog is drifting in from the Gulf of Finland, St Isaac's, the Kazan Cathedral and Peter and Paul already rubbed out, the Admiralty spire a faint pencil sketch. And having recovered, I stroll slowly through the streets, looking at people and buildings, observing, absorbing. It's like somewhere in Italy: its designers, mostly Italian – Rastrelli, Rossi, Trezzini, Quarenghi – created a planned, larger Venice, diverting rivers and criss-crossing them with bridges and networks of canals. All the façades are delicate pastels – pale blue, apple green, buff, russet, pink. Beautiful.

To the Kirov for *Il Trovatore*. A more gracious opera house than Odessa's, not so sumptuous, all good-taste blue and gold and acoustically excellent; though I'd forgotten how hard are its seats. With a very sore bum after two weeks of diarrhoea . . . I haven't seen *Trovatore* since 1951 at the Garden. I was fifteen. And what a concoction of non-sense it is with its gipsies and auto-da-fés, mistaken identities and missing brothers; but I've wanted to see it again for a long time now – because a decade ago I made passionate love with an opera singer, *Il Trovatore* in the background on his record player. I can never hear the Miserere Chorus and Manrico's 'Ah, che la morte' without thinking of . . . no, I cannot reveal his name. He was gorgeous, and terrific in bed but not keen on a second meeting: in any case, I was soon to spend a year in San Francisco. On my return I was told he'd come to my house while I was away; he was hoping to stay with me for a few weeks, 'resting.' Fuck! Yet another door into a rose-garden I didn't open . . .   In contrast to Odessa's *Aida*, the singing, the production, the sets and the costumes are just fine. The set for the Miserere Chorus is almost exactly the same as I remember Covent Garden's; darkness, a dim and distant tower at the top of which is a lit window. Child Roland to the dark tower came . . . I did . . .

In the country outside St Petersburg are the three summer palaces of the Tsars – Petrodvorets (the Peterhof), which is Peter the Great's mini-Versailles built by Rastrelli on the Gulf of Finland; and, close to each other at Tsarskoye Selo, Pavlovsk, built for Paul the First by a Scottish architect, Charles Cameron, and the Catherine Palace, Rastrelli again, for Peter's daughter, the Tsarina Elisabeth. All three were looted and vandalised – nearly destroyed – by the Nazis, but they have been rebuilt exactly as they were, though restoration is not yet complete. I comment that almost nothing has been done since I was here in 1987: and I'm told that because the state pays restorers so badly there are very few of them left; instead of earning useless roubles they manufacture tourist grot, which they sell for dollars, pounds, and deutschmarks. None of these buildings has the scale of the Winter Palace, but they are nonetheless spectacular pieces of architecture with, inside, the usual vast amounts of malachite, lapis lazuli, marble, gold, etcetera; the Grand Salon of the Catherine palace is quite breath-taking, as is the Throne Room at Petrodvorets (chandeliers of smoked crystal) and the silk-lined walls of the Partridge Room. The Amber Room at the Catherine Palace, once floor-to-ceiling amber, must have been the world's costliest boudoir, but the Nazis stole the amber and it's never been found; it's so expensive – and rare – that the room has only been partially restored. One can work up a torrent of anti-German feelings by just going round these palaces . . .

The great glory of Petrodvorets is its gardens, but it's October and the Versailles-like fountains have been switched off. Raw damp autumn; dense fog. And it's *cold*. The white and yellow of the palace looms indistinctly through the mist, and the Gulf of Finland is invisible. But fog and falling leaves have a certain charm, a pleasing melancholy. Outside the main entrance a flautist and a cellist in eighteenth-century costume and with huge, full-bottomed wigs are entertaining the tourists with *Eine Kleine Nachtmusik*. Not for many weeks longer . . . Some of the pools are now empty, as if the whole place is preparing itself for the great winter ice.

I too must hole up for the winter. Prepare for ice. I'm not

well. My travelling days, though not over, are, I think, numbered.

October 1991

Packing It In

Saturday, ten thirty p.m.; I've just finished reading *The Lost Language of Cranes*, a novel I've spent most of the day with. It's incredibly quiet, indoors and out; the only sound is snow-flakes pattering against glass. Then footsteps, a man's I think, scrunching along the pavement. I'm safe and warm inside my house, and alone; *cocooned* in safety and warmth and aloneness. I look up and acknowledge my things, all placed exactly where I want them to be; the books, the ornaments – souvenirs of trips abroad, of lovers, of my children when they were children – and the chairs, the TV (silent the whole evening), the pictures on the walls, and my work-table strewn (no, not strewn; I'm a tidiness freak) with letters to be answered and manuscripts of half-finished essays, held down by paperweights and Aids medicines. Nothing has moved in the hours my inner eye has been observing Leavitt's lost cranes. There's no one here to move anything.

The phone has not rung since this morning: Denis, asking if I'm OK. Saturdays and Sundays my phone hardly ever rings; the calls, if any, are outgoing. Friends have other preoccupations at this time of the week. They have other preoccupations most of the week, in fact; lovers, husbands, wives. Not long ago I said to Dorothy that if I dropped dead one night my body wouldn't be found for days: the sort of instance one reads in the press, neighbours becoming suspicious because the curtains haven't been opened for a week and the milk is piling up on the door-step. I should give her the spare key, she said. I did. I talk to her on the phone every other day; we see each other perhaps twice a fortnight, and perhaps twice a month she and Tony come to dinner, or I go to their house. The same with Denis. Other friends I talk to on the phone, but rarely see. This, apart from writing, domestic chores, the garden, holidays, trips to London for work purposes (books, publishing) is how I live.

This is real, true isolation. I'm happy with it and I'm horrified by it; a paradox I often think about but cannot resolve. Aids is its cause.

The first floor of my house has two rooms. They were the children's bedrooms: empty for years now. Stephen's I use as a guest room; he decorated it himself and the carpet was his choice – I see no reason to alter things here, for he has good taste, good colour sense. The five paintings on the walls are family portraits – my grandmother, my mother, me thirty years ago, Jenny, Adam. We stare down at friends who stay overnight, or for a few nights, and I hope we don't disturb them, though I suspect lovers making love in this bed could think the watchful eyes of four generations of my family a bit intimidating. It's two years now since my mother's death; I inherited the picture of her. As she willed my share of her estate to my ex-wife (a punishment for being gay), I've been trying to steel myself to destroying it. The idea, however, of burning a work of art appals me. So it remains.

Adam's room needs redecorating. His technique was more careless than Stephen's, and his colour sense bizarre. I could do up this room and have a lodger – it's quite big. It would solve the paradox: put an end to the hours, the whole days, of silence. I'd be horrified no more. Maurice has a lodger, an old friend of mine I call Fru-fru (he calls me Daphne) and they get along splendidly. They care for each other and bicker with each other like an old married couple. I'd like that too. But I'd lose the silence, the isolation; the grip I have on the reality of my own existence. I can't do that.

I go upstairs, look at both rooms, survey the relics of Stephen and Adam – the things they left here when they grew up and went off to lead their own lives. It's still snowing hard, in my garden, which I can see from Stephen's window, and in the street, which I can see from Adam's. Is it snowing in Dublin, where Stephen lives; in Amsterdam where Adam lives? Probably. The snow is general all over Europe. And in my mind. *In these empty rooms children would play*, so runs the old Abba song . . . *Breaking up is never easy, I know, but I had to go* . . . I rarely listen to that record. It's too depressing.

196

Sometimes I feel like packing it in. Aids, come on, come on! Stop pussyfooting around, come and get me! But a moment or so later I shoot that thought right out of my head. I'm like Vladimir in *Waiting for Godot*, who cries out, "I can't go on!" Then, after a pause while he contemplates the awful alternative: "What have I said?" He goes on. As most of us do.

Work, more than anything else, sustains me, and for that I value the silence, cherish the isolation. But there's not much work to complete now. No novels or short stories gestating; the life I live has nothing in it that could be the material of fiction, and the life I once lived has been used in the books already published. I could go on churning out essays, travel pieces in particular, but the reader would soon tire of that: another mountain noticed, another solitary dinner eaten, another flower scent sniffed, another medieval church assessed. I shan't stop travelling while I'm still able to, that's for sure, but . . . writing about it? There's nobody more boring than an old fart of a writer with nothing left to say. As Pope observed:

> Who shames a scribbler? Break one cobweb through,
> He spins the slight, self-pleasing thread anew.

But if I wrote nothing I'd go crazy. I wouldn't any longer think, like Vladimir, "What have I said?" I would be packing it in.

One of these days I will have to pack it in. I fear it more than anything else, more than dying of a nasty, lingering Aids-related disease. (The thought of deafness fills me with a similar fear.) In *The Lost Language of Cranes*, I found Rose the most sympathetic character: a middle-aged straight woman, who has never thought much about homosexuality apart from acknowledging its existence and being vaguely aware that a few of the people she works with are so inclined. She discovers that her husband and her only son are gay; she has to deal with this at a time when she is being forced to quit the apartment she has lived in for twenty years. We're not told what happens to her, but we don't need to be told – we can safely assume she survives.

197

She has spent all her adult years protecting herself by escaping into her work, cocooning herself in it; she will go on doing the copy-editing she has always enjoyed. I can identify with Rose and her isolation. But I'm not sure how much longer *my* work will be a protection, a cocoon. It may be a fragile, empty shell.

This house, which I love, is also a cocoon. Unlike Rose I can't be forced out, unless my ex-wife, with whom I jointly own it, wanted to sell. It isn't probable. *In these empty rooms children* . . . But is it enough?

I put Schumann's Piano Concerto on the record player. One of the great piano concertos – perhaps the only great piece of music Schumann wrote. It shuts out dark thoughts; again, an escape.

Midnight: the snow has muffled the cathedral's clock. As I look from Adam's window the drifts are beginning to smother the street's familiar shapes. The touch of snow is like feathers or gentle fingers; I can see the wind's eddies building it against walls, doors, and smoothing away footprints as breath blows dandelion seeds. Another cocoon: no one is out walking in this. Absolute silence. I go up to the second floor of the house, my bedroom. I'll sleep well – I usually do – for tomorrow is *not* another day. Despite the snow, it's the same day. If it ever should be another day, it would mean I really am packing it in.

> Vladimir: That passed the time.
> Estragon: It would have passed in any case.
> Vladimir: Yes, but not so rapidly.

However . . . I want to end as I began, with Auden's *1st September 1939*, lines from which I used as the epigraph to this book; for the eighties, like the thirties, have been a low, dishonest decade; and, though the reasons are obviously quite different, the unmentionable odour of death offends our night as much as it did his:

May I, composed like them
Of Eros and of dust,
Beleaguered by the same
Negation and despair,
Show an affirming flame.

February 1990